b-mother

b-mother

MAUREEN O'BRIEN

Harcourt, Inc.
Orlando   Austin   New York   San Diego   Toronto   London

Requests for permission to make copies of any part of the work
should be submitted online at www.harcourt.com/contact or mailed
to the following address: Permissions Department, Harcourt, Inc.,
6277 Sea Harbor Drive, Orlando, Florida 32887-6777.

www.HarcourtBooks.com

This is a work of fiction. Names, characters, places, organizations, and events are
the products of the author's imagination or are used fictitiously, and any resemblance
to actual persons, living or dead, events, or locales is entirely coincidental.

Library of Congress Cataloging-in-Publication Data
O'Brien, Maureen, 1960–
B-mother/Maureen O'Brien.—1st ed.
p. cm.
1. Teenage mothers—Fiction.   2. Single mothers—Fiction.
3. New England—Fiction.   4. Child welfare—Fiction.   I. Title.
PS3615.B7625B56   2006
813'.6—dc22   2006003703
ISBN-13: 978-0-15-101398-2   ISBN-10: 0-15-101398-5

Text set in Minion
Designed by April Ward

Printed in the United States of America
First edition
A C E G I K J H F D B

For Tim: who laughs, who listens

one

1

Had you spotted me on the railroad tracks that autumn morning, you would have thought I was an ordinary teenage girl in thigh-tight jeans surrounded by the tassels of dried summer grass. But I wasn't listening for the distant freight train whistle. I was waiting for Shell, my best friend, who suddenly pulled up alongside me in her old station wagon. She smiled her snaggle-tooth smile, one front tooth pressed over the other like the folded wing of an origami bird.

"You're not okay, are you."

"Not really," I admitted.

"Hop in, hon. We're gonna find out for sure."

We drove out on Route 26 past the Oxford Plains Speedway as the sun poked through the bleachers. The cool air brought everything into sharp focus. The sugar maples were speckled with salmon leaves. Every fall Shell would usually *ooh* and *ahh* over the foliage. Instead she glanced at me more than the trees along the road. I cracked the window to drink in the wind, trying to calm myself from gagging. I had been moving through the hallways of my high school, wide-eyed and tender, clutching my junior year notebooks in front of my swollen, aching breasts. Between class bells, I rushed to the girls' bathroom, checking my underwear in the haze of cigarette smoke. Each time the cotton crotch was white.

"I could have been wearing white pants every day like the Man in White," I joked sarcastically. The Man in White was an old lunatic who wandered all over the county in starched button-down shirts, white trousers, and white dress gloves.

"Yeah, all you need is a steel plate in your head like his." She glanced over at me. "You gonna puke?"

"No. I'm okay," I muttered. Relieved, Shell turned on the radio, tuning the dial to WOXO. "Brown-Eyed Girl" came on. Shell's song. She hated when boys recited the lyrics to her, flirting. But with me, she sang loudly and off-key, each verse lifting her mood like a cold Coca-Cola. "Thank god I have brown eyes with hair this white," she said.

It was a joke with us. "I know, I know, otherwise you'd be an albino."

We passed over a river that frothed yellow foam from a paper mill. "The town of Gray. Such a lovely place to find out for sure if you're knocked up."

"Did you tell Miles?" Shell asked.

"He hasn't written me in over a month. Maybe I was just a summer fling."

"Maybe not. Maybe you'll end up together."

"Miles did cocaine. Didn't you notice how he was always racing around, disappearing into the bathroom? There it is." I pointed to the stucco building. "Gray Family Clinic."

The receptionist handed me some papers. Shell and I sat down on hard plastic chairs in the waiting room. Three other girls kept their eyes downcast and didn't take off their jackets. A nurse with greasy hair slicked back under a headband opened a door from a back hallway. She called my name. The other girls shifted in their chairs. My face reddened.

She led me to a bathroom that smelled of roach spray, glanced at my forms, and asked, "Last period?"

I whispered, "Late July." She instructed me to pee in a cup. Then Shell and I waited in an examining room. The nurse knocked and didn't wait for an answer. She flipped over a paper. "Your urine has tested positive. You're pregnant."

I knew. I had known each time I had checked my underwear.

The nurse wrote on a clipboard and spoke as if I had been arrested and she were reading me my rights. "A counselor will speak with you before you leave. You have options. If you want an abortion, we can perform it here. You're about three, three and a half weeks shy of the twelve-week mark. So you really need to decide soon. If you want to go full term, we provide prenatal care in a separate part of the clinic."

An hour later I found myself naked from the waist down, my bottom wrapped in a crinkly paper cover. I swung my legs and stared at the dark pink posters, urn-shaped drawings of the uterus, while Shell kept braiding and unbraiding her hair.

The doctor was young and direct. "Is this your first pelvic exam?" she asked, snapping latex gloves over her hands.

"Yes."

She guided my feet into stirrups that were wrapped in dingy terrycloth and rubber bands. A desk lamp shone between my legs. "Do me a favor and scooch your bottom down." She checked me for sores and warts. After that she greased up my belly and skated a small black box over me. I heard static, and then, like the gusting of a helicopter landing, the room suddenly pulsed with a whirling, bright-yellow sound. "That's the heartbeat," she said.

"Oh my god," Shell burst out, "there's someone in there."

Tears pooled in my eyes, making the room shiny.

"You okay?" the doctor asked me. Then the room was silent. "Meet me in the office next door."

I dried my eyes with the paper cover and wiped off the cold jelly smeared on my stomach. My legs trembled. Shell helped me slip my underpants back on.

"I'm not telling my mother," I said to the mountains on the way home.

"Does she have to know? That woman said everything could be, you know, private."

"She won't know a thing if I get an abortion. My brother dying was enough, now this?"

"I feel sorry for your mom," Shell sighed. "She used to be so pretty."

We bounced over the speed bumps of the school parking lot. The rows of buses, jocks wearing their numbered shirts to promote school spirit, cheerleaders in saddle shoes, all of it choreographed to the swish of the heartbeat. *You really need to decide soon.*

"Shell, are you ashamed of me?"

"Nope. Definitely not."

"Will you stick with me? No matter what?"

"I double-pinkie swear," she said, just like when we were in fourth grade.

Pinkies linked.

———

My high school lay wedged between the dump and the Dead River Company gas station. Going east you passed a gold-leafed sign—WELCOME TO PARIS!—next to the graveyard that sprawled all the way to the McDonald's, near the dark stink of the leather tannery.

If you head west through the town of Norway, straight down Main Street, past the fire station's Smokey Bear cutout, the empty Woolworth's, and Woodman's, where they sold night crawlers and rifles, then hung a left at the bog of Lake Pennesseewassee, you'd come up the steepest hill in town. On the left is Pike Hill Cemetery. That's where my brother is buried.

The cemetery is ringed with small hemlocks and a rugged stone wall. Maybe fifty people are buried there, most of them teenagers and children. Many of the names of the dead are rinsed away, their markers askew. That first winter Birdy was gone, I crawled on top of the fresh snowfall on his plot and swiped my arms and legs in perfect snow angels.

My mother went, too—alone, during the day while I was in school. If she noticed my angels, she never mentioned them to me. She left boot marks all over them, and yellow rose petals.

My brother died when I was twelve, the day before Thanksgiving. I spent that winter trudging in slippery, tangled shadows. I'd fall, ripping holes in my tights. The chimes of the town tower clock carried up through the woods as I'd hurry home, the scent of wood smoke hanging like a pork smell in the air, stirring my hunger. The beaded lampshades of our parlor radiated through the front windows, throwing a rosy glow onto the whiteness of the snowbanks. But inside, no afghan or fire in the fireplace could touch the chill of Bird's absence. It soaked through us.

I pushed open the back door those nights without saying hello or good night to my parents and headed upstairs to run a scalding bath and strip off my blood-crusted tights.

Birdy was supposed to come home that Wednesday.

"Mr. Donnelly, is Hillary Birdsong in your class?" The receptionist's voice crackled through the two-way speaker at the front of the science lab. Our seventh grade class was making homemade batteries. Mr. Donnelly was picking on the derelicts in the back—around town they were known as the Street Rats—because several wires were missing, stolen to be used as roach clips.

"She is."

"Please have her report to the office immediately."

I mouthed to Shell, *Talk to you later.* Mr. Donnelly, one of our few male teachers who never had sweat stains under his pits, spread his arm wide, opening the door. It's strange the details I remember of that day—that his underarm was as crisp as the rest of his purple pastel shirt. I headed down the hallway, which was quiet without all the twerps slamming each other into the lockers. I thought maybe Bird had come to surprise me, home from college a few hours earlier than planned. Outside the shop class in Hall C, the air was pine sweet, hazy with sawdust.

I froze, heart suddenly beating wildly, at the sight of my Uncle Billy's massive head and hunched shoulders. Through the glass partition the principal, Mr. Parker, wiped his hand over his jaw line. When Uncle Billy turned to me I felt sick. I knew something was horribly wrong. His chin quivered in soft, ugly shapes.

"You need to come home with me," he gasped, pulling me roughly into his soft red sweater.

"What is it?"

"Your parents want to be the ones to tell you."

Uncle Billy barely braked at the four-way stop signs. As we cut through town black-and-blue crows were hopping, dancing together on the rims of garbage cans. Rushing up the steps of the side porch and looking in the window, I saw Mr. Phelam, the high school football coach, standing in a ring with my mother, father, and Aunt Iris. The metal door slammed wide open against the siding. Voices went silent as Uncle Billy danced me forward, my feet on his as if I were a rag doll. We hesitated in the doorway of the pantry underneath Bird's chin-up bar.

My mother lunged toward me. "Bird's gone."

"Your folks got a call this morning. There was some sort of accident." Uncle Billy swept me up, gathered me in his beefy arms, and cradled me. My parents closed in around me. I couldn't breathe with the dark pressure of their bodies.

"Poor little thing. Jesus," Mr. Phelam said in a low voice to Aunt Iris. "I know how much she worshipped Bird."

"It must have been his time," Aunt Iris sighed.

"His time?" My mother unwrapped her arms from around Uncle Billy's wide waist. "His time? Those idiots killed him. He was eighteen. And you're hitting me with your born-again shit?" I had never seen my mother's mouth open so wide. Her incisors were bearlike, jagged, pointy white.

My mother and my aunt usually spent days preparing Thanksgiving dinner. But Bird was dead. Aunt Iris poured the biscuit batter into the sink and washed it down the drain. She stacked the canned peas back on the pantry shelf, then snuck the turkey away, naked and slippery in Saran Wrap, shiny with olive oil and smelling of chopped celery. Instead of our sit-down meal with Irish lace and big spoons at the dining-room table, townspeople swarmed in the house, holding paper plates with rolls, roast beef, black olives, and potato salad—everything cold. Women stood in wool coats, squeezing lipstick-caked tissues. Men blinked as if ice fishing, blinded by a bitter wind. By nightfall the house was jammed with Bird's friends, football players to the end, standing in a huddle with their arms around one another.

Sunrise on Friday, my mother's tears began while ironing the white, button-down oxford shirt that Bird was going to be buried in. He had been shipped from the university straight to Lowell's Funeral Home. The shirt had to be delivered to the funeral home by seven. She sprayed it with Niagara Spray Starch, steering the tip of the iron around the buttons. Pan-icked that she had starched it too much, my mother washed it all over again, her arms wrapped around the washing machine while it chugged through the spin and rinse cycles. With her face pressed into a warm pile of dish towels, she wept while the shirt, all alone, rose and fell in circles inside the dryer. My mother ironed until my father gently pried the shirt from her fingers.

"Jan, Jan, honey, "my father coaxed. "Janée? You can give it to me now."

The mortician had shellacked Birdie's bowl cut so his hair would stay straight-banged across his forehead while he lay on his back in the casket. My father stroked Bird's jacket lapel as if he were smoothing out a feather. I wanted to touch my brother, too. I placed a hand on his elbow. He was so stiff I jumped back from the casket as if I had scalded myself. "You all right?" my father asked. I never touched Bird again.

Shell, a blonde shadow by my side. I don't remember her face from the hours I spent near Bird's closed eyes during his "viewing." I could hardly breathe in that windowless room. What's clearest in my memory are the white polka dots on my navy blue dress, the exact size of wafery paper circles falling from a three-hole punch.

The first winter storm arrived that Saturday, just as the weatherman had predicted. At Bird's burial, soft flakes blew slanted from the sky. My mother, frail in her black Chanel suit, shuddered. "That thin shirt isn't enough with just a suit jacket. He's going to be so cold." They lowered him deep into a shiny clay hole. A friend of Bird's from college, Tom, was the final person praying at Bird's grave as my parents and I entered the stifling heat of the limo. Snowflakes swirled into the spaces in my mother's black veil.

I received a letter from my brother that afternoon, mailed a few days before he was supposed to come home.

Dear Hill:

Greetings from the north country, it's three in the afternoon. I just got out of the physiology of exercise lab, and I have no more classes today so I thought this would be a good time to get this in the mail. I've made a lot of new friends and I am pretty sure I am going to join a fraternity. I really miss you. See you in a few days!

Love you, Bird

My father and I trekked to Orono to gather Bird's things from his dormitory. Tom was the only boy brave enough to greet my father and me. He shivered in the fluorescent light of the hallway, the same hallway where less than a week before EMTs had carried Birdy out on a stretcher.

"I just don't know how it happened." Tom steadied himself on the cinderblock wall as if he were dizzy. He had very dark curly hair and a smooth, tanned complexion. "I'm sorry. I really am sorry. We were just trying to have fun."

The other boys would not come out to meet us. Bird died trying to become their "brother." But he must not have succeeded, because the boys who had come freshly aftershaved to the wake now closed their doors, breathing on the other side, listening, waiting for us to be done. Dr. Higgins, the president of the university, led us through the corridor. He reminded me of Ichabod Crane—a big Adam's apple in a long drooping neck.

Dr. Higgins unlocked Bird's door. My father carried in a stack of cardboard boxes and we tucked Bird's deodorant and toothpaste into his toiletry bag as if we were packing him for a vacation. Those objects seemed beautiful to me. Four bars of Ivory soap, still tightly wrapped.

Summers, Bird and I smelled as sweet as big-headed babies. Our lake cabin had no shower, no bath, so we lathered ourselves up with Ivory soap, standing ankle deep in the lake in our swimsuits. We shampooed with liquid Prell, green liquid so thick a pearl would sink slowly through it.

I plucked a photo off the mirror: he and my dad and me flexing our muscles on the rocks of Step Falls. In the back of Bird's closet I dug out his cleats. Dried patches of turf slipped off the spikes. I carefully put the wafers of grass into a box— we would bring home every piece of him. Notebooks barely written in, packets of oyster crackers. Dr. Higgins's hands trembled as he piled up Bird's textbooks. "I know this must be hell for you. I want you to know that the entire Greek system on this campus will be seriously investigated."

My father bit his lip and looked down.

It was a slow procession as we carried out the boxes to my dad's pickup.

I had to pee and whispered to my dad, "Where is there a bathroom I can use?"

Dr. Higgins called out, "Tom, can you take her to the girls' dorm next door?"

That dorm was pulsating with songs overlapping from several stereos. The doors were all open. Two girls wearing fluffy pink slippers trotted down the hallway.

"Hey, Jenny, this is Brad Birdsong's little sister," Tom said shyly. "She's going to use the ladies' room."

"Sure thing," Jenny said.

I figured all the dorms were replicas of one another. Bathrooms with two shower stalls on the right, four sinks, three toilet stalls. How could so many boys have fit into a space this crammed? The yellow tiles shone in the bright fluorescent light.

It was a relief to pee. I sighed as I settled myself onto the toilet and then I saw my underpants: a maroon oval. I stared at it, shocked that I had finally gotten my first period. I flushed, washed my hands, and looked deeply into my reflection in the mirror. I looked tired, and I noticed a juicy-looking whitehead on my nose that I hadn't seen before.

The door opened a crack. Jenny poked her head in. "You okay?"

"I need a pad," I whispered.

"Oh! Wait here."

She came back and handed me a pad. I turned it around, inspecting it. She asked, "You haven't ever used one before?"

"Not really."

"Hold on." She returned to her room, came back with two tiny safety pins. "When you go home have your mom buy you a belt. But use these for now." She paused. "Listen, I just want to tell you. I am so sorry about your brother. We had U.S. history together. He was real sweet."

"Thanks."

She turned and adjusted her short hair in the mirror, smoothing it back behind her ears. She studied my reflection. "Take care of yourself, okay? It's gonna be hard."

My cramps began as Tom escorted me back to Bird's dorm, where my father had carefully pulled off the decorations taped to the door. He grinned at the article that Bird had taped there. "Cow-chip bingo," he said.

I had to smile, too. "He actually won one hundred dollars last summer. The cow walked mooing all over the bingo board and then pooped right on Bird's number."

My father yanked the sheets off the bed, rolled them into a ball, and laid them on top of the laundry bag. We were done packing. My father and Dr. Higgins shook hands near our pickup. Dr. Higgins said, "A *full* investigation into this." Groups of students stood at a distance, watching us. I could not see their faces clearly; they might have been at the funeral. My father sat staring into the steering wheel, like he had forgotten something and couldn't remember what it was. Then he said, "Wait here. I'll be right back."

I knew he had gone into the bathroom to see the tiles where Bird had died. I pressed my hands into the soft spot below my belly button, trying to warm away the pain. Hanging from a window of the lounge in Bird's building was a spray-painted bed sheet, dated the day Bird had died.

DK HAPPY HOUR / NOVEMBER 24 /
LAST PARTY BEFORE VACATION

My father returned and tried to muffle his sobs with his hands. His body shook. I patted the top of his bald head, where a few strands of hair floated. He inhaled deeply and said, "Okay," then circled out the driveway.

With Bird's boxes rattling in the back, we drove through the dark, arriving home at midnight. My mother pulled an all-nighter unpacking. She placed her son's deodorant on top of his dresser, as if he still had underarms.

Many nights after visiting the cemetery I listened to the sound of Bird's voice on a tape I had made the last New Year's Day we were together: 1976. I had slipped quietly into a corner of the cellar so no one could hear me singing with the radio turned low to WOXO. Like a cricket along a shadowy trail, I suddenly ceased my music when I heard the door squeak open.

"Hill? You down here?" Bird called on the tape. I remembered how his high-top sneakers appeared as he peeked sideways under the stairwell, the Red Sox baseball cap clamped on his head. Always that cap on his head, turned backward, covering his baby-fine, straight hair. He spied me huddled under the Ping-Pong table. "What are you doing?"

"Nothing."

"Nothing? You are too." He gleefully vaulted over the stairs and snatched the tape recorder from my hands, pressing the REWIND button. He held the tape recorder aloft like a basketball and I leaped up, a losing opponent. He pressed PLAY and my voice warbled, "You fill up my senses like a night in the forest." I was alarmed at how off-pitch I sounded, because when I was recording I thought I sang near perfect.

He laughed that deep-pitched giggle. "John Denver?"

"So what. Shell likes him, too."

He clicked the RECORD button and the brown circles of the tape began spinning. "Ladies and gentlemen!" He spoke with his lips close to the mic. "Here we have the lovely Miss Hillary singing—and I use the term loosely—her top-10 hit!"

Then the hollow sound of a Ping-Pong ball bouncing faster and faster.

"Birdy, stop!" I whined.

My mother yelled down, "Brad, did you find your skates?"

"No, Mother."

Our dad raced down the steps. For an overweight, barrel-chested man he was surprisingly light on his feet. Bird pretended to jump into our dad's arms. "Catch me, Pop!" Bird, at seventeen, still curled up in Dad's lap sometimes.

Then the tape ran out.

Sometimes we had stayed down there entire Sunday afternoons, competing in one of the silly contests Bird was always making up. Blowing Ping-Pong balls across the table into empty Sugar Smacks boxes. Throwing my mother's old sling backs through the broken basketball hoop and racking up points if the heel got caught on the rim. Bird loved games, any games, official sports and sudden, ridiculous contests that he would spice up with bets.

Fast forward to New Year's Day, 1977. Bird dead a month. I played this tape until Valentine's Day. I wore it out. Had Bird been alive, he would have laughed at how demonic the slowing recording made him sound. One day the little wheels churned, and a long, shiny brown strand knotted up. The first day of spring came, and I couldn't hear him calling to me anymore.

2

The day I met Miles was what we called a scorcher. The giant thermostat that spun outside Norway Savings Bank read ninety-two degrees by eleven in the morning. Cicadas vibrated high up in the trees. Shell had greased herself up with so much coconut oil that I had to squint to look at her, her bronze shins reflecting like mirrors in the sun. We dozed on my dock wearing each other's bikinis. Suddenly, at the end of the lake down near Crocket Ridge, a sleek, furiously fast blue boat rocketed toward us. "Holy shit," Shell exclaimed. "Who the hell is that?" We shaded our eyes and followed the plume of white spray shooting out from behind the motor, until the boat disappeared west by the totem pole. "Who needs such a speedy boat on a lake only eight miles long? And that includes the bog," Shell said. But it was sparkly and glamorous, and I ached to ride in it with the throttle opened.

Later that afternoon Shell passed her driving exam and inherited her uncle Zee's old station wagon. Just in time for us to race out to the annual Waterford World's Fair. With booths of homemade rhubarb pies, it resembled a 4-H fair, except for the drunken jerks mooning people and the generators cranking to keep the gears of the Tilt-a-Whirl running nonstop. I

paid one dollar to view the Biggest Pig on the Eastern Sea-
board. I felt horrible, peering into the tiny circular window, the
giant brown pig stuck on its side, feeble, as if in a coma, flies
shining on its tail and filthy face. Shell had warned me not to
look. "Please don't do it, honey, it will just get you all upset."

But my feelings brightened as I heard the microphones
getting turned on, screeching with feedback. Shell and I eagerly
climbed the steps into a big barn. People began pairing off,
dancing as the old farts with the wooly gray beards sweated in
their flannel shirts and sawed away on their fiddles. In his rock-
star black blazer, one boy stood out in the sea of overalls.

"That's Miles, my cousin," my friend Billy shouted in my
ear. "He's up from New York City. You seen that blue boat on
the lake yet?"

"God yes. Is that his?"

"It's his, all right. It's called the *Blue Blazes*."

Miles looked over at us and shrugged at Billy as if he were
asking him, *Why have you dragged me here with these hicks?* He
stared at me and then stalked over and held out his hand. "You
polka? 'Cause I can't."

I fell in love the moment I cupped my hand on his thin
waist just above his hipbone. If not at that moment, then in
the next one when he grinned and put one hand on my back
and wove his fingers through mine.

"Like this," I instructed. "One, two-three and one, two-
three."

We spun laughing into the traffic of dancers like a car
gunning onto a freeway. Our knees banged, but when we
slipped into form we were smooth together. Liquid. Afterward
we talked, alone, in a ditch, a dried-up creek bed at the edge of
the fairgrounds. He made a crown for me from soft thistles he

plucked from the weeds. When he kissed me I thought, *A city slicker with a butterfly tongue.* From that night on everything seemed tinged with blue. Miles was metallic, his eyes the color of scratched chrome, his hair very black with blue highlights, like the wings of a dragonfly.

And, like a dragonfly, he darted out of sight and back to New York the next day, and the lake became bleak with weak little seven-horsepower putt-putt engines on the backs of old rowboats.

I spent my sophomore year sitting on boys' laps in drivers' seats while I steered all over the shoulders of back roads and they pressed the gas and brake pedals, trying to sneak their hands under my shirt. Then we parked. In the dark front seats, I awakened when boys filled my mouth with their breath. Boys' names flowed like a poem. Marcel Colette, Eddie Frechette, Vinnie Chute, Anthony Durgess, Michael Parnell III. The year passed and I began ignoring my curfew, and my parents said nothing as I tiptoed past their door long after midnight. By the time I turned sixteen, Shell and I had stopped wearing bras, our nipples poking in shadowed circles beneath our tee shirts. We set up a little private tanning area in the field behind her house, sunbathing nude inside refrigerator boxes, protected from sight. In May, just as the lake was turning from ice to liquid, we plucked our eyebrows into slivered moons.

Miles sped back into town on the summer solstice. Shell and I were at a party on a roof that overlooked the Weary Club, a tiny house on Main Street where old men played checkers. Billy must have clued him in on where I would be, because Miles left his red Mustang convertible idling and a moment later I felt him tap me on the shoulder. "You polka?" We ran down the stairs and then tore away with the top down.

"You're wild," he said, hours past my curfew. I grew wilder under his gaze, daring him to drive his hot little car up the rutted road to the old quarry on top of Singe Pole. Abandoned years ago, the flat surface of the pond was black and deep. At dawn the water was so tranquil our reflections barely quivered. Miles moved behind me, buried his hands into my hair, and commanded, "Look."

My eyes in the morning light were the color of polished cherry. Miles ran his hand over the sloped contour of my forehead and the auburn V of my widow's peak, across the pale freckles on my cheeks to the small hollows under my cheekbones. He traced the pronounced M of my top lip.

Later, completely undressed, I jumped off the sandstone ledge, shrieking into the black water twenty feet below. It was breathtaking, free falling naked. "I will never ever see a sight as beautiful as that," he said. He kissed me, waited until I dried, dressed me, and then unwrapped a tiny tab of acid, tucking it under my tongue. At first I just felt nauseous as we waited, overlooking the turquoise furrows of the valley, a view that spread open all the way to Mount Washington. The dead scrub pines began to move, kicking their branches like legs. Then the white down of the clouds became the profiles of men and women kissing; the women all had swanlike necks and thick wavy hair piled on their heads like in Victorian valentines.

"Oh my god, Miles what is that?" I shouted, pointing up at the kissers.

Miles cracked up, covering his mouth with his hand. "Hillary, it's the sun. God, you are such a rush."

Suddenly I remembered what the blinding ball was named. I was too stupid to even recognize the goddamn sun.

Since my parents and I stayed in our cottage in the summer, Miles and I used to go make out in our house in town.

Miles opened the yellowed sheet music to "Moon River" on our upright piano in the parlor, and played a few chords.

"Come on," I whispered one night, pulling him up the stairs. "Up this way."

"Why are you whispering?"

"I don't want to disturb the ghost."

"Hillary, I don't really want to go up there. Are you going to make me go into his room?"

The door stood halfway open, as if Bird might have been in there, and we stepped into the room.

"Don't you ever go in here?"

"No, only my mom, to dust." I realized that in four years I had never stepped over Bird's threshold. Even our cat, Lucky, never curled up on his bed to sleep.

Our faces were reflected in the rows of trophies glittering on his dresser. Little gilded football players getting ready to pass, baseball players crouching for a pitch.

"Your brother was some athlete, huh?"

"In this town he was. He went away to college and never came back."

Miles blurted, "I can't believe he died of a heart attack. You usually think of that happening to some old geezer."

"Old geezers don't try to get into fraternities. I'm not sure of everything that happened that night. My mom won't talk about it. I know he drank something and that he was forced to do something." I ran my finger over a brass championship plaque. All the words just got mixed up in my head. It was like a theme song playing over and over. Freak accident young Bird-man, accident freak young Bird-man.

Miles laced his hands in mine and began moving me in no particular dance, just motion. He hummed. Then he pressed his hands on my back. It felt delicious to be touched softly on my spine. I began to whisper, "When I saw Birdy I knew he was dead. There was none of that 'oh but he looks so good.' He was gone."

Miles pulled away, cupped my face. His tenderness made me shy, and I looked away. My brother's Brut cologne was still three-quarters full on his bureau.

"Screw this," I said. "Let's get the hell out of here." I knelt down in the plush of the carpet and erased the footprints of my sandals.

We would drive the *Blue Blazes* out into the middle of the lake, and then we'd cut the engine and watch the shooting stars while kissing with our eyes wide open. There was no rippling around us, just the occasional splash of a leaping bass or the sound of a lone car carried over the water, at the end of Crocket Ridge.

"Come with me to New York!" Miles demanded as we skinny-dipped, treading water as one.

"I've already been to the Twin Cities."

"Twin Cities?"

"Yeah, Lewiston-Auburn," I drawled in a deliberately ex-aggerated Maine accent. "The bustling metropolis."

And just for a joke, we drove one afternoon through Lewiston-Auburn, and I sneered at the smokestacks filling the sky with white discharge. "That's so ugly."

"In a way, it's not, though," Miles said. "If you didn't know it was pollution, it would be beautiful." We watched the smoke, thick yet feathery, light, and free, filling the horizon with long, tapered clouds.

We were in a tacky bungalow at Old Orchard Beach. The scent of fried dough blew in as if it were the true smell of the ocean. You had to stand with your feet in the water to breathe the water's salt. Otherwise you inhaled sizzling oil with every gust of wind. There were hairy potbellies slung over Speedos everywhere you looked. THE ALL-AMERICAN MEAL! signs read along the pier, A HOT DOG AND A COKE FOR $1!

"Check that guy out." Miles pointed with his chin. "You think when he was little he was like, 'oh, when I grow up, I want to be a psycho at Old Orchard'?"

I turned toward a man who stood near us in the line for a slice of pepperoni pizza. In the eighty-degree heat, he was tucked into a trench coat. He had a stubbly face the color of a cornfield, with thick, round stalks of hair. He flicked the bow on his fiddle to the theme from *Star Wars*.

It was like a sci-fi movie, so many humans in the cramped boxes of the cabins. Sitcoms blaring—Archie and Meathead bickering—sirens, children tantruming and parents yelling with clenched teeth, sloshed women falling off their sling-back sandals. The sounds of everyone outside comforted me like rain as I lay in the bungalow, and I was happy. I was in a tawdry town with misfits, all of us gorging on fried food in red-and-white paper baskets. And I was with a fine-looking boy who was in love with me. His skin was pale white and cool to the touch. On a saggy bed covered with a nubbly bedspread, I pulled my bikini bottom to the side and he cradled me, pushed into me, and those warm moments sang very bare and sweet.

Afterward, we lay shocked that we had actually finally done it, pulse points fluttering in our necks. The town had stilled, and once again began to move. Outside the window there was a hiss like an hourglass: the landlord pouring sand out of his shoes.

Miles was with all of us on Billy's party barge, a flat, open boat like a floating porch with a motor on the back. Shell was already testy, realizing her hair was full of snarls. Sloppy Joe wore a big, puffy life vest as a joke. He was bitching about everything. The warm beer. The mosquitoes. Then he was pissed when we reminded him that since he lived in a swamp what could be so bad about a refreshing night-water breeze? He had refused to bring his mandolin even though we begged him. Miles had white powder in his nose and wouldn't stop fluttering his hands on the metal picnic table.

Shell and I settled in cross-legged in the front of the barge. "What was it like?" she murmured. "Did it hurt?" But Miles, ever restless, joined us. When Billy suddenly rushed off his stool from behind the steering wheel to fake-punch Miles, the weight of the four of us sank the front of the boat. We hooted, shocked from getting our bottoms drenched. Billy quickly stepped back, and the boat righted itself, perfectly parallel to the water. The indoor-outdoor carpet was soaked; the empty beer cans floated like buoys.

But Sloppy panicked, shrieking like a girl, "Take me back to shore. Now!"

"What a pussy." Miles and Billy mocked him.

"You're an asshole, Billy." Sloppy marched off the boat with his six-pack. We got a whiff of the acrid burn of his sweat. "You're all a bunch of assholes."

I was the only one who knew why Sloppy was acting like an idiot: He was petrified of drowning. Even Shell didn't know that Sloppy couldn't swim.

We went to check on him the next day. Sloppy's trailer was right at the tip of the hairpin turn along Harrison Road on the back way to the lake. As we neared his trailer, I heard the old-world sounds of his mandolin. I was always surprised that such big, hairy hands could get such a lovely sound out of the instrument. He stopped playing when he saw I was with Miles. Miles apologized as Sloppy spread his toes, showing us the blisters he got between his toes from walking all the way home in his flip-flops.

"Okay, so I was a wuss," Sloppy said reluctantly. "You guys didn't have to be such pricks about it. That's why I prefer winter when the lake is frozen."

Miles and I slapped at the mosquitoes biting our ankles. Sloppy was immune. He must have built up some sort of swamp antibody, because no bugs hovered around him. "But think about it, Slop," I said. "Snowmobilers race across when the edges are getting mushy in early April. We've had people fall right through the ice. Remember those people from Mechanic Falls a few years back? They almost died of hypothermia. And what about ice fishing? You could slip through the hole."

"I wear a life vest."

"You're kidding. Under your parka?"

"Yeah."

Miles smirked. "And you wonder why people give you shit?"

"Look," Sloppy said. "Everyone is afraid of something. I just admit it. Come on, Miles, what are you afraid of?"

"Well, there is something," Miles admitted reluctantly.

"What? C'mon." I was curious.

"Elevators. I'm afraid of the cables breaking."

Sloppy guffawed.

"Hey, in New York City you're in elevators all the time. I go on them like five, six times a day just going in and out of my apartment. Those cables could snap. It's happened, you know."

"I've never even been on an elevator," Sloppy realized.

"What about you, Hill?" Miles asked.

I remembered how one autumn Shell's uncle made us go every Tuesday to Flanner's stables. How terrified I was. "They look so beautiful from far way, but up close I'm afraid of being trampled or bitten."

"By what?" Sloppy wondered.

"Horses."

"You're a crazy wench to go there," Sloppy Joe warned me the afternoon I told him of my plan to find Miles. He was the only one besides Shell who knew I was pregnant. I knew he could keep a secret. He had once been busted for ten pounds of reefer. When he had applied for a job at Ames and they had given him a polygraph test, Sloppy lied through his fingertips. The store detective had asked him, "Have you ever been arrested on drug possession?" Sloppy answered no, and he passed.

"I plan never to leave Maine," he boasted. "And I will never ever set foot in New York City. I wouldn't go if I were you. You could get shot." We sat at his kitchen table as Sloppy's iguana, Mr. Wizard, was hanging upside down from the wire mesh top of a giant glass aquarium, scratching on the wire to get out. Mr. Wizard's toenails produced an atonal noise like the broken zither Shell and I played in Mrs. Unger's fourth grade class at recess. That iguana was a mean SOB. He stared at us nastily from the green creases of his face.

"Seems to me I have more of a chance of getting blown away here. Marcel was stomping around the woods with his rifle just the other day. He wants to beat his record from last year."

"But it's not bobcat season yet."

"Exactly my point."

We watched as Mr. Wizard's toenails slipped from the wire. He fell through the air on his head, then righted himself and pushed himself up with his long tail back onto his drift-wood perch. I couldn't stop wondering why Miles hadn't written, and I took a certain delight in watching Mr. Wizard plummet.

"Do me a favor when you get to New York?" Sloppy urged.

"What?"

"Don't get inside any elevators."

The enclosed air on the Peter Pan bus smelled of bologna sandwiches. As we moved down through New England and then into Connecticut, my pulse quickened at the thought of seeing Miles. The landscape was turning man-made. Steel girders and concrete walls were spray painted with messages in an unfamiliar alphabet I didn't understand. Vowels with snow-capped tops, consonants burning, names on fire.

We headed into New York. The trees became more stunted as we got closer to the city. The ride took seven hours. As I stepped off the bus at the Port Authority terminal, the first whiff I got was of dried pee on concrete mixed with the driver's aftershave as he offered his hand to me. My stomach lurched at the lack of fresh air. I swallowed hard and closed my eyes, fighting a sudden flood of nausea. I simply stayed in the mass of people and then we all rose up on an escalator. The nausea finally passed as a shaft of sunlight like a gang-plank poured in a straight line through the windows.

The homeless people limped by in tattered strips of cloth-ing. I slipped dimes into their cups; when I looked into the eyes of one old woman, they were bright blue but creased and tired and I thought of the Man in White. His crispness wouldn't last long in Manhattan. He would be dingy and dis-graced in no time.

The broken people disappeared as I neared Miles's ad-dress. The shops of Fifth Avenue were one long reflection of tinted pale copper. The women reminded me of my mother when Bird was alive. They were dressed in camel-hair coats and tortoiseshell sunglasses and strode with a confident, al-most arrogant bounce in the cold bright air. I felt dizzy won-dering if I might bump into Miles. So this was where he was from: taxis honking; older women with cotton-candy hair spun into airy helmets; tiny, brittle dogs on rhinestone leashes. Miles's building was guarded by a black doorman with golden fringe dangling from his shoulder pads. I panicked. What if Miles doesn't love me anymore? Why had he stopped writing?

I shouldn't have come, I thought. *I'm an idiot, a total idiot, standing here.*

"Can I help you?" the doorman asked.

"No. Thanks."

I spotted a phone booth and walked toward it. I dialed. After letting it ring a while, I spotted Miles, arm-in-arm with a girl. I hung up the phone and watched as he rubbed his finger lightly under her chin, like he used to do to me before he kissed me. He kissed her. They pulled apart as the doorman hooted and patted Miles on the back. Then Miles stepped inside the revolving door.

The girl didn't even feel me staring as she floated by in soft black leather, as if under a spell. Her big green eyes shone. She had very long, skinny legs and walked like a ballerina, with her feet pointing out at the ankles. Her head of long, dark curls disappeared around a corner.

I dialed the number again.

"Hello."

"Miles. It's Hillary."

"Hillary? *Whoa.* I can't believe it's you. How are ya?"

"Oh, just terrific." Dried leaves and torn Styrofoam scratched over the sidewalk, whirlpooling around my feet.

"I'm sorry I haven't written in a month. Don't be pissed, okay?"

"Why would I be pissed?"

"I don't know. You sound like you are."

"You have a new girlfriend."

"Sort of."

"Sort of," I repeated mechanically.

"I couldn't help it, Hillary. She says she's in love with me, and she's beautiful—"

"You said *I* was beautiful." The desperation in my voice embarrassed me. "You said you loved me."

"I think I do love you. I never met a girl like you. Talking to you now, I feel confused, like what am I doing with Tina?"

"I'm pregnant."

There was a long pause. "Oh my god. What a rush." He practically giggled.

"A rush?"

"I just can't believe I have, you know, the capability to be a father, that's all."

"You don't even know how to be a boyfriend."

I heard the swish of his thumb on the flint of a cigarette lighter. He must have smoked half a cigarette before speaking again. "So you know what you have to do, right?"

"Me? So there's no 'us'? It's up to me?"

"What do you want me to say? I mean, it's a mistake. I'm assuming you're going to get an abortion."

"I don't know what I'm going to do."

"What do you mean?"

"I heard the heartbeat, Miles."

He was quiet again, but breathing hard. A cabinet squeaked open in the background, then whined shut. "Hillary, I'm really sorry. Where are you anyway? I assume no one can hear you talking about this."

"I'm calling from the phone booth on Main Street," I lied.

"Hillary, I did care about you—I still do. We had some good times. But this is really messed up. You need to get the abortion. I'll send you the money you need."

"I don't want money."

"How much is an abortion up there? Two, three hundred?"

"I don't want your money."

"Okay, then, I'll go with you to a clinic. I'll come up."

"You do that," I answered coldly. "We could all go to-gether. You. Me. Tina."

I ended up in the Bowery. I had heard of the Bowery in some old Frank Sinatra song my dad played. The garbage cans, like scabs, leaked a metallic dried-blood odor, and people like full garbage bags were passed out in piles along the buildings. Frightened, I scurried to the middle of the deserted street, swiveling my head around, knowing in that moment who I was: a lost girl who had wandered too far and had ended up in a dangerous place.

I collapsed on the steps of a bead boutique. I must have been crumpled in the orange neon light for ten minutes, face pressed against my thighs, hot tears soaking my jeans, when I felt a tap on my shoulder. "Hey, I'm Patricia. Take this." A bony claw reached under my armpit and placed a clean, flat tissue over my fists.

I lifted my head up to find a tiny, skeletal woman with a giant Band-Aid covering half her face down to her throat and around to her neck. I never knew they made Band-Aids so big. The situation suddenly struck me as absurdly funny. I balled up the tissue over my lips and laughed. "I am so pathetic."

"Who isn't?" The woman shrugged. "Why so sad? No, wait, don't tell me. A fella." Her voice gurgled as if she held no breath inside her raspy lungs. With spindly legs in tiny tights, she reminded me of the dark green drawings of Rumpelstilt-skin in a picture book I had as a child, except that her eyes were slits, not bulgy. "I make things out of glass," she spoke out of the side of her mouth. Her Band-Aid puckered. "Broken glass is easy to come by. Especially Heineken bottles. I used to paint in oils, but I can't afford them." She coughed and cackled, pointing to her neck. "Throat cancer."

We watched an old drunk snap grungy boxers on his head, flattening the tattered legs so the underwear draped sideways, like he was Lawrence of Arabia. He flirted with his plaid reflection in the window of a parked taxicab and flicked his antennaelike eyebrows.

"See that?" Patricia asked. "That's a welfare motel. Look at those poor little babies."

Through a third-story window, children jumped on a bed. One wore a diaper; the older ones were naked. Two women shared a cigarette. A quart of milk balanced on the windowsill outside. "That's their refrigerator. But it's not cold enough out. I'm sure the milk goes sour." Patricia shook her head and looked right at me. She pursed her lips to the side, wrinkling her Band-Aid. She said in her dry-sounding voice, very sadly, "It's an imperfect world." The children somersaulted.

She unwrapped a man's handkerchief. "I want you to have these. Sea glass. Broken pieces washed smooth by waves."

"Thank you." I slipped the cool glass stones in my jeans pocket. They clicked against my loose change as I strode back to the Port Authority, following Patricia's directions.

As I headed home on the bus, the billowing smokestacks brightened the night skies of Bridgeport with thick smoke, blowing up slowly, in snaky figure eights.

No doubt about it: It was ugly.

Shell, of course, wanted to strangle Tina. "Rich city bitch," Shell hissed as I watched her during gymnastics practice. Steadying herself on the lower bar, she leaped up, feet spread-eagled, and whipped around on the uneven parallel bars, her hair spinning like the whorls of a seashell. I was lamely spotting her a few days after I returned from my New York trip. Shell had the opposite of a fear of heights: She craved them, swirling and uninhibited, endlessly airborne. She dismounted and rubbed her sore palms together. "So what's the deal? Miles just breezes into town," she lowered her voice, "knocks you up, and never returns? I still don't know why you didn't take his money." She moved to the mat and pulled her bare foot up behind her, stretching herself into a bow.

The day before I had received a letter from Miles. "Please take good care of yourself," he had written and he had included a money order for five hundred dollars. I had taken a black marker, written "What a rush!" on it, and mailed it back to him.

"I want nothing to do with him."

"You've thought this through?" she asked.

"Screw you."

Shell draped her arm around my neck. "Please, honey. I'm on your side, remember? I was only suggesting the money might help. You're sticking to your guns and I'm proud of you."

With her face so close to mine, I could see her chicken pox scars, small nicks like the shadows of raindrops. When she was three, Shell and her parents had all gotten chicken pox. It was a freak thing. Both her mother and father had died of it at St. Stephen's Memorial Hospital. Her uncle Zee had gotten custody of her, and he was too distraught to remind her not to scratch the blisters on her face. She rarely talked about the fact that she was an orphan.

"You think I'm being too intense," I said.

"Of course you're being intense. It's one of the things I love most about you." Shell bent over to touch her toes and then lifted her head. "Hill, just remember, you don't have much time to decide. You need to think about it now if you're going to call the lady at the clinic and schedule an appointment."

The gym was empty. I still whispered. "I think you just want me to party and have fun."

She dropped into a perfect split and looked up at me. "I do. I'm having a hard time with this."

"Tell me what you're really thinking."

"I can't. It will piss you off."

"Tell me!"

Like an open pair of scissors, she slowly closed, slid to a standing position, and sighed. "If only you had been on the pill we wouldn't be talking about this—"

"Oh, spoken like the niece of a pharmacist. Very good."

"—I'd be measuring your bust to sew our gowns for the Halloween Ball."

I said sarcastically, "Maybe I could go as a bride."

Shell smiled softly at me. In kindergarten, we insisted on dressing alike, buying cheap boxed Halloween costumes in the basement of Newberry's. Dressed in shiny, fire-retardant fabric, we marched, two brides holding hands, parading with our school down Main Street. I remember how chapped my hands were, and Shell gushing excitedly, "Oh, so that's how freckles feel!"

Shell curled herself into crunches. "I used to think . . . I would have made a . . . great bride for Bird."

"I know."

"I daydreamed about marrying him." She exhaled loudly and flopped back on the mat, little dime-sized circles of sweat on her leotard underneath her arms. I settled in next to her, cross-legged.

"If I keep this baby, will you help me?"

"I'll do what you need me to." She rolled over on her stomach, rubbing a bit of chalk out of her eye. Suddenly I recalled a game she and I used to play in kindergarten.

"Do you remember those baby lion cubs?"

"Oh lord. We'd hide behind your couch and take turns squeezing the stuffed animals down our pants. Your mother burst a gasket when she found us back there doing that."

Giving birth out of our waistbands.

Shell had given me a deadline: I was to tell my parents by New Year's. I walked home from sledding as the tower clock gonged midnight. Cars on Main Street honked gaily, like limos after a wedding. The weeks had passed—Halloween, then Thanksgiving, and I had never called the clinic back. I felt a strange buzzing, a tickle in my belly, as I shivered behind the old maple tree in our front yard, waiting for Uncle Billy and Aunt Iris to finally leave my parents' New Year's Eve party. Finally at one in the morning, my hand nervously squeezing the sea glass in my pocket, I greeted my mother in the kitchen. She was scrubbing the chicken fat out of a roasting pan, listening to the swelling orchestra of my father's Dean Martin record: "When the moon hits your eye like a big pizza pie, that's *amore*."

"Happy 1981," she said, not turning to me.

I followed the wings of her shoulder blades furrowing, then flattening, as she rinsed the remaining dishes.

"I have something to tell you."

She froze, sponge in midair. Then she squeezed the dishwater out and placed it gently next to the faucet. "I know. I thought so."

I lunged at her apron. "You knew and you didn't say anything?"

She held up her arms to shield herself. But I didn't rip her frills off. Instead, I twisted around and banged my fists on the kitchen table. I wanted to hurt myself. "Jesus Christ!" I wailed.

My father turned the stereo down. From the silence of the parlor he called out, "Janée? What's going on in there?" His broad shoulders filled the doorway.

"Have you noticed," my mother demanded, her voice going cold and low, "that your daughter has been wearing your button-downs?"

He scanned to the white, billowy tails of my shirt. "Yeah. It's a teenage fad, I guess." Suddenly realizing why I was hiding myself, he collapsed on a chair and placed the heels of his palms against his forehead, eyes shut.

My mother folded and unfolded a dish towel. "I assume it's Miles's."

I refused to answer. My father rubbed his colorless wisps of hair. His mouth was pressed into a frown. He looked out the window into the blackness. "Is it that boy Miles?"

After a long pause I admitted, "Yeah."

"Does he know?" my mother asked.

"He knows and doesn't care."

"So you've spoken with him?"

"Yep. I did. I saw him."

"He was back up here?"

"No. I went to New York."

"New York City?"

"I took the bus right before Halloween."

"You lied to me about where you were."

I crossed my arms over my newly big breasts. "You never asked. As usual."

"Does Shell know?'

"Of course she does."

My mother turned to my father. "So Shell's been lying to us, too. She's known and hasn't told us." My mother spun her wedding ring around on her pudgy finger. "In our day, a boy did the honorable thing and married the girl. Isn't that right, Ray?"

My father moved the salt and pepper shakers on the red-and-white squares of the tablecloth.

"Ray?"

"Nineteen fifty-nine was a long time ago," he murmured.

"Or else girls gave the baby up," my mother continued.

I looked over at Bird's chin-up bar, still in the doorway. I remembered the afternoon when he put it up. He didn't have the right amount of tension, and I had run up to it, swung, and fell with the silver bar clutched in my hands. "Or kept them," I hissed.

She didn't hear me. "It's clear what needs to be done. You have to consider the option of giving the baby to a nice couple who could really provide for the child."

"I don't get it. You knew and you never said anything to me."

"I have my own problems, Hillary. Not everything is about you."

"About me?" I shrieked. "Nothing is about me. Are you kidding me? I've been losing my mind these past months and you never even tried to help. So fuck you."

"Don't you dare talk to me that way. I am your mother."

"No. No, you're not. You're not really my mother. You're still just *Bird's* mother."

In the darkness of my room I wept into my nightgown sleeves as my mother raged on and on at my father through the night. Through the wall I heard the boards under the braided rug creaking as she walked back and forth. "Wearing your shirts. Don't you think I was mortified when I realized? I kept thinking, maybe it's not true, maybe this isn't happening. She waits until New Year's Eve? Until she's too far along? There are clinics. I could have taken her far away from here; no one would have known. It would have been kept quiet. Now, everyone will talk. There's no hiding it anymore. She's showing."

I heard a low mumble from my father.

"I'm sorry, Ray. I know. It's harsh. But the whole town is going to think our daughter is a whore. She's making our family look like trash."

The next morning my father asked me to go with him to check our cottage for possible New Year's Eve break-ins. My father and I fit our boot treads into the ribbons of snow compacted by snowmobiles along the unplowed camp road. He wiped his nose on the back of his glove as we checked around the woodpile: no footprints in the snow. We shimmied the doors and windows and then followed the white cones of our breath into the cabin. Except for a few mouse turds on the counter, everything was exactly as we had left it when we closed up. I flopped down on my father's red La-Z-Boy chair and stared at the dark pine knotholes swirling like birthmarks on the walls.

"You okay?" he asked.

"Dad, what the hell am I going to do?" I searched for a clue in his face.

He took a deep breath as if he were pulling the question into himself. His summer golf tan had long faded from his face, exposing the wispy fuchsia threads of the capillaries in his cheeks. Dry flakes of skin fluttered in his eyebrows. He nodded in the direction of the door and went outside.

The ruts of the road were too narrow for us to walk side by side. It was sunset, and the woods had grown quieter as the few birds still around quit flying. The freezing air was clear and sweet. A small stream snaked nearby, water twitching. I yearned for the surprise of one of his "I love you"s that were like the sudden shock of a cold spring electrifying your legs when you swam in the dark water of the lake. He would tell me this sometimes, with his eyes right on me, willing himself not to be swamped by his shyness. He delighted in finding those words. He was silent so much of the time, his feelings quietly eating away at him, burning hot ulcers into his insides.

We reached the pickup parked by the paved apron near Crocket Ridge. My dad unlocked my side, looking right into me. Was he about to tell me that he would take care of us? Me and this baby?

He looked down at his boots, ashamed. "I don't think I could handle raising another baby at this point. I'm sorry. I just don't have it in me."

As we drove home I kept my face turned from his as I stared at the birch trees and pines flickering by. Sure, the pines are green all year, like summer. But most trees stand gray and bare in a winter that goes on and on. The wind chill had dipped below zero, and it was hours till supper.

———

My mother made phone calls, whispering as she tried to muffle her voice in the upstairs linen closet, and then checked in with Aunt Iris to report. I made calls, too, feeding dimes into the pay phone on Main Street, reading the numbers I had circled in the *Advertiser-Democrat.* The Woodman's albino porcupine, stuffed to look like it was begging for a treat, lurked in the window, glass eyes watching me dial the Shop and Save—*Cashier's pay is minimum wage, $3.35 an hour*— and Moosewood Realty—*Yes, it's a one-bedroom, three hundred a month, no heat*—and Lollipop Daycare—*Full-time care for infants? Ninety-five a week.*

One sleety afternoon I came home and heard my mother upstairs talking at regular volume, finishing a conversation with Aunt Iris. "Of course, yes, I'll call immediately." The rotary dial spun seven times, and I softly picked up the downstairs phone to listen in.

"SMFS, this is Kate, how may I help you?" a woman answered.

"Yes, I have some questions about adoption."

"Relinquishing or are you looking to adopt?"

"My daughter is pregnant."

"How far along is the mother?"

Mother? Oh my god, I'm the mother.

"She's due late April, I believe."

"The baby's father—is he agreeing to an adoption plan or do you think he will want custody of the child?"

I cut in. "See, the thing is, I'm not really sure I want to . . . I think I might want to . . . keep it. I don't know."

"Hillary," my mother snapped. "Please hang up."

Kate said, "She's how old?"

We both answered, "Sixteen."

As Kate tried to figure out what to do with us, she said, "Perhaps I could speak confidentially to the young woman?" My mother slammed down the phone, then banged her bedroom door shut.

Kate continued. "What about your parents?"

"They won't help me with it."

"Are you sure? You discussed it with them?"

"Look." I got bitchy. "My dad isn't the 'discussion' type. They don't want a baby around, okay?"

There was a long silence between us. Then she spoke kindly, "Are there any other questions you have for us today?"

"My best friend told me something. I was wondering if it's true. Would I be able to choose my baby's parents?"

"Absolutely. At Southern Maine Family Services, we support that decision."

There was another question I struggled to find the words for. "Is there a moment . . . a final moment, a moment when someone actually gives her baby up? Does that happen?"

The woman on the other end took a deep breath, then let it out. She answered gently, "It happens all the time."

3

My mother's whispers led to my being sent away.

My father carried my bags out to the car. "It's only for a few months," my father assured me, blinking nonstop. "After you come back, we'll start over. Start fresh." He hugged me good-bye.

"Yeah." I pulled away. "We can act like nothing ever happened. It works real well for us."

My mother sighed and stretched her leather gloves over her scaly winter hands.

I flipped down the mirror on the visor and spoke to my reflection, unused to my new round face. "We don't say 'give up' anymore." I was mocking the pamphlet that my mother had received. "We say 'relinquish,' and it's not shameful anymore, either. Why, it's an act of 'empowerment.'"

"They'll take very good care of you at La Rosaria," my mother insisted. "Your Aunt Iris assured me that these sisters are kind."

Just after suppertime, under a moon three-quarters full, we careened into a long driveway. Ice crystals whipped around the bumpy meadow. Dark bones of driftwood poked out of a snowbank. Flooded in the glow of a white spotlight, a Mary statue stood with her stone thumbs pressed into a prayer, all of her fingers chipped off.

The windowpanes of the main house glowed with a golden light, and I suddenly longed for a mother, some long-ago mother shading me, whose thighs I could hug, throwing her off balance with my love. Instead, my mother walked with her back to me as I toddled gingerly on the black ice, alone with my suitcase.

A circle of women greeted us in the vestibule. A gray-haired woman with small, round glasses said, "Welcome. I'm Sister Joan. This is Sister Catherine and Sister Marguerite; they supervise the girls' home."

My mother compensated for her embarrassment by speaking in a voice too loud. "Hillary's father and I will be back in two weeks for a visit. Please don't hesitate to call if she needs anything." She touched my cheek with the tips of her fingers, still wearing her gloves. I refused to speak again. She left with a long sigh. I watched, yearning out the wrinkled glass window until her taillights disappeared into the tunnel of pines.

Sister Catherine lifted my suitcase and escorted me to the building closest to the ocean cliffs, clumping my suitcase onto the porch, then welcoming me to "the home." At the top of the stairs we headed left down a long hallway of tiny identical rooms. Mine was at the very end.

"Here we are." Panting slightly, she flung my bag onto a single bed with a metal frame and patted the sweat from her thinning hairline. The square room held a desk, a lamp, and a crucifix hanging in the middle of a bare wall. But instead of an open-armed Jesus in the center of the cross, a painted, jade-colored butterfly hovered with dark blue antenna feeling the cool drafts.

"You must think I'm a real slut."

Sister Catherine shrugged. "Nope. I really don't see it that way. If you want to know, I think you're brave to do what you're doing." She flapped open the down comforter and tucked it around the mattress. "I'll pray for you, that things will seem better in the morning."

"Don't get your hopes up."

She laughed. "You want to come down for dessert? Fudgesicles tonight."

"No."

"Okay. Oh, the bathroom's down the hall."

When I settled under the comforter, the scent of frankincense wafted out from the heavy feathers. Around ten o'clock, I heard doors closing, water running, slippers scuffing past in the hall. As the building quieted and darkened, I could feel the baby rolling over inside me. I wished it could stay inside me forever. My window looked out onto the ocean like a two-way mirror. I sat up all night, watching the waves break and tumble on my face.

In the morning I waited until I sensed complete quiet in the hallway, and then I peed quickly in the bathroom and leaped back into bed. I refused to open the door when someone knocked.

"The bacon is ready. Nice and crispy," Sister Catherine said.

"I'm not hungry."

"How about pancakes?"

"I said I'm not hungry."

———

I stayed rolled up in the comforter all afternoon. Dusk seeped out of the ocean. By dark, my stomach growled when the aroma of stew floated into my room. I slunk downstairs in sweatpants, with a greasy ponytail, not bothering to brush my teeth.

A girl with a big belly carried a bowl of hot rolls, the word "Rodney" doodled in black ink all over her hands. "Hey, you're up. I'm Sunny." She smiled, exposing dull gray braces that made her teeth appear rotten. She resembled a little troll with very round eyes with bags under them, and her nose spread wide on her face. "That's Wanda." She tilted her chin to point at another big-bellied girl. "Grab that loaf of bread, will you? You can sit here."

I slid over on the bench. The kitchen reminded me of my aunt Iris's house: red-and-white-checkered curtains, mason jars full of dried peas.

I gobbled down two helpings of the beef stew, listening to the conversation around me.

"These potatoes are wonderful," Sister Catherine beamed, nibbling off a bit of the brown skin.

Sister Marguerite ripped open a roll and dipped it. "I used the same amount of Worcestershire as I did when I made it for the Feast of the Epiphany."

"Did you fry the onions first?" Sister Catherine peered into her bowl.

A long pause. "Yes."

"How much pepper?" Sister Catherine asked.

Another pause. "Half a teaspoon. This mulligan stew is quite good," Sister Marguerite decided.

As more baby carrots were ladled into my bowl, I wove my hands together and bowed my head. But I wasn't saying a longer *Bless us O Lord* than the one the nuns and girls had already recited—Wanda praying with her middle fingers raised. Oh no. I was trembling with laughter. How the hell did I end up here?

When I finally lifted my head, I could feel my cheeks glowing hot, and my mood had been blown, galloping like a horse weathervane in the opposite direction. I gritted my teeth, straining not to cry. Sunny stuffed her cheeks with stew meat and stared at me. *I know,* her look said. *Boy, don't I know.*

The sisters wore turtlenecks, but never pants. They sported panty hose, thick wool skirts, and practical L. L. Bean boots. A photo tacked up on the refrigerator with magnets showed Sister Catherine and Sister Joan dressed up in habits. The dark blue dresses accentuated Sister Joan's petiteness and Sister Catherine's plumpness. Their headpieces fell to their shoulders like straightened dark-blue hair.

"You used to wear those?" I asked Sister Joan.

"Our order gave up habits over ten years ago. That picture is from the Halloween party last year at the seminary."

"You mean those are costumes?"

"Yes."

Nuns dressing up as nuns for Halloween.

Sister Joan, the old lady, was my favorite. She was always telling us how there was suffering in the world. "And yet," she'd continue, "there is hope, don't you agree?" She commanded so much respect that even Wanda resisted an obnoxious answer. I think it was because when Sister Joan said "hope" her mouth formed a perfect little "o," as if the word itself could be spelled on her face.

Sister Catherine was filled with a light and cheeriness that enraged Wanda. She chased Sister Catherine around like a kid after a firefly, wanting to put Sister in a jar with the smallest of air holes punched in the lid. No matter how rude or cruel Wanda was, Sister Catherine's magic emanated. Sister remained free, beyond Wanda's reach.

Sister Marguerite was the youngest of the nuns, the hippie, the oddball. Wanda said Sister Marguerite became a nun because she was too "god-awful ugly to ever do anything else." I wasn't so sure that was the reason. The truth was she had an eerie connection to Jesus. Strolling the beach alone one afternoon, I followed the sound of a guitar coming from behind a dune. I peeked around the crest of sand and discovered Sister Marguerite strumming away, her eyes closed, thick lenses askew on her long face. She was singing her heart out to God. I was completely embarrassed at finding her like that, so exposed. When she opened her eyes she didn't stop, as if she were under a balcony, madly serenading her lover.

Hungry seagulls wheeled at high tide, finding no clams. They screeched at us, pleading for crusts as Sunny and I pinned cold laundry to the lines set up on the cliff behind the main house. We had chores and rules at La Rosaria: no sleeping on top of your bed just so you didn't have to make it every morning, lights out by ten P.M., no flicking your cigarette butts on the ground.

"So," Sunny asked me, "when are you seeing your boyfriend again?"

"What do you mean?"

She reached up on tiptoes to clip a clothespin around an underwear waistband. "I mean I can teach you how to sneak out at night so the buzzer doesn't sound and wake Sister Catherine."

"You do that?"

"I haven't gotten caught yet."

"Where do you go?"

"I'm waiting for Rodney. We keep getting our plans mixed up. He says to meet him behind that Mary by the entrance, to look for his van. But we get messed up on the times."

"So he comes to see you here?"

"Kind of. I'm still waiting. He—you know—he has to work a lot."

"I don't know why we don't just use the dryer. I don't care if it is a February thaw. It's still so cold that all this shit just freezes."

"So do you know who the father is?" Sunny asked.

"Of course." I licked my chapped lips. They tasted of salt.

"Wanda doesn't. She doesn't have a clue. She won't eat; she doesn't care about the baby at all. And Jill? She had her kid a few weeks before you came. Jill claims she never even had sex. She's calling it an immaculate conception. Pretty amazing, huh? Me, I'm pretty lucky. Because Rodney loves me. And he's going to marry me."

I felt a stab of jealousy that her boyfriend stuck with her. "Then why do you have to be here?"

She shrugged. "I still might give the baby up."

"But how could you still be with him, if you have a kid together, somewhere out there? Won't that be too weird?"

She smiled her silly little troll smile. I envisioned Sunny with lilac hair, stiff and tapered above her head. "Love conquers all."

"No matter what I decide, I'm never going to see the father

of this baby again." I clutched the empty wicker basket against my hip. The springs of the clothespins squeaked as I spread them open over the fabrics, pinching them on the clothesline.

"And you don't think that's weird?" Sunny demanded.

I surveyed the silky bikinis: my purple ones, Sunny's red ones, Wanda's camouflage ones, the nuns' white, high-waisted briefs. The clothesline sagged, dragged by the wind. I remembered when I touched Miles, cupping my hand on the fly of his underwear. I had never been that curious about a boy before, and I was thrilled to find out his bulge was so cozy in warmed cotton.

"Yeah," I decided. "It really is."

Sunny and I peeked through the hanging clothes at a cancer-survivors' retreat group descending the stairs to the beach. Some were lifted from their wheelchairs, cradled by the sisters. There were bald chemo heads and faces hidden by oxygen masks with clear tubes connecting to tiny red tanks. Down to the water's edge they went, shuffling slowly in the damp air. The tide was receding finally.

"You think we could find some sea glass?" I asked Sunny.

"Like those little stones you keep on your dresser? Maybe. Yeah."

We carried our baskets, following a flock of women in head scarves blessing themselves as they walked down the warped boards of the stairs. Thrown off balance by our big bellies, we gripped the weathered banisters. Thick splinters poked into our palms. Sunny and I stood together, plucking them out like gray thorns.

The home whistled: The wind never stopped blowing through the salt-stained storm windows. Wanda whined, "It's driving me mad!" To cover up the whistling she played her tinny little clock radio and lip-synced in her mirror. She ripped open a seam of her faded maternity top and slid the neckband down over her shoulders, exposing her cleavage and shimmying her big boobs to "Funkytown." Wanda's belly was the biggest, and then Sunny's, then mine. The three of us couldn't all fit in one of our tiny built-for-a-monk rooms. Sister Catherine's eyes twinkled when we danced in the hallway. After slipping a pile of fresh towels into the closet, she'd grin and shake her head in wonderment at our movements. "That's joy in the Lord," Sister would announce, her index finger pointing skyward. Wanda mocked her, pointing up to the Lord with her middle fingers.

Wanda loved to do the bump, the early disco dance Shell and I used to do in the darkness of her house's shadowy eaves when her uncle got pie-eyed on sloe gin fizzes. It's a simple dance: Partners bump hips together on the beat. Only Wanda's version involved bellies springing off one another like sumo wrestlers.

"Ow!" Sunny moaned one night. "You're too wild, Wanda. You're going to hurt the babies."

"Big fuckin' deal." Wanda shrugged. She was one of those big-boned girls who didn't know her own strength. She chain-smoked Newports and ate Humpy Dumpty potato chips for breakfast and lunch.

Sunny and I scoffed at the idea of prom as the season approached. Wanda, of course, would never participate in something so all-American. With her combat boots that she called "shit kickers," her faded overalls, her spiky punk haircut—no, she wouldn't be caught dead in a high school gym stapled over with tissue-paper carnations.

"Who cares about a wrist corsage?" I snarled.

"How wimpy," Sunny agreed, blowing her gum into a pink bubble and letting it pop into an empty sac on her cheek. "Lilies on a bracelet. Those poor little idiots worrying about buying matching shoes for their gowns. It's so inconsequential. Save all that effort for the real thing: a *wedding*." She sighed dramatically, accidentally farting. "Whoops!"

"Besides, who would even want to kiss us if they knew we had these belly buttons?"

Sunny slapped my palm in a high five and cackled, "Oh god, I will never let Rodney see mine." She imitated the nasally tone of our prenatal nurse. "It's very normal when you begin the third trimester for your navel to change in size and color."

Sister Catherine called up, "Hillary! Your friend Shell is here to see you!"

I dashed down the hallway. The edges of my thighs, where they connected to my body, were sore. The ligaments are stretching, the nurse had told me. Sunny shouted, "We used to have cute little innies! Now we have these disgusting mocha outies!"

Shell was perched primly on the rocking chair in the living room. We hugged as we always had. She put her arms around me; I kept my arms at my sides with my hands raised so I could squeeze her biceps and say, "Hey, Miss Muscles!" I smelled her shampoo, then pulled the hassock next to her so I could play with the long, cottony waves of her hair. Despite my cynicism with Sunny, seeing Shell made me crave my old life. I wanted it back.

"Has anyone asked you to junior prom?" I asked Shell.

"Nah. It's too early. If I don't get a boyfriend soon, I'll just go with Billy, as friends."

"You should wear a shell-pink dress. And crimp your hair like a mermaid's." A dark look flickered over her face. "What is it?" I asked.

She kept her voice low. "It's just so hard seeing you here. I've never seen you anywhere else but home."

I let go of her hair and crossed my arms. "Well, get used to it. I don't know where I'm going to end up."

"What do you mean?"

"I don't know, I don't know what's going to happen. To me. To my baby."

"I thought you were just going to be here until you had the baby. Then you'd give it up and you'd come *home*."

I looked into the familiar circles of her eyes, brown with lighter tan flecks, and saw that Shell also just wanted things to be the way they used to be. She and I, girls together. *Come home.* She made it sound so simple.

The Mary statue guarding the front lawn of La Rosaria wasn't the only religious symbol missing pieces of itself. Throughout the retreat house and the home there were wax guardian angels with feathers lopped off their wings, porcelain baby Jesuses with intense gazes, thick ankles, and no feet. An angel blew into half a trumpet. Near the front door a headless stone cherub cradled its own snowy head.

My mother came for a visit after Sister Joan invited her up to have a "talk." I didn't hug my mother hello; I didn't even look at her face. I kept my eyes on the cross-eyed ceramic angel that hung in the reading room of the retreat house where the three of us met. My mother settled next to me on the couch; dust motes flew out as she sat down heavily. "I ran into Betty Ciliberto in the A&P. She went on and on about Darlene's National Merit Scholarship."

"Uh-huh," I replied absently, noticing how the angel clutched the purple star. "Darlene's really smart."

"A brain," my mother agreed. "Speaking of school, how is your homework coming?"

"Okay, I guess. Sometimes it's hard for me to focus."

"We all have to do things we don't want to do," she sniffed.

I faced forward stiffly, pretending I was riding with the cross-eyed angel on the Peter Pan bus, both of us staring out the window, wearily engrossed in the landscape. Ladylike Sister Joan perched on a chair with her back perfectly straight and tidied the pleats of her skirt.

"Thank you for coming, Mrs. Birdsong. Hillary is a wonderful girl. A tad feisty but wonderful." Sister waited for my mother to grin. She didn't.

"My daughter," my mother began, "is beyond miserable. Vicious would describe her more accurately. I don't suppose she shared with you that this past Thanksgiving she called me a—I'm sorry—I don't want to say it. I don't wish to offend you." My mother waited for me to admit to what I said. I just kept breathing shallowly. My mother sighed. "She called me a fat bitch. Of course, ever since my son died, the holidays have been a horrible time for us. Even though it's been four years. I tried to go through the motions. I always spent the whole week before Thanksgiving cooking. So I still sautéed, lightly browned, and baked. Every thought was 'Four years ago today I was chopping celery when—'"

Sister Joan raised her hand as if she had just heard the beep during a hearing test. "Did you have any idea Hillary was pregnant?"

I waited to hear what she would say.

"I had my suspicions around the holidays. My daughter did look plumper. But then she always gains a little baby fat in the winter when she can't swim laps in the lake. I suspected Miles had broken up with her because Shell phoned to check on her literally twenty times a day. Anyhow, Hillary shrieked those horrible words at me and so—well—I'm not proud of this, but I threw a pan of stuffing on the floor. Buttery mush everywhere. Oh yes, happy Thanksgiving. Hillary disappeared for two days. Ray drove everywhere searching for her. I stayed home and ate semisweet chocolate and pumpkin right from the can."

Sister's wiry, never-been-plucked eyebrows raised up, but she didn't flinch. I imagined the humming bus floor and pretended I was just passing through, stuck next to a lunatic who spills her whole life story to strangers.

Suddenly my mother's voice trembled. She held back tears, whispering, "When I realized Hillary was . . . I was ashamed. I didn't want to believe it was true. The whole town has been riveted on our loss for years. Oh yes, those poor Birdsongs." Her voice became louder, more bitter. "Poor Ray, his wife really let herself go. My son's death is like a door always open, people gawking at the sordid details. And then my daughter ends up pregnant."

I watched the cross-eyed angel as she spun a little in the cool draft. Right below her wings, she had a dark, deep hole in her back, probably from being baked in a kiln.

"You're very angry at your daughter," Sister Joan offered.

"I'm just glad her grandma Maud isn't here to see this," my mother said.

"But what about the boy?" Sister asked. "The father? Are you angry at him?"

"Miles was in love with her, I saw that. Besides, Hillary hasn't obeyed her curfew in years."

"You never worried?"

"I wasn't concerned when she came in at three in the morning, if that's what you mean. The cottage is so teeny, I always knew what time she sneaked in. Besides, last summer she was happy. I found her one afternoon, helping in the vegetable garden. She was working quietly alongside Ray. I could tell by the little grin on Ray's face he was so content to have her near. His little girl, picking the night's dinner salad, pulling weeds without complaint." Finally, my mother exhausted herself.

"'His little girl,'" Sister Joan repeated. "Don't *you* think of Hillary as still being a girl?"

My mother simply twisted the tissue that Sister handed her. Sister Joan asked again, "Don't you think of Hillary as still being a girl?" My mother shrugged her right shoulder. She moved her lips, but formed no words.

"Do you have anything to say, Hillary?" Sister Joan prodded gently.

I refused to turn toward my mother. I kept her on the edge, a blur in a dark suit. I spoke to the smudges on the window, smears of lips where bratty Wanda had kissed the glass. "I never meant for this to happen."

The three of us sat silently. The room grew colder. "I have an idea," Sister offered. "Your family has had so much heartache. Maybe, just as a beginning, between you both, you could each share a memory. Something lovely."

"Well," my mother said after a moment. "I used to love the Fourth of July Cove-to-Cove barbecue. I loved that first bite of summer corn. I remember Brad with small kernels stuck to his chin. Hillary preferred to fill the colander with fresh peas. She liked peas better."

That wasn't true. Bird and I had shucked dozens of ears for the barbecue. He'd make it into a contest, who could be first to fill up a brown paper bag with corn silk. Then later we had butter races, racing our shrinking pats of butter around on the hot kernels.

Sister Joan prodded me. "Hillary?"

I could feel my mother turn toward me. I let my eyes drift a little higher to the burnished gold of her big-link necklace. But I had reached my bus stop. I stood up and walked out. This was where I was going to get off, to follow the fleck of movement out the window: Sunny and Wanda on the snowy hill. Sunny snapped a pine bough and picked off the needles one by one. I could read her lips: *He loves me*, pluck, *he loves me not*. Wanda ignored her, smoking and contemplating her bright orange ashes. Wanda took one last hard suck down to the filter, then smirked, flicking the butt.

We should have seen it coming.

Wanda's baby wasn't due for almost three weeks, but she had been waking us up at three A.M. for several nights with her nightmares, crying out that her room was getting broken into. Water ran in the pipes all night from her flushing the toilet and dashing cold water on her face. She gave herself black eyes by rubbing her mascara in with her fists.

She slammed through the home like a typhoon, destroy-ing anything that wasn't pinned down. Sunny and I were downstairs peeling carrots for stew when we heard crashing. We charged upstairs to find Sister Catherine unable to get close to Wanda. Wanda had knocked over her desk and was hurling bottles of black nail polish, pens, slippers. Then she unscrewed the nail polish remover and flung it on Sister Catherine. "Set yourself on fire, bitch," Wanda snorted.

"Quit it, right now!" Sister Catherine demanded.

But Wanda was unstoppable. She ripped open her pillow and let the feathers snow in the air. She ran down the hall into the bathroom, tore the shower curtains off the rings, and shattered the bathroom lightbulbs with a toilet plunger. Then she deliberately stomped on the broken glass.

"You think you're so perfect, so good, so pure," Wanda shrieked, smearing bloody footprints on the floor tiles. "You don't give a shit about me! All you care about is this baby. 'Don't smoke, Wanda, it's bad for the baby. Eat your fruits, Wanda, the baby needs good food.' I'm just a fuckin' breeder for you. You don't love me. You just want my baby."

Sister Catherine spoke softly. "Sunny, go into the downstairs bathroom and get the Bactine and some Band-Aids."

I stood very still as Wanda pulled her Newports from her tee-shirt sleeve and lit one, burning the center of her palm with it. I never would have thought that burly, stiff Sister Catherine could lunge so fast. But she did, grabbing Wanda's arms and twisting them around her belly, putting her into a hold. Wanda began crying harshly. But not a single tear came out. The tip of the cigarette sizzled in a spot of blood. Smoke faded.

"Oh fuck!" Wanda gritted her teeth with Sister Catherine wrapped around her, restraining her. "This really hurts!"

"I don't want to hurt you," Sister Catherine said calmly.

"It's not you. It's these killer cramps."

———

Turned out Wanda had been in labor all day. Sister Catherine got her to the hospital just in time for Wanda to give birth to a baby girl. She weighed four pounds.

I wanted to join Sunny in upholding the tradition of La Rosaria girls visiting one another in the maternity ward. So the next day after our tutor left, we asked Sister Catherine to give us a ride to see Wanda and her daughter.

Sister Catherine's brow popped with little circles of sweat.

"What is it?" I asked her. "Is Wanda okay?"

"Oh, I'm afraid we have to really pray for her. I got a call this morning."

"From Wanda?"

"From the head nurse. Wanda . . . ran away."

Sunny exclaimed, "Where did she go?"

Sister shook her head slowly from side to side. "We don't know."

I pictured Wanda stumbling on the rocky shoreline in her shit-kickers, laces untied. "So . . . she took her baby?"

"No."

"So what happened to the kid?"

Sister looked out of the bay window facing the cliffs and said dully, "Wanda never signed the paper releasing the child. She doesn't have a legal name. The social worker simply nick-named Wanda's daughter 'Tiny.' The baby's been placed in foster care."

"Foster care," Sunny repeated incredulously. "What the hell."

"I know," Sister Catherine said.

The sea wind blew, high pitched, like a whimpering dog.

4

Wanda took her little radio, but not her baby. While helping poor Sister Joan clean up Wanda's dumped desk drawers, I claimed a pair of her shorts. Sewn of the same spongy polyester material as my high school gym suit, these ugly maternity shorts had been handed down from girl to girl forever, according to Sister. I lay on my bed as I waited for the social worker to arrive to start the interview process to find a mother for my child and watched my belly. When the baby rolled and kicked, the pilled material of the shorts popped, like deep, dark water beginning to boil.

My "adoption liaison" appeared in the doorway. DeeDee Moore spent her working days lugging around manila folders overflowing with paperwork. She put down a stack of files from couples wanting to adopt. "You don't need to rush into anything." Her glossy chestnut bangs gave her face a very soft expression. She was ladylike but not prissy. I doubted she had ever shrieked at anyone in her entire life. If she hadn't had such pink, pretty lips, the triangular lids of her eyes would have made her expression very sad.

DeeDee unclipped the forms I had to fill out while she asked me what sort of adoptive parents I might consider. Did their race, ethnicity, economic status matter to me? If they owned a house, if they believed in God, if they had other children? For the first time I understood that I was coming toward a certain bridge and that unless I really wanted to turn around there was nothing else I could do but cross it. I picked lint off my shorts. "So, did you ever give away a child?"

"No."

I eyed her silk sleeves, pear-cut diamond, and gold band. "You got any kids?"

"I have a daughter."

"And a husband, I bet."

She hesitated. "Yes."

"Is he the father of your daughter?"

Again, she considered for a moment whether to answer. "Yes."

"So," I continued. "You have a cute little family and probably a house. I'm knocked up. Most likely giving up my baby. Temporarily banished from my home. Anything in this picture seem just a little bit unfair to you?"

She felt the sadness seeping out of me. She didn't get angry. She patted the folders with the tips of her burgundy fingernails. "Just look through these. See what you think. I know this is hard. No, I haven't been through what you are going through. But I'll do what it takes to make sure your plan of adoption is what you want."

Plan of adoption.

Right.

Like sketching out the blueprints for a houseboat, building it, letting it go. Moving on with your life as free as a turtle ripped from its shell.

The fact is: I was shopping around for parents for my kid as I flipped through the pages of letters from prospective parents.

Dear Birthmother,
We are a loving couple, married for twelve years and have been unable to have children. We live in a 3,000-square-foot house in a town with an excellent school system and would raise your child with Christian values.

As DeeDee and I entered the Howard Johnson, the loving couple was already positioned in their booth, smiles secured on their faces. They had coffee; I had hot chocolate while we viewed photos of their house and "lifestyle." I suspected that the Larkeys redecorated just to impress b-moms like me. From the looks of it, their house must have smelled like stiff, new bolts of cloth at a fabric store. Their couches with their brass buttons shone like band uniforms. Glass tabletops were free of any fingerprints. Formal. Neat. Polite.

"Call us Chrissie and Howie," they insisted. Yet they called each other Christine and Howard. They were more like roommates; they even looked alike: feathered dark-brown hair and brown eyes, straight white teeth that shone when they smiled on cue.

I was afraid my baby would grow up in a house with no romance. This couple would make fine parents, but not for my baby. My baby needed more than a mother who wore perfect pearl earrings. More than a dad who wore docksiders without socks and ironed creases in his blue jeans. What clinched it for me was a photo on their "family" page: Chrissie and Howie were perched on a dock with the lake a cherry orange from the sunset, arms around each other, heads tilted together. They looked tame and posed, though Chrissie made a point of telling me, "The best man at our wedding took that. We didn't even know he was there!" Christine and Howard had no real spark between them. Commitment, sure. And Christian values, whatever those were. But no juice.

With them, my kid would grow up lukewarm, with name-brand everything and impeccable manners. This was not enough. As DeeDee and I drove off, I turned around and saw the smiles drop from their faces. Christine wrapped her coat tighter and got into her car, sitting there alone, while Howard lit a cigarette.

"They're not the ones." I had already decided.

"You're sure?" DeeDee asked.

"What if I gave my kid to a couple that just ends up getting a divorce?"

"Why would you say that after meeting them?"

"DeeDee, come on. I may be only a kid myself, but anyone can see, that's a woman who doesn't even french kiss her own husband. You know I'm right."

DeeDee laughed, her glossy hair swinging over her shoulders. "Oh lordy," she said. "God bless teenagers."

DeeDee arranged several other interviews. No one felt right to me. "I'm sick of this," I muttered to DeeDee as we parked near the orange roof once again. The waitresses were used to us by now, brought me hot chocolate with extra whipped cream without my even having to order it. "Besides, what if I change my mind and don't want to give the baby up?"

"We've been over this, Hillary. Nobody is forcing you to do anything."

And then I had to shake hands with yet another couple: the Horgans.

I didn't even bother to look at them. I was too busy observing a ponytailed mother (and wife, I saw her wide gold band) a few booths down. She was singing along with her daughter and a friend, both toddlers. Something about a blankie being very yellow. She babbled nonstop baby talk, swinging her ponytail from side to side and clapping her hands.

Shut up, I felt like screaming to her, *the whole restaurant can hear every goddamn word you say.*

"How's that milkshake?" she asked brightly. "Mama'll do it for you. Hot? Oh, heart? Is that what you said, baby? Heart?" When she took the kids to the bathroom, all three of them passed by me, skipping merrily.

I don't remember Mr. Horgan's face, but I remember his fake, hearty laugh when he wished me luck with my decision. I complained on the way home, "It's the same every time. All these people seem okay, but I can't feel much for them. New love seats, good jobs. Who gives a shit."

"What are they supposed to do," DeeDee asked, "photograph dirty socks on the sofa so you can observe their natural habitat? They're nervous." She spoke in her honest, level-headed way. "And your snottiness makes it harder for them."

"Whose side are you on, anyway? You don't think they look down on me, 'the little tramp'? Plus, if I choose them, then they're terrified I'll change my mind and keep the baby. They desperately want what I have and they hate me for it. They're so secure, so good, so normal, and they can't get pregnant. Meanwhile, I spread my legs a few times and voila—a baby."

"Please don't call yourself a tramp. You don't deserve that. Here, I have a couple of new files for you to look at."

"Great. More golden retrievers. More loving couples praising me for how *brave* they think I am." I flipped open the folder and read out loud, "'We are a Christian couple, financially stable, open to paying for your medical care if needed.' I'm glad I don't have to suck up to any of these people about the medical bills. At least La Rosaria takes care of that. Did you know that Doc Pearson gives us big lollipops after we get our checkups?"

She laughed. "He's very committed to helping you all."

I didn't need any doctor to tell me that my baby was amazing. Below my right rib I constantly felt that incredible, familiar bump I knew was my child's tiny heel. But whenever I touched it, it quickly darted away.

I had an uncanny feeling about Lola Vining the moment I read her letter. It was handwritten in square, pleasant penmanship, whereas most other letters were neatly, perfectly typed.

Dear Birthmother:

In writing to you, whoever you are, the first thing I think I want to say is that there was a silence in my body after I gave birth to my own daughter, Natalie, three years ago. I had felt her move all those months and it was music. Music. But she was born way too early and never even cried. She lived four days. I am hungry to be a mother. I can feel it in my arms. So can my husband, James—to be a father . . .

All the couples DeeDee had helped me contact had special phone lines set up should a birthmother choose to call. I always made DeeDee make first contact. I knew they had peppy outgoing messages, trying not to sound too desperate or eager. I asked DeeDee if I could call Lola Vining myself. I was taken off guard by the beginning of the answering machine message, the intro to a corny Barry Manilow song: "Her name was Lola, she was a showgirl . . ."

My first thought when I spotted Lola in the Howard Johnson was *Why would someone so beautiful cover it up like that?* She stood near the cash register looking around for us through oversized black eyeglasses. They were the unflattering shape of those joke glasses that come with plastic noses attached. DeeDee waved, and as Lola approached with her husband, pink rhinestones sparkled in the corners of her glasses. She was taller than she appeared in her file photo—around five foot ten, plus the height added by platform loafers. Her hair was cut so short and bleached so white that she looked like she was sprouting soft feathers. I followed the graceful lines of her long neck down to her skinny, flat chest where I spotted a tiny silver pin on her jacket.

"Is that a Barbie shoe?"

DeeDee nudged me and put out her hand. "Hi, Lola, good to see you. I'm DeeDee. This is Hillary."

Lola shook our hands and said to me, "It's a real Barbie shoe. I dipped it in silver. This is my husband, James."

The olive green of his eyes reminded me of Birdy's old Boy Scout pup tent. James was shorter than Lola and wore a flannel shirt and jeans. "Hey, Hillary," he greeted me. His handshake was strong. Everything about him seemed level; even the deep melody of his voice had a steadiness to it. Once again, there I was, settling into a booth, facing prospective parents. But my face felt flushed. For the first time in my whole life, I ordered a cup of coffee. I sounded older to myself. The waitress just nodded.

DeeDee opened the files, turned to the "Our Home" page. I expected Lola to apologize for having such a small apartment, to tell me they were on the verge of buying a house. But she didn't.

"So, Hillary." Lola unbuttoned her brown-and-red-plaid coat. I stared at her massive ring, shaped like a roller skate wheel. It hovered like a lunar moth in the center of her long, thin hand. "You're from Norway. We've never been up there."

"Uh-huh."

"Do you like living there?"

"I guess. The tourists think it's grand. And you're a . . . I'm sorry . . . I already forgot what your bio said."

"A metalsmith," Lola said. "I design jewelry."

Beyond the starkness of her black frames and jarring hair, her complexion was perfectly creamy, her face very innocent. I thought, *It's like she's protecting herself.* I wondered if, close up, she smelled airy, perhaps like White Shoulders. I asked, "You made that ring?"

"This one was part of my BFA project." She slipped it off and handed it to me. "Spin it."

When I flicked the yellow and blue wheel molded onto the plastic band, it turned deep green as it spun. DeeDee and I laughed. I reached across the table to hand it back to Lola. She was holding hands with James. When they unlocked their fingers, he poured two sugar packets into her coffee for her. A strange image flooded me: my baby napping in a wicker

bassinet. I sensed breath just barely puffing out the baby's nostrils. Then I heard the sound of snaps on a tiny pair of overalls and pictured Lola's hands.

I caught a deep breath in the place below my breasts.
"DeeDee," I flicked my thumb at her as if hitchhiking, "DeeDee
reminded me what I'm supposed to say about what I want.
Updates every year, pictures of the baby."

"I could do that," Lola said quietly.

"And," I continued, "I want the information available
so that the baby would be able to come find me if he or she
wants to."

DeeDee interjected, "That wouldn't happen until the
child turned eighteen."

I shot her a look. "I *know* that, DeeDee."

Lola nodded. "I guess we all know how this goes. Now
here's where we're supposed to ask about your health history
should you choose us to—"

"Make a plan of adoption?" I asked sarcastically. "DeeDee
is brainwashing me. She doesn't like when I say 'give my baby
away.' 'Making a plan of adoption' is so much more sanitary.
And for your 'health history' information, I got kinda shit-faced
on New Year's Eve, but I've been mostly straight otherwise."

They didn't ask what "mostly straight" meant. I felt
ashamed for being so obnoxious and mean. "I'm sorry,
DeeDee." I was suddenly very hungry, my mouth watering at
the smell of sizzling bacon fat.

"It's okay," she assured me and began tidying up her papers. A black-and-white picture I hadn't seen before caught
my eye. "Why do you have Marilyn Monroe in your file?"

"Actually," James said proudly, "that's from a series of pictures I took of Lola the first year we were married."

I leaned in for a closer look. Lola's hair was dirty blonde, curly, and past her shoulders. No glasses, no jewelry; she wore a black strapless push-up bra and smiled slyly into the camera. "Wow" was all I could say. "You look really different."

"It's the false eyelashes," Lola said.

A few days later, I read and reread the menu, waiting tensely for Lola and James. OUR ORANGE ROOFS ARE MADE TO BE SEEN FROM THE HIGHWAY, the laminated cover told me, TO BE EASILY RECOGNIZABLE TO THE WEARY TRAVELER.

I don't know why it shocked me that the direction of a baby's life could be altered in a place as common as HoJos. Maybe it was fitting that my child's life with his or her adopted parents would begin in a family restaurant jumping with hungry children waiting to be fed.

I asked DeeDee if I could be alone with Lola and James. Lola strode into Howard Johnson's without her glasses, her hair covered by a leopard-skin pillbox hat.

"Is that real leopard?" I asked.

"It's old. Yeah."

James sat across from me. Lola sat by my side. We all ordered waffles.

"You know why I wanted to meet you. I think I want you to be the mom and dad to my baby. I'm pretty sure I'm going to give the baby up."

Lola wrapped her long fingers around my wrist lightly, like a loose bracelet. "There's something I need to tell you."

"What?" I asked. "You don't want the baby now?"

"That's not it. There's just something I want you to know," Lola said. "DeeDee said I don't have to disclose this to you. But I just don't feel right keeping it a secret. After

I lost Natalie, I went . . . I was really depressed. I had to be hospitalized."

"You mean like a nuthouse?"

"Yeah."

"Oh."

"I had to tell you. Even if you think I'm unworthy to take the baby now."

"But you're okay now, right? I mean, you seem fine. How long were you there?"

"Two months. But I've been okay since. That's not to say I don't have my bad days when I feel sad."

The waffles came. We poked our forks into their steaming centers, spread a thick layer of butter over them, soaking them in syrup.

I didn't bother waiting to swallow. I was talking with my mouth full. "I've never known anyone in a mental institution. But I know crazy people. When my brother died, my mom lost her mind. I don't think she has it back yet."

"Lola and I saw that in your profile . . . that you lost a sibling," James said. "That must have been . . . still be . . . so hard."

"Listen," I assured Lola. "I don't think any differently of you."

"Maybe you want to think it over, what I told you."

"No. I'm just as sure. If I give the baby up I want you to be the mother."

Lola swept her willowy arms around my back. I flinched, and then I let her hug me. But I didn't hug her back.

We cleaned our plates. Then Lola said, "Birdsong is an un-usual last name."

"We're the only ones in the whole state of Maine. All my

dad's family is from down South." I looked at her. "But you wouldn't keep that name for the baby, right?"

She held my gaze. "No. I don't think so. The baby would be a Vining."

"Yeah, that's what I figured."

"Does that bother you?"

"Why should I care? Birdsongs are a dying breed anyway. That's what my mother said, when she lost my brother."

"What was your brother's name?" James asked softly.

"His real name was Bradford. But I couldn't say Brad when I was little. I called him 'Bird' and the name stuck."

"Bird," Lola enunciated slowly, as if sounding out the word for the very first time.

"You can't gab on the phone too long," Sunny chastised me. "Rodney's going to call." Every night after our dessert, Sunny plopped in the rocking chair by the pay phone, waiting. I had been wrong to be jealous of Sunny; Rodney never ever called. But Shell did. Cooped up in the home, I waited and waited for her to come visit again.

Though I was completely banished from my town, it comforted me to know that Shell wasn't changing, only me. She brought me photos of her in the sports section of the paper. Whole features on her, the supple star.

"The balance beam is driving me crazy."

"But you're so good at it," I reminded her.

"Out of spite. If you ask me, it's the meanest of all the apparatuses. I can never really let loose without feeling the edge. I can nail that double somersault now, in the floor exercises. Oh my god, I feel so free."

I pictured her buoyant in the air.

"Hill, there's something I have to tell you."

"What?"

"Priscilla Nix is pregnant."

Priscilla and Shell and I used to spend indoor recess figuring out all sorts of cat's cradle tricks with shoelaces: Jacob's ladder, witches' broom. "Who told you that?"

"She's showing. And she's got the balls to still come to school!"

"She's not . . . going somewhere?"

"No. Her mother is going to raise it for her."

"You're kidding."

"Nope. Priscilla is gabbing every morning in the back of homeroom. 'My kid' this and 'my kid' that."

"Who's the father?"

"Ricky Pisani, supposedly."

"Oh, gross."

"I know."

I pictured Priscilla. She was a little runt of a girl who still wore stringy pigtails.

That night I swept back the kitchen curtain and watched Shell drive away. Priscilla's mother was going to raise it for her. In the beam of Shell's one headlight, I could see that in the long harsh winter both of Mary's hands had cracked off.

Miles of broken white lines and freshly paved blackness led to the Lamaze class at the YMCA in Portland. I had asked Lola, "Would you be my birthing partner?" She replied, "I'd be honored."

With cushions on the floor, I leaned back into Lola. Together we practiced panting: *hee-hee-hoo.* "I remember this from when I had Natalie," she sighed.

The instructor didn't bother to modify the class just because an unwed mother was there. "Okay, wives, what I want you to do is picture your vagina as an elevator. Squeeze, then go up several floors, fifth floor, sixth, seventh, now squeeze and hold. Now the elevator is going down. And squeeze."

When Lola drove me back to La Rosaria, I kept calling her "my hubby." "Going up?" We broke into fresh hysterics. "Now squeeze!"

"Miles's biggest fear was elevators," I told Lola. "Actually, now that I think about it, I guess he wasn't that afraid of *my* elevator." And we cracked up again. The setting sun turned the marshes orange. The light spread like fire on the surfaces. Someone had poked the wire legs of a flock of pink plastic flamingos along the edges of the bay. With their silly necks curving into big beaks, the flamingos stood, and I pretended for a moment that Lola and I had flown far away, all the way to Florida.

Despite the tutor who came every morning and struggled to get us to fill in worksheets at the kitchen table, I learned nothing from my schooling at the home except for two words that weren't even proper vocabulary words.

The first was "Golgotha." Though the sisters never forced us to attend services in the chapel, I ended up there one afternoon during Lent. They were talking about how Jesus was brought to a place called Golgotha. Pronounced *Gawl-gu-tha.* It was the loneliest sounding word I had ever heard. Will giving my baby away be like Golgotha? When I said it a hollow darkness expanded from within me.

The other word I learned from the possums nesting in the cool clay and dried leaves near the laundry line. I skimmed them with the beam of my flashlight one night while I was carrying out a bag of trash. They were like rats, with long triangular noses and absurdly long tails—the ugliest animals I had ever seen.

"They're marsupials," Sister Joan said.

"What?"

"Marsupials. Like kangaroos. They carry babies in a pouch. We actually welcome them because ever since they moved under the house we've had no mice caught in the traps in the basement."

Soon there would be spring possum babies, completely delirious, dozing all day inside their mothers' pockets. Marsupials. I lulled myself to sleep some nights by thinking of names for a rock and roll band, should I ever join one. The Golgothas. The Marsupials. The Golgotha Marsupials.

Lola and I took a day trip, heading up the coastline. "Hey, check that out." I pointed to a bumper sticker ahead of us. It read: BORN IN MAINE, LIVING IN EXILE. "Whatever that means," I said. "I don't know. But it applies to me."

At Fort Point the fog enveloped the old bell that hung completely silent, outdated. The Coast Guard used automated foghorns now. Once a full, vibrant bell, it hung mute without a tongue.

Lola and I watched the fog lift. First the line of low pines came into view, then telephone poles and wires. When we could finally see Penobscot Bay, I stammered, "Could you . . . maybe tell . . . tell me . . . what happened to your baby?"

She rubbed her hand over her lips and then said, "I only got to hold her as she was dying. That's when they unhooked her. And we could finally cradle her without any tubes getting in the way. We spent a long, long time with her; even after she died we held her for an hour. A few days later James carried the coffin to her grave. The box was so small, shiny white with brass handles. It was so light he could walk with it all by himself. One pallbearer. That was him."

My stomach tightened, picturing James.

"You know the tight little caps they put on newborns? I held it to my face the whole time we were at the cemetery. I could still smell Natalie in that hat. A pure smell. A sweetness. I ran the hat under my nose. It was all she left behind. Her belly-button scab hadn't even fallen off. That takes a week or two. She wasn't here long enough to use anything we had ready for her. She never came home to use the bassinet or the cradle. I never used any of the clothes I got at the baby shower. Beautiful outfits with bears floating like bubbles."

She looked at me, dry-eyed. "I want you to know I gave them all away. This baby isn't getting any of the stuff meant for Natalie. I guess I'm just superstitious.

"That hat was all I had. About a month after she died I panicked when I could no longer smell her. The hat was just dusty and dry. I blamed myself. I had sucked all the scent out, used it up. I lay on the couch curled around the hat and couldn't even move."

"Is that when you went to the hospital?"

"Yes. The shrinks told me I had to make peace with the fact that she was gone. And so was her scent. So I decided that it had disappeared inside me. That's what I decided to believe. That my bones were like nets. And I caught her somewhere inside me."

My throat had a big lump in it, the size of Natalie's hat. "I wonder if we're having a boy or a girl," I said.

She shrugged. "It's an old wives' tale that it will be a boy if you carry big and low like you are."

"I'd like to name him Tom if he's a boy." I said it more to myself.

"Why?"

"It's kind of dumb but when Bird died, this kid Tom was nice to me." I picked up a plain brown rock near my shoe. I struck the bell with it, surprised that the vibration quickly spread up and around the lip. The giant bell buzzed a long while. I could only imagine the sound of its voice when it had been complete with its clapper.

I awakened to the rhythms of hooves, like clusters of gourds blowing. When I peered out the window, two chestnut horses stood stamping right in the empty spot where Sister Joan usually parked her car in the lot: Sunny had gone into labor in the middle of the night.

In St. Michael's maternity ward, the gray tiles on the floor made the off-white walls seem even more dingy. The long hallway was bleak, opening onto a wide window and the nursery where all the babies slept. Stepping into Sunny's room, I realized that I had never looked closely at a newborn before. Sunny tilted her son, swaddled into a pod, toward me. He had her exact nose: wide, troll-like. He seemed to be using his tiny, soft tongue to smell the new air. He was amazing.

Hours after giving birth, Sunny, so odd-looking that she was cute, had become beautiful, flushed and radiant in her hospital johnny. She flashed her braces in a smile as I handed her a bouquet of tulips, buds shaped like fat, red tears.

"Rodney's coming to see us," she gushed. She had named her baby Rodney Junior but what did that matter? As soon as he was adopted, his name would be changed to Daniel or Nick or Stephen, and a new birth certificate would be issued as if Rodney Kendall Junior had never existed in Sunny Findlay's arms at all.

Sunny returned to La Rosaria to pack up and squiggle herself into her old jeans. "It all happened so fast." She held her breath on her bed with her stumpy legs in the air, trying to force the zipper all the way up. It wouldn't budge.

"I thought they told us it takes a while for the uterus to shrink back to size," I reminded her.

"Oh, screw it." She tugged her shirt down to hide the bump of the stuck zipper. "Rodney never got to see our kid. He had to work overtime. I don't get it, though; he had time to sign the papers that my social worker had. But I don't care. I'm out of here." She sprung up breathless and slipped her feet into her Candies. The stiletto heels made her take little baby steps, like a kindergartner dressing up in her mother's party shoes.

"I gave an amazing gift to that couple. Maynard, their name is. Boy, were they old! The dad looked about fifty!" She unwrapped a square of Bazooka gum, popped it in her mouth, and worked her jaws furiously. "But I made them very happy. I made them a complete family. I really am quite brave."

Oh my God, I thought, *she's like a baby doll. Pull her string and watch her go.*

"I don't want to say good-bye to you," I said.

"Okay," she agreed, blowing a giant bubble then sucking it back in her mouth. "Let's just say 'see ya.'"

"See ya."

But when would Sunny and I ever meet again? La Rosaria was not a shelter any girl returned to. There were no giddy class reunions. The home was a tunnel you passed through, an underlit archway where you and your baby got dumped.

Lola and I snuck back into Norway in April so I could show her where our baby was from. We drove up Pike's Hill.

"This road takes you back around the town if you follow the ridge. The cemetery is at the top."

Lola slowed the car down and pulled into the dirt driveway behind a maroon car.

"Uh-oh."

"What?"

"My mother is here."

My mother stood at Bird's grave in her black wool coat. I opened the door and called out. With the plucked arch of her eyebrows and the point of her nose, my mother looked like a barn owl blinking at me.

"Hi, Mom. Fancy meeting you here."

I zigzagged unsteadily through the rectangles of plots. She went to kiss my cheek, not quite touching me, pecking air. She looked toward the road nervously. Someone might see me. "What are you doing in town? I was planning to visit on Sunday."

"I'm showing Lola around."

Lola inched her way through the slush, taller than the monuments in her platforms. She wasn't wearing her nerdy Buddy Holly glasses, and the leopard-skin hat disguised the jarring shortness and brightness of her hair. The hat framed her face so she looked very young, almost like a teenager.

My mother said, "I love your hat."

"Thank you."

"Do you do volunteer work at the retreat house?"

"No." Lola looked to me, waiting to see if I was going to tell my mother that Lola was the one who was going to be the mother of my baby.

I could not find the words to tell her. I stared at a plastic holly sprig poking out from Bird's marker, fake berries rattling in the wind. It had been years since I had swept my legs and arms in the snow. Could I let go now? Would the imprint look as it did when I was younger, or would I leave behind a pregnant snow angel?

Lola broke the silence. "I'm sorry for your loss. I lost a child too."

My mother blinked at her. "I'm so sorry." She suddenly seemed to want to be closer to us. "Come have some tea, warm up," she offered. "Daddy's home. He'd be so glad to have you home, even for a short minute."

It was hard to realize that my mother was inviting me to my own home. What used to be my home. She'd probably want me to sneak onto the porch wearing a disguise.

"No thanks, Mom, we have to get back. I'll still see you on Sunday?"

"I'll be there."

"Nice meeting you," Lola called out. I followed Lola's footprints in the melting slush. They dug deep as horses' hooves.

"Hillary?" my mother called as she was opening her car door.

I turned around hopefully. "Yeah, Mom?"

But she looked momentarily confused. She had lost her thought and just shrugged.

As my mother drove off, the Man in White stepped out of the woods, wearing unbuckled galoshes and carrying his briefcase.

"Who's that?" Lola whispered.

"The Man in White."

He clicked open the briefcase and removed a wire brush. I watched him scrubbing stiff green lichen off a crooked headstone and said to Lola, "Your adopted baby will have an . . . uncle . . . who died."

We headed back. "My mother had an incredible fur hat collection. She had this one hat I loved. I think it was fox. It was so soft, it looked like a halo. I was always proud of her when she was the prettiest mother. You know, I used to beg to paint my mother's fingernails, coat after coat. She never hugged us much. That's all she allowed me to touch: her fingertips."

Lola glanced at me. "She's still pretty, in her own way."

I looked out the window. That's what everyone says about heavy women. Before Bird died, my mother was as cool as a Hitchcock blonde with trim ankles in silky Evan Picone hose. She never forgot her clip-on earrings. She collected tiny sequined purses called "clutches" and arranged them in her closet by colored rows like a box of fresh pastels. She wore face powder even when shoveling snow. Pulled her hair into a chignon, smelled of White Shoulders, ironed everything.

My mother no longer drove to Boston to shop at Lord & Taylor. The best she could do was black tent dresses and wide-link gold jewelry to draw attention away from her blubbery belly and up to her face. Her graceful neck had disappeared. Even her shoulder blades were puffy with fat. She settled into her body like a big old Cadillac. Heavy and wide, she was less apt to be crushed. She complained about being ugly and queen size, and that she was becoming like the trash who bought their sneakers at the A&P. Sometimes strangers even asked if she was pregnant. Only a moron must have been able to ignore the weariness on her face. Her big body was not carrying life. She was holding death, and it filled her; it blew her up wide.

Stretch marks trailed down the skin of my belly and my upper thighs like the rivulets of rain on my window. I slapped the bathroom tiles with fat paddle-feet until the end of April, waiting with a sore back, eight, ten days past my due date into May, then eleven days past, then twelve. Did my baby know that every day overdue was one more long, ripe day we had together?

My water finally broke, a hot surprise soaking my black shorts on the afternoon that a flash-flood warning was issued for the southern coast of Maine. As I waited for Lola to come and get me, Sister Catherine and Sister Marguerite helped me pack my things.

"We have a little present for you." Sister Catherine handed me a small plastic box. When I opened it, out popped a recipe card for mulligan stew. I burst into tears.

Lola arrived and the contractions began, painful waves zigzagging at the base of my spine and working around to the front like hot bolts of lightning. I counted the minutes between them.

As Lola and I drove through the storm, I couldn't recall the rule about thunder and lightning. If you see the lightning, count the seconds until you hear the thunder? Several loud booms exploded around us as I began hee-hee-hooing.

The blackest part of the storm had blown out to sea by the time we reached St. Michael's. We pulled into the emergency lot just as Shell squealed around the corner.

"Sweetie! How are you?"

But I could only collapse into a wheelchair panting hee-hee-hoo. Shell exclaimed to Lola, "I did eighty miles an hour all the way down from Norway with only one windshield wiper."

Who needed to rush? The contractions grew fierce, but the clock barely moved.

"I'm Dahlia," said the nurse with deep brown skin who helped me change into a johnny as I crawled into a birthing bed. Dahlia showed Lola and Shell how to follow the contraction monitor as the needle squiggled over the unrolling paper. It was as if I had to pass a lie-detector test. As the pain grew more intense, Lola steadied me, giving the breathing pattern. But nothing could douse the piercing fire as I rode up and down on searing red waves of pain.

Strange flickering visions reminded me of my acid trip with Miles: A silver wolf with the softest fur and yellow eyes carried me lovingly on her back. Then each contraction was an endless heavy black chain, and a circle of seagulls helped me carry it, lifting it with their beaks. I dug my fingernails into the palm of Lola's hand. Shell wiped my forehead with a wet washcloth and Dahlia gave her small ice chips to tuck into my mouth between breaths. "Is that okay, hon? You want another one?"

A long night of wild orange pain.

The doctor came only at the end. He felt inside me and declared I must push. *Push! Push!* Gritting my teeth, bearing down, and battling to move the mountain. A useless struggle, full of sudden pee and loose farts and freezing sweat. "Go go go go," the doctor called up between my legs. I bore down down down. "There it is," the doctor called out.

I heard Shell say, "Look! The baby has hair!"

"Okay, let's do it again," the doctor urged. "Go go go go!"

"You're doing great," Lola and Dahlia assured me.

"She's amazing," Shell agreed.

Bearing down upon roundness.

I let out a deep, low, animal growl as I pushed on the mountain and felt it move through me. I pushed and felt the mountain become a head. I pushed and felt the mountain slide out, shoulders, a body sliding, and the doctor lifted the baby. "It's a boy." Suddenly the entire earth swelled with my son's first sounds, the rhythm of his first shocked breaths. Between his plump, shiny legs I saw the rosy beauty of his balls. My son: I loved him instantly.

Dahlia weighed Tom. "Seven pounds, three ounces." I pushed out the blob of placenta, and the doctor sewed up the edges of my body where I had torn. Dahlia wiped Tom up, tucked a little hat around his head, and lowered him into my arms.

"My god, he smells sweet!" Shell and Lola pressed their faces together as they leaned down and counted his fingers.

"What's the baby's name?" Dahlia asked.

"Tom," I said. I looked closely into his eyes as he squinted, shocked by all the newness of light as James entered snapping pictures, laughing. Shell stepped away, and he hugged Lola. They nuzzled their faces into each other's necks.

"See if he'll latch on," Dahlia suggested. I didn't care that James saw me half naked. He was Tom's new father. I guided Tom to my right nipple. His dark little eyes looked so serious it made me laugh. He began sucking away, tugging on me. His mother.

That night, in the brown darkness of our hospital room, I lifted my baby up close to my face. His eyes were cloudy, still adjusting to being outside me, but he was listening. I whispered to him for hours. I only stopped talking when the nurse came in to lift my gown and refresh the icepack between my legs, and to cuff my arm to check my blood pressure. I told him of beauty: how lady slipper blossoms bulge pink and full in the shade of the birches. I sang a Mother Goose rhyme I suddenly remembered: "Little Tommy Tittlemouse lived in a little house. He caught fishes in other men's ditches." I promised him he was getting a wonderful mommy and daddy and that my love for him would be forever bigger than the sky. "I love you, little guy. Thank you for coming into the world." My baby boy nursed and drank in my words.

I didn't want to stop holding him, feeling his dark peach fuzz tickling my face. I had only forty-eight hours. If I was lucky, maybe seventy-two. I refused to let the nurse put him in the nursery or near me in a plastic bassinet. I heard people in the hallway, checking my chart. "She's La Rosaria."

"So?" a voice answered.

"So, she's probably giving the baby away. Why bother nursing him?"

"Because she is," the second voice answered.

"I don't understand those girls. Why do they just make it worse for themselves?"

But his mouth, tugging hard on my nipples, was exquisitely warm. He was so white, he glowed in the dark. His smell surrounded him like a halo.

My mother visited on the second day. She approached us very slowly, tiptoeing. She only took her eyes off us when I opened my gown to nurse Tom. No milk then, just colostrum, but he sucked eagerly.

She spoke more to herself than to us. "I loved the smell of babies. I could smell you and Bird strongest after you had been tucked in for a few hours. Bird always slept on his back with his arms flung above his head. He was so active during the day that he slept like a little rock at night. When I kissed him he took a deep breath and blew it out his nostrils in a high-pitched whistle. You? You were such a light sleeper. Grandma Maud advised me to stop checking on you at night because my footsteps always woke you up."

I nursed Tom on both sides and then closed my gown, picking a bit of crust that was as soft as mica from his head.

"Do you want to hold him?" I offered.

She looked stricken. "Oh god, no! I better not. He is beautiful though. I mean, he really is."

She couldn't bear to cradle a grandchild already signed away. How the hell did she think *I* felt? She didn't think about it. I sighed in relief when she left. The nurses wheeled in my dinner tray, and that spaghetti remains the most delicious I have ever had. The meatball slightly burnt, perfect.

Shell, my parents, Lola, James, and DeeDee assembled in the maternity ward corridor.

"I want to leave like a real mother," I whispered to Lola.

"But you are a real mother."

"No, I mean I want to leave the hospital like the other women I've seen. The ones taking their babies home with them. Their husbands push them along in their wheel-chairs."

"I'll push you," Lola promised.

"I need a few moments alone with Tom."

I shut the door to our room. I lay him on the bed and tenderly slipped off his tee shirt and unpinned his diaper. I just needed to gaze at him naked one last time.

I pressed my ear on his warm chest, careful not to brush my chin on the bandage tied over his belly button, listening to the perfect flapping of his heart. I dabbed my tears off his skin with a flannel hospital blanket. He quivered as I dried him.

I cupped his head inside my hands. He looked into my face, one eye squinting, locking his gaze on my eyes at the sound of my voice. "I just want you to remember me as loving you." As if they still were floating within me, his tiny hands glided through the air, slow and smooth. Circling his wrist was a plastic hospital bracelet: BIRDSONG BABY. But even in those closing moments while I was weeping a lullaby to him he was already VINING BABY.

Lola pushed Tom and me into the elevator, a blue helium balloon tied to my wheelchair. Everyone filed in. No one made eye contact; no one spoke. I pushed up the sleeves of my sweater so I could feel the soft cloud of Tom's blue fleece suit on my bare skin. Bells rang. The elevator took us down. The door slid open. Lola cautiously steered the wheels over the cracks, trying not to jar my sore, stitched-up privates.

A moist wind blew as we reached the shadows of the overhang outside the front entrance. The plan we all had made would happen. I would hand him over.

DeeDee chirped, trying to rupture the silence. "It's a lovely spring day."

"Yes it is," my mother quickly agreed.

My father handed James the snowy teddy bear that the nurses had given to Tom. "I just want to say thank you. You and your wife seem like real decent folks. I wish you well. All three of you." He bowed to Tom. "Good luck"—his eyes filled—"small fry."

My mother broke down, choking into my father's wide shoulder. "This is harder than I thought it would be."

I stood up, cradling Tom. *Should I take him, crush him to me, keep him, and run?* I couldn't bear to kiss him good-bye. Lola bent down to hug both Tom and me, the three of us united like a family. I wish we could have both grown up, Tom and I, with our faces in the sweetness of Lola's faux-leopard plush.

Is there a moment?

I knew he was Lola's now. I began kissing Tom's sleeping face. He yawned. I kissed him again and again and again. He sighed and kept dozing. "This isn't good-bye," I sobbed. I lifted him up, and placed him into Lola's long, spotted arms.

It happens all the time.

I grabbed the big blue balloon from the wheelchair, snapped it off, and began to run, sore nipples chafing, sweat pouring, legs buckling under me. Shell and I squealed out of the parking lot, tires laying a long hot patch. I needed a quick getaway, as if I were a criminal.

She had a fat joint rolled for me in the ashtray of the car. Shell's long blonde-white hair whipped in my face, blasted by the wind from the open windows. Loud, snotty, vicious, we screamed along to the Rolling Stones on the radio.

I was completely wasted by the time we cruised down Main Street past Smokey Bear. I pushed the balloon out the window. It rose higher and higher, getting smaller and smaller, until it disappeared into the cool spring day, but the sunshine was thick, like the days I spent with Miles, days I would never get back under a silky summer sky.

two

5

Aching between my legs, I followed Shell upstairs. When I peered in at the nubbly bedspread of my parents' bedroom, I inhaled the scent of the Pond's Cold Cream that my mother moisturized with every night, her pillowcase scented with the coolness from her face.

Across the hall, Bird's Brut stood on his dresser, still three-quarters full. I lifted up my storm window and lowered the screen to inhale the early May breeze. My milk let down, gushing and filling my breasts. Though the nurses at the hospital had told me to put packets of frozen peas on my breasts to keep the pain at bay, it didn't work. The milk was dribbling into big milky wet spots on my tee shirt.

The first nights home, I couldn't sleep. I perched on the edge of my bed, opening my legs wide and repeatedly banging my thighs against each other like clumsy wings. It didn't matter that I was still bleeding and sore. I was nauseous, flooded with anxiety because I couldn't hear Tom breathing, snuffling, fussing. No matter how many blankets I wrapped myself in, I could not get warm without wrapping myself around my baby.

I stared all night long at a plastic A&P bag caught in the

leaves of the old maple tree. The handles had slipped themselves through two twigs so that the bag resembled a white
camisole beaded with rain. When a lighter wind blew, the bag
filled like a breathing torso.

My mother and father tiptoed around the house, afraid of
disturbing me. They closed closets quietly and only ran the
dishwasher and washing machine when they thought I was
awake, when they could see the smoke from the cigarettes
Shell brought me wafting from under my door. They knocked
and when I wouldn't answer, they left plates of linguini and
bowls of Frosted Flakes for me. I would not eat. The cereal
turned to mush. Fruit flies hovered.

Eventually I grew so weary I curled into a tight ball and
slept. I dreamed of a naked baby without any covers. Lost.
Howling in a crib at the end of a hallway. I ran and ran, trying to reach the baby's round, empty mouth. But I could not
get closer. I could not reach it. All I could do at the other end
of the long, dark hallway was listen.

I woke up sobbing uncontrollably. Bottomless cries that
rose out of my belly, twisting through me. Suddenly my parents burst into my room with Shell. My parents were useless
as Shell held me.

"*Shh, shh,*" Shell soothed me. But it made me writhe more
violently. She tried to quiet my legs as they banged open and
shut. She wrapped her arms tightly around my thighs like
twine. It helped. Stillness alighted for a moment, then I inhaled and the wailing began again.

"Jesus!" my father cried out. "Help us."

WOXO played nonstop Beatles songs from three until six
in the morning. Every night for weeks those were the hours I
ran dry of tears and became very still. Those simple, clear

songs did comfort me somehow as I lay pretending that Tom's tiny hand was curled around my pinky.

Wrapped up in my nest in a flannel nightgown despite the high humidity of a rainy summer, I welcomed the sudden and dangerous storms. Bird and I used to believe thunder really was the angels bowling, winged creatures wearing white crinolines like my mother's dusty prom dresses in the back of her closet. And the faces of the angels? I imagined they had dainty noses and shiny nylon hair like the screw-on head of the jar of bubble bath my father had once surprised me with, an airport gift.

Lola. Lola snapped the final photo of Tom in my plump arms. I could see the hands of my wristwatch forever frozen at ten until two. I kept the Polaroid safe under the coolness of my pillow.

"Hillary, honey." Shell plopped down on the end of my bed as if she were ending a routine on the trampoline. She had unbraided her hair and was combing her fingers through the long crimps. "Please. Listen to me." She flipped her hair behind her shoulders. "Honey, when was the last time you showered?"

"I don't know. Wednesday, I think."

"Of which week? It's Wednesday again, sweetie."

"So what. I don't have anywhere to go."

"Do you want a fresh shampoo?"

"Not really."

"You need to get some help. You can't continue like this."

"Just because I'm not washing my hair obsessively like you?"

"It's not okay to just . . . disappear like this."

"I can't face anyone."

"I know you feel shitty."

I refused to answer her.

"You haven't left the house since you got back from the nunnery."

I glared.

She kept prodding. "It's after the Fourth of July."

Finally I exploded. "Like I give a damn about the demolition derby."

"Sloppy won."

I hugged my knees. A scent of sweat, tart as soured grapefruit, billowed out from under my sheet. "Did he?"

"He was a maniac! By the time he was the only one left out of fifty cars Sloppy had four flat tires and two broken ribs. Plus he smashed the shit out of Billy Morgan's car. Took the bumper clean off."

"He's called here a couple times. You know my mom can't stand him. So he doesn't visit. She thinks he's a fuck-up." I paused. "Don't you get tired of me being a fuck-up? Aren't you fed up yet?"

Shell sighed. "I get tired of you seeing yourself as a fuck-up."

"I'm crazy, too. I hear Tom crying and I can't stop it. It's like a mosquito buzzing next to my ear."

"If he is crying, Lola will go to him. She'll be a good mom. You've said so yourself a thousand times."

"So he's just fine without me, right?" I began yelling. "It's just like square dancing, switch your partners, do-si-do." Spit flew out of my mouth onto Shell's cheek. She held my gaze with her big brown eyes, then calmly wiped the spit off with the back of her hand. How could I yell at her like that, when I loved her so much? "It's not ever going to be the same, Shell. It's impossible. I've changed."

The bag-camisole twisted sideways in the tree, like hips playing dodge ball. She said quietly, "Everyone is asking me if you had a kid. Your mother made me swear to keep it a secret. Everyone asks me where you went. 'Oh, Hill went away to do grief work.' Like anyone knows what the hell that even is. And how do I explain that you came back worse than when you left? You're supposed to be cured or something, but now no one's even seen you. And you should know something else. Billy told me that Miles wigged out when he got that call from DeeDee telling him you were planning to give the baby up for adoption."

My heart skipped faster, hearing about Miles. "Miles had his twenty days to petition the court about it. No one heard a word from him. What do you mean, he wigged out?"

"Miles disappeared for a month. They finally found him strung out in some nightclub. I guess he had been freebasing coke nonstop."

"Did Billy say if Miles is—"

She looked down. "Miles ran off to L.A. Hollywood, I guess. He's gonna be the next James Dean, according to Billy. Come on. Let's just focus on today, huh?" She grabbed the wide-tooth comb off of my dresser and began to rake through my snarls. "Well, one good thing about not washing your hair is that the natural oils are like a conditioner."

"Shell, cut my hair. I'm sick of it. I've had it this style since I was a freshman."

"Hon, no way are you cutting it. Girls kill for waves like yours."

"Come on. If you don't, I will."

"Why not go to Rosemary? I'll call and make an appointment. She did Ally's hair. It looks cute."

I stood up in the steamy air and examined my extra-curly hair in the mirror. "I'll cover it up with a hat if it looks bad. How hard would it be to just cut my hair?" I grabbed a handful on the side, like a pigtail, and snipped it off.

"All right, I'll help you do it."

Shell demanded that I take a bubble bath while she shampooed and conditioned my hair, like a real salon. Bold blue veins still mapped my breasts, even though they were shrinking back down without milk. She said nothing, just wrapped me up in a fresh, white towel. Then she took my mother's black-handled sewing scissors and I settled in a chair, bowing my dripping head. She tugged and snipped. "Shorter," I demanded. In my bureau mirror was the outline of my new little pea head. I had hoped to look pissed off, maybe even punk, and tough. Instead, I still looked like I did that first night I was with Miles, only sweeter, a glitter fairy, not the barbed-wire bitch I wanted to be.

The sky suddenly blackened. Another storm began whipping, filling the waist of the bag-camisole with wind. Shell let the rain blow through the screen window. "Ahh," she said. "I love that sound. It's the one clear memory I have of my mother. She was holding me as we hurried under a black umbrella to the neighbor's house."

I drew closer to her as the rain came though the window, landing on our faces. Shell never talked about her mother. The thunder cracked loudly right above us. The lights and radio flickered out. The summer's Top 40 love songs went dead.

Next to Betty's Bakery with the gingerbread men in the window was a park of dirt and crabgrass with one broken bench. Sloppy hung out there, and Quentin Cilberto, and kids

younger than I. Street Rats they were called, from the High
Acres Trailer Park, the dropouts who used food stamps. I was
shorn, defiant in the streetlight as Shell and I followed the
sound of Sloppy's mandolin and a few guitars being strummed
by the other silhouettes in the park. It was my first time out.
The group was singing. Everyone nodded a greeting at me,
then kept on with their harmonies. *Hick music,* Miles had
called it. But the gentle chorus of the Street Rats singing
"Peaceful Easy Feeling" soothed me.

"Isn't she cute as a button with that hair cut?" Sloppy
grinned. The temperature dropped, cooling my nape, and I
shivered. I felt so bare, my stomach flip-flopped, like spinning
into high speed on the Tilt-a-Whirl.

In all my years in Norway, we never had loons. But after my
milk had finally dried up, and I was back to wearing my old
bras, loons crashed into the smooth, cold surface of Lake Pennesseewassee. The loons became *Advertiser-Democrat* front-
page news: WINDBLOWN LOONS PRODUCE A CHICK. I waded in
the night shadows all summer, listening to the birds' trilling,
cuckoo noises flooding the pre-dawn with sadness and longing. Like the possums, I became nocturnal. I knew exactly on
which branch in which pine tree the great horned owl perched
every night. In the moonlight along the railroad tracks, the
Man in White passed me, going the opposite direction, silent
as a lunar moth. And I discovered that Shell's rage also revealed itself at night, a wild furtive creature.

She bolted away from me one August night, running bare-
foot down Main Street, making noises like Wanda had made,
guttural sounds like the sound of a rusty pump handle on
a pump that had no more water. She ended up outside St.

Stephen's Hospital by the emergency room, screaming her head off.

"This place sucks! It sucks, I know it, and the whole town knows it." Nurses came running out to quiet her, but when I couldn't get her to stop, they called the cops.

"Should we sedate her?" the nurses asked. All I could picture was her being shot with a dart, like some crazy dog wild with distemper.

"No, no, she'll be okay." I squeezed her hand really tightly as the blue and red lights from the police cruiser reflected in her big eyes. They did not arrest her for disturbing the peace. Even if they had, and her name ended up in the police log of the paper, what difference would it have made? All the mothers in town pitied her for being an orphan. They would just sigh and say, "Oh, Rochelle. That poor Carlton girl." As if her full name was ThatpoorCarltongirl.

I made her walk for hours up along the ridge. We followed the raccoon families through the freshly mown meadows back to the lake. Finally exhausted, she slept inside a canoe by the boat landing. I hoped she was spinning a lovely dream as I watched over her. I tried to fan the mosquitoes off her face all night, but sometimes they tangled in her hair. She whimpered in her sleep as I pressed my thumb along her hairline, killing the mosquitoes before they could pierce her.

I hid my wide thighs in the August moonlight but when the day after Labor Day came, I had no choice but to stuff myself into brown corduroys and cross the lime stripes of the football field back into Oxford Hills High School. Nothing had changed in the hallways: still the same metallic slamming all around me. I fit more easily into the desks without a baby inside me. How could I be the same Hillary Birdsong who had answered "here" last year in the A-D homeroom?

I wasn't "here." I went through the motions of trying to look like a "normal" teenage girl. Growing my hair out, spraying the thick waves to make them look even fuller. Taking vocabulary quizzes (*quagmire, quintessential*). Bumming Humpty Dumpty potato chips at lunch from girls I had grown up with, who begged me, "C'mon, Hillary, come to the dance with us Friday night, we're getting wasted at Diane's first."

They didn't know that only the grungy Street Rats were willing to tap me on the shoulder and ask me to slow dance. Marcel Colette, who once sang every single word to the six-minute long "Bohemian Rhapsody" with me, now laughed along with Tasha Lynn Randall when she clucked, "*Mmm-hmm*—slut," as they surrounded me at the water fountain. And I said nothing, now repulsed by the syrupy smell of Marcel, his mouth still filled with a thick gob of Juicy Fruit.

I played my counterfeit good-girl role until hunting season, and then I couldn't fight the dizzying sensation of being sucked into a whirlpool anymore. I had always hated the dead deer that hunters paraded down Main Street, the beautiful wild animals slung on the tops of passing pickups. It was the law that hunters had to transport them in full view, not covered, not concealed. It pushed me to rage, seeing their eyes still open, round velvety pupils black as the centers of whirlpools.

I remember my strong brother Birdy peering over the side as my mother rowed us out to the totem pole, my chest plump with an orange life preserver. Droplets fell from my mother's oars, circling in the warm summer air, and small, spinning holes formed on the smooth, cool surface of the water.

"Could those holes grow bigger?" Bird demanded.

"You two sit in the middle of the seat. You're making the boat tippy."

"Has there ever been a whirlpool on this lake?"

"No. There's really no such thing. Same as quicksand. We don't have that here."

My mother. Tan in her crisp, white blouse and a white bracelet clinging to her wrist. It was one of the few times I remember her barefaced. Free of mascara and eyeliner, her hazel eyes looked more like Bird's. She rowed efficiently, strongly, concentrating on keeping the oars in the rusted oarlocks. Then the rotting old boathouse came into view, built over the water so that a motorboat could dock right into it. No one even knew who owned it anymore. No people ever came to that water-garage, with rooms to live in above. No other camps were nearby, the totem pole making that isolated property on the lake even more sinister.

The top of the totem pole was carved into a severe, angry eagle face. The hooked nose was a dull yellow and the wide wings had been washed white by storms. Of course the eagle never blinked, never looked side to side, just stared, furious. Bird and I shuddered as we glided along the shoreline, the little holes in the water darker in the shadows.

"Bradford." My mother jerked the boat sharply. "Don't be such a baby. There's no such thing as whirlpools here in Maine."

But whirlpools did spin in the dead deer eyes all November—except on Sundays, the only day of the week hunting was not permitted and I could hike through the woods without having to worry about being shot. It was bad enough that Daryl Perch eyed me in school as if centering my breasts in the middle of his cross hairs. During the week he cut through the woods on the way to school, where I climbed the pines, and he called me a tease and plunked himself down on the roots and waited for me to come down. He chased me through the dried, prickly undergrowth, twisting handfuls of my sweater.

I hesitated to confide in Sloppy. But as he helped me gather up the summer tools in the cottage shed and bring them back to town, Sloppy asked, "I hear you missed two days of school this week. You got that stomach thing that's going round?"

"No." I decided to tell him the truth. "It's Daryl."

"What the hell?"

"Daryl pushes his crotch against me in the hallways, and pinches my arms. He knows about the baby. Everybody knows." I shrugged. "Some of the boys think I'm easy."

"Really? I'll take care of him."

I knew what that meant, and I was pleased that he wanted to look out for me. Sloppy Joe may have walked duck-footed, and never played contact sports, but he was scrappy, a bully and a hair-puller. Daryl could expect some bald patches on his greasy pig head.

I turned the wheel on the padlock and swung open the doors to Dad's shed. I saw the ax, the hammer, and the needle-nose pliers he used to yank fishhooks out of the faces of wide-mouth bass.

"Let me see that ax," Sloppy demanded. It was a cold, depressing day, the trees plucked of leaves. Sloppy held the handle, and then threw it with all his strength. It spun and landed with the tip lodged in the edge of an old pine.

"Let me try." The ax was heavier than I expected, nothing like a hammer. The metal blade felt silky. I threw it fiercely and it landed with a musical *fwop* in the bark.

We took turns playing with the ax, working on our aim and deepening the depth of the blade in the trunks of the trees. Cedars were the softest.

"Let's go for a more challenging target," I suggested.

I wrapped the ax in an old wool blanket, and we tramped through the dead undergrowth of the woods to the totem pole. The lake frothed, choppy with the autumn wind, the pewter clouds hanging low. The eagle was exactly my height; its wings as wide as my open arms. I stepped back, then chucked the ax into the back of the eagle's head and a ruffle of splinters rose like a cowlick.

"Ten points!" Slop cried, just like Birdy would have, my happy-go-lucky brother. Carefree. I was the serious one, they said. The defiant one. My mother said I was the handful.

I began amputating the wing. I stood behind the totem pole so no one across the lake could see me. I didn't worry about the sound carrying across the water. There were so many of those sounds in the fall, the whine of saws and then a crashing and a thunk that you could never really tell which direction the sounds were coming from.

The wood crackled, stiff with varnish. But I got a rhythm going. Wood chips sprang from the curved shoulder. I chopped a notch, then widened it, whittling away. I grunted and sweated. "Come . . . on . . . geez . . . *uggh.*" Finally the wing, pulled down by its own weight, began to split from the body. I hacked some more and kicked it hard, bruising my heels. The wing hung suspended, connected by the feathers in the armpit, then dropped slowly, making a heavy thud on the moss. It rocked, and then lay still.

"Whoa," Slop said. "That's trippy."

I hurled the ax one last time. The eagle would stare forever at the spot where the ax disappeared into the lake, as it cut its own splash. I pushed the wing over the silky carpet of dry pine needles, straining my back, but succeeding in shoving it into the water. It sunk for a moment, and then bobbed to the surface, like a child learning to swim, starting with the dead man's float. It began to spin in its own slow whirlpool.

The next week's front page of the *Advertiser-Democrat* showed two photos of the eagle: one before, one after. Under the still-glaring eagle the headline read in bold print, NORWAY LAKE'S BELOVED LANDMARK DESECRATED.

My stomach lurched as I stood at the newspaper stand outside the drugstore owned by Shell's Uncle Zee. Carlton Drugs sold toiletries and moose-decorated souvenirs for tourists, and had a soda fountain that served breakfast until 11 A.M. At seven years old, Shell had buttered Wonder Bread toast and cracked brown eggs before school. The regulars at Carlton's loved how her brightness balanced out the weight of Uncle Zee's perpetual scowl.

Uncle Zee had insomniac's bags under his eyes and jet black hair that he Brylcreemed into a side part. He was a decent father to Shell. He took the job of raising his sister's child seriously. Because Shell and I were inseparable, my father and Uncle Zee became friends, ice fishing in a little plastic shack for hours on the surface of the lake.

Shell and Uncle Zee lived on an overgrown lot at the edge

of Oxford County, in an unfinished little bungalow that never received any direct sunlight. The stairwell up to Shell's room was murky, decorated with drawings of cowboys that seemed to follow you hungrily with their eyes no matter how far up the stairs you ran. When the snow melted at the end of the winter the whole house leaked, and tin pots had to be strategically placed under the cold drips. When I slept over at Shell's, I always awoke to find daddy longlegs underneath me, flattened like cartoon characters under a steamroller. I was always tickly, thinking they were exploring my palms and face with their light, wispy legs. Despite the sour reek of cat pee in the corners, I always begged my mother to let me sleep over there.

Maybe because of the dankness and the daddy longlegs, Shell grew obsessed with washing her feet every night after brushing her teeth. Then, in the summer before seventh grade, my mother said we could shave (Uncle Zee had little confidence in his ability to raise a budding teenager, so he frequently turned to my mother). Shell groomed her legs every night in the bathroom sink. She'd get in an extra hamstring stretch, one leg lifted under the mirror, flexing her toes under the faucet as she lathered her long shin. "Mmm," she'd hum, sliding her smooth legs into a cool fresh bed as if she could taste it.

But she wasn't saying "mmm" in the dark mauve dawn when I confessed to her out on the back steps near the Dumpster that stank like sour milk jugs.

"I wish you hadn't told me. I don't want to know, okay? Every customer who has been in here drinking coffee was chattering about it. Including Officer Lerman." Shell was so angry with me that her hands quivered as she lit her cigarette. "Who, by the way, showed up to ask me questions. He said an eyewitness saw two people shoving the wing into the water. But this witness was too far away to be sure of anything. There was no positive ID, according to Officer Lerman, but if he had his way, he said he would put the guilty party away, make sure they were sent to Juvi in Lewiston."

"How can he be sure it was a teenager?"

"What grown-up would do such an immature thing?"

"Well, Sloppy, for one."

She rolled her eyes. "You are messed *up*, honey."

I wrapped my arms around my knees for warmth as I sat glumly in the frosted shadows. "The wing washed up on Sandy Shore. They're not going to be able to reattach it."

"Like you care?"

"I know it was stupid. I feel horrible."

"But it didn't feel horrible when you were chopping away, did it?"

"No." In fact, it had felt exhilarating to destroy with such aim and precision.

"You need to get a grip, Hill."

"Like *you* never go schizoid."

She stubbed out her cigarette in a Coke bottle and let the screen door slam behind her. I followed her back inside and watched her break open some brown eggs and start whisking them.

"Scrambled eggs. Your favorite color, right?" That was my attempt at an apology, reminding her how much she loved soft yellow.

The Man in White sat at the counter, counting out dimes from his change purse. He loved to tip Shell. Every morning she filled and refilled his coffee cup with the same tenderness with which he tended the Pike Hill gravestones.

Priscilla Nix's smarmy face poked around from the corner shelves of souvenirs: red lobster decals, tee shirts with moose. She still wore stringy pigtails as she pushed her son, Jason, in a wobbly, duct-taped stroller. Shell and I exchanged a look, shocked that she was in the store that early and wondering if she had been eavesdropping.

I heard my mother's voice in my head, *That Nix family uses food stamps at the A&P.* Priscilla bent down to offer the baby a marshmallow chick, deliberately showing off, talking baby talk to him. "Need some num-nums?" I could not bear to look at her baby's face.

I sneered. "Does little Jason-wason know about the spectacular show his mother put on Friday night when he was with Gramma?"

"Shut up," Priscilla snapped at both of us. She hurried down the first aid–feminine products aisle.

"You didn't know I was there that night, did you? The whole town is admiring your ability to mud wrestle."

"Back off, Hillary," Shell whispered.

Two weeks before, Sloppy Joe had taken me out to, in his words, "have some kick-ass fun." It was kick-ass, but not fun. Priscilla had been on a roped-off stage in the Pub, paired against Baby Jane. Both of them were extremely drunk, goopy, and brown as they spun each other around in the mud. Steve Pyne led the sold-out crowd in chanting "Go Puss-illa!" But Baby Jane had massive speed-skater thighs in her cut-offs and kicked Priscilla's butt.

I hissed, my voice slithering through the drugstore as I enunciated clearly, "Puss-illa."

Her pointy chin jutted out in anger. She thrust the stroller briskly past the Man in White and pulled open the door. She looked at me with fear in her eyes. "You're crazy. Crazy. Just like Daryl says. Like everyone says."

Maybe I was.

I ran to the trees, with a hundred restless birds sailing around squawking.

I left the store that day and climbed a pine tree at the top of Carpenter's Crest. I shimmied to the top and began shifting my weight, bending the trunk down, then letting it spring up. I rode the tree, back and forth, whipping through the air, just missing the dead bristles of the other trees. My palms grew raw and blistered from the rough bark. I didn't feel free. I never felt free. But I imagined that Tom could see me, his crazy birth-mother, blowing into the clouds like a smoke signal.

Sometimes I skipped school just to wander around the baby clothes in Ames. Newborn. Three months. Six to nine months. Twelve months. I bet he's pudgy by now, I thought, solid in Lola's arms. Soon I would receive Lola's first letter. Was my baby walking? Had he had his first real barbershop haircut, not just a trim of the bangs from Lola? I lingered with Shell among the onesies and Pampers, trying to choose Tom's birthday present. We walked past rows of smiling little dolls with round heads and no arms, rubber duck families, and water-filled teething rings. I didn't want to give him hard plastic. I wanted to give him warmth. And softness. I decided on a giant plush white unicorn, stuffed just right, so that when you hugged it, it hugged you back. I imagined his perfect little hands reaching out to squeeze the sparkling silver horn.

Before I addressed the box—to DeeDee's agency, which I hoped would forward the package to Lola—I kissed the unicorn's silver hooves all over. I folded the present into balloon wrapping paper, and I wrote on the tag: *To Tom, I love you baby boy and miss you baby boy and think of you every day. With love forever and ever and ever from your birthmother.*

My mother knocked on my door. "Hill? I have something here for you."

"Just leave it."

I heard a heavy sigh as my mother slid the envelope under the door. I recognized Lola's square handwriting.

His photos were here.

Should I tear the envelope to bits? What good does it do to look at him? I can't touch him. Can't smell him. Can't feel his breath on my breasts. He probably eats off a small spoon by now.

I had once heard that you should never burn a photograph. That something toxic is released. Why not just burn Tom's pictures? Didn't I let him go?

In the old days some unwed mothers didn't even get this much. They pushed their children out, and a stranger in a mask cut the cord and whisked the baby away forever. It must have been like going blind, not ever seeing your own child.

At least I got to hold him with all my senses. And he had held me, too.

I could not burn his pictures.

I opened the envelope, slid out one of the pictures, felt the cool surface. But I didn't look at it. I slipped it into my bra over my left nipple, though I hadn't had any milk in a long while. I left it there for ten minutes. Then I took the photo and tucked it into my right bra cup, switching sides.

I looked. Tom had more hair, blonde like my mother and Bird. He was lying on his belly, laughing into the camera. The front of his onesie was soggy with drool. He had four white, square teeth: two on top, two on the bottom. His nose was still shiny and his smile reminded me of Miles. *He's crawling all over! And took a few steps already!* Lola had scrawled on the back. There were two other photos. I stared at the whorls of his ears and the faint hair of his eyebrows, thinking that his cheek was so creamy it looked like I could just reach out and stroke it.

Then I found the letter.

Dear Hillary,
First: I think of you everyday.
I've been composing this letter in my head for a month, and I still don't know what the right thing is to say. I can't believe it's been a year since I saw you. James and I do want you to know that Tom, at one year old, is doing great. I think you are an amazing person, Hill. I need you to know that I am keeping the promise that I made to you: I am raising Tom the best I can.
Love,
Lola

My mother knocked again. "Hill? Dinner will be ready soon. Pork loin."

"Fine," I answered. I could see the shadow of her shoes underneath the door. She was waiting.

"What did Lola's letter say?"

"Tom's crawling."

"May I come in?"

"It's unlocked."

She held Tom's pictures for such a long time that she sat down on my bed to rest. "My goodness," she sighed. "He looks so much like your brother." I smelled the sharpness of coffee on her breath. "I know you might not want to believe me, but I miss Tom."

"You have no right to miss him."

Stunned, she answered, "He's my grandchild."

I could feel the grief spiraling in me, the way it had the first few days without Tom. I did not want to break down in front of my mother. She had seen enough of me being so raw. I needed to cut her so she would just leave before I lost it.

"Some grandma. You barely looked at him." I plucked the photos from her hand. "And now you miss him."

She stormed out of the room just as I broke down, muffling my choked sobs in my pillow. *I miss you. I miss you in my arms. I miss your heat. Your skin. Your breath. Your wet diaper. I miss you, Little Tommy Tittlemouse. That's all I am: All I have become is missing you.*

6

With the weight of Tom's absence bearing down on me, I could no longer handle visiting Bird's grave. But Shell told me that the Man in White still tended Birdy in Pike Hill and everyone buried over in the Old Dam Church cemetery out on Route 26. The Man in White had to reach up on the tiptoes of his white bucks to clean my grandmother's headstone that was shaped like the Washington Monument with an angel on top. I always felt bad that Shell's parents had thin little tablets for markers that blended in with the graves from the 1700s. She felt bad too, I think, because she made fun of Maud's headstone, saying it looked phallic.

My mother's mother, Maud Wright, spent her whole adult life trying to prove that she had moved far beyond her childhood, during which she had languished for several years in the Otisville Poorhouse. Maud's family had been supported by the town, and all the "inmates" had to work: caring for the aged residents, growing corn and beans in the summer, feeding the chickens, cows, and pigs all winter long.

It always gave me the creeps when we drove by it. "There's the poorhouse," my mother would mutter. It's not a dark misshapen building, but a simple one-story farmhouse, abandoned, set back from the road, with pickup trucks rotting near the barn.

"She only lived there a few years," my mother would tell me. "It's not like she spent her whole childhood there." But I disagreed with my mother: I don't think Maud ever got over the shabby dresses, the stench of humid privies, the daily succotash.

Her family finally moved from the poorhouse to a shack farther up Swampville Road, and at seventeen she married my grandfather. He was an ordinary carpenter in a canvas apron. He didn't object to working two jobs to support her extravagant taste in fashion because he loved to pose her in various settings, photographing her endlessly.

My mother spent her childhood in party dresses that required the utmost care. All the black-and-white photos of her feature a serious-looking girl posed on the lawn. Even the hoods of her snowsuits were fashioned with real fox fur. When I found a photo of her wearing a dress with a black velvet top and a taffeta skirt, I asked my mother, "Did you have gym in school?"

"Oh yes," she answered. "Every day we did jumping jacks in the gymnasium."

"Did you wear that dress doing jumping jacks?"

"I sat out," my mother told me. "I didn't care if I got to play. I felt beautiful."

Though she died when I was young, I remember Maud clearly: an auburn-haired, softly freckled woman who slipped her slender bare feet into stiletto heels all summer. When we played dress-up in her giant closet, Shell would coil Maud's silk scarves into a swami turban; I would put a satin half-slip on my head, pretending to have long white hair like Shell.

———

There were three things Maud hated: being embarrassed, anyone from Sloppy Joe's family, and pigs. While she was in the
poorhouse, the town of Otisville refused to pay for residents
who needed to be sent to the Maine Hospital for the Insane.
Instead they were kept in cages on the town farm. Sloppy's
grandfather lived there, and it was my grandmother's job to
bring him his morning oatmeal.

"He was a beast," my grandmother told me. "All those
Lombards are a pack of loonies. Your brother should steer
clear of Sloppy Joe. His father? Frank? You know he's completely loco."

But I was fascinated with Sloppy's father. He claimed to
have been abducted by a spaceship while walking through
Bridgeton one snowy night—actually, a mere mile from the
old Otisville "farm."

Maud refused to eat pork chops, bacon, or ham sandwiches. "People think that pigs are all sweet and pink. But my
god, the flies that cover them. The horrible grunting they
make, like monsters. The way their snouts move around. Wet.
Shiny. Dark brown, not pink like ribbons. Disgusting, scary
creatures. But at least you could sell them and make a profit.
Not like us, the pitiful people. The dregs.

"When your mother was born, I never wanted her to have
to see anything ugly. I wanted her to have luck and beauty. So
I picked the most beautiful name I could find: Janée."

My grandfather died before I was born. Maud died when
I was ten. She spent the last years of her life as a stylish widow
who retained her graceful figure until she died of skin cancer
that was discovered only a few months before she passed away.

"She was photogenic to the very end," my mother bragged.

———

Though I looked just like her, I did not inherit Maud's fear of embarrassment that filtered deeper into my mother the months after I received Tom's pictures.

"Your grandmother would have been appalled by your be-havior. Simply appalled. I overheard Daryl Perch in the drug-store say, 'That bitch is nuts!' To think he was talking about my daughter! Oh, if your grandmother had seen you whip-ping back and forth through the trees she would have had a stroke. It's not enough you hang out with that loser Sloppy Joe. No, you have to go and befriend the town fool. How do you think it looks, you and the Man in White, skipping down the railroad tracks hand-in-hand?"

By the time I graduated from Oxford Hills, she held her tongue about the Man in White. Because, despite my truancy and lackluster grades, he had, oddly enough, helped me get into Tremont College, a school in Ithaca, New York, which based much of its entrance requirement on the application essay: Write five hundred words on a person whom you admire.

This is what I wrote:

> In the sharp curve of railroad track where Norway becomes Paris, a crossing signal with vivid red lights and deafening bells lowers white gates, warning that a train approaches. But years ago, before the signal, the road intersected with the track in complete darkness at night. Two newlyweds were driving home after a performance: She was celebrated for her expressive soprano voice; he was admired for his melodic tenor. They were struck by

the night freight train. She died instantly; his head was sewn back together with a steel plate inside. When his hair grew back, it was completely white. No one is sure how old he is, but he has been wandering my hometown forever.

He is without a voice and can walk in the hottest sun without sweat, brushing the ants off his wife's grave without shedding a tear. What I admire about him is how he dresses all in white, not black. Not in the color of mourning, but in the color of a bride. He lives on disability checks but makes it his job to clean headstones. Not just his wife's, but headstones throughout the town. He scrubs the tombstone of my grandmother, and other family members as well.

When I was small I was fascinated by the idea that he had a plate in his head. Because he uses only dimes to pay for things—shiny, dazzling dimes—I pictured the plate as thin as a dime and with "In God We Trust" printed on the underside. Though my mother always made me hurry across the street to avoid him, I have recently come to understand that he isn't crazy. He's really quite brave. I think it's pretty amazing that he is able to return to the exact spot where his wife died. I hope that now that there are signals, he feels a lot safer.

The first time he reached out for my hand I was scared. Usually he ignored me, or simply nodded. But I came down from climbing trees one day and there he was with his arm outstretched. I thought I would help him, if that's what he needed, though I had never stood that close to him for that long.

His grip was surprisingly strong. There was nothing creepy about touching him. Nothing gross. My hands were sore from the scratchy tree bark.

People say he's an idiot, a simpleton. But his glove was cool and soothing in my hand.

The last August night before I left for college, Shell treated me to the circus, where we sucked root beer out of cool unbroken mounds of snowcone. "You and your root beer," Shell joked. "Like that bottomless cup you invented for your Barbie." I sipped the snow until the plastic monkey cup was empty. I had forgotten how Shell and I used to hide in my backyard in the honeysuckle. How I pretended my doll had a thimble full of soda that never went dry.

I had not expected to be among so many babies covering their ears, screaming in fright at the sound of motorcycles riding around and around inside a metal sphere. It seemed as if Shell and I were the only ones there without a small child.

"That elephant is depressed." I pointed to a drooping baby waiting its turn to join the others lumbering around the center ring.

"How do you know?"

"I can just tell." I had received Tom's unicorn in the mail that day. I wasn't surprised. I had known that the agreement with SMFS forbid any contact with Lola or James or Tom for eighteen years. The flow went only one way: Lola, to me. It had taken months for them to send the gift back to me with a note saying, *Southern Maine Family Services is not authorized to contact the party to whom this was sent.*

She shrugged. "It's the circus." Shell couldn't take her eyes off the contortionists. Their flexibility astounded her. "Look at the duration of those handstands!" Tiny muscled women sprung up off long elastic sticks and assembled into a human ladder.

Enormous sinewy tigers came leaping out of a cage. They growled with fierce open mouths and beautiful ragged teeth while sitting on their seats batting the air with their paws. Every two seconds people applauded the tiger trainer, some guy with a German name, who looked like the Incredible Hulk with a whip. Then the tigers ran away in single file, orange stripes vanishing through a swinging black door.

The elephants trotted out again, this time with purple plumes bouncing on their heads. They looked moronic, standing with their giant flat feet on yellow stools.

"This is b.s.," I shouted into Shell's ear. "Look at these elephants sitting on their butts, waving their arms in the air."

"It's just the circus," Shell answered with an edge in her voice. "The animals really are amazing."

"I'd rather see them in the wild."

"So would I, but this is the closest we can get for now."

"They lead miserable lives."

Shell grabbed her sweater and stormed out of her seat and up the stairs, taking two at a time. "Getch yer souvenirs heah," the vendors beckoned to us. I chased her, grabbing her elbow near a souvenir cart full of purple elephants dangling from sticks.

"You're mad?" I asked.

"I'm not mad."

"Then why won't you look at me?"

She turned to me, eyes blazing. "I'm confused, that's all. I just wanted you to have *fun*. This is our last night before you go off to college. I wanted it to be special. I brought you here to have fun. Remember? Fun? Laughing, joking, being like a kid again? This is the circus. You know, clapping, cheering. Would it hurt to just have *fun*?"

"Just because I don't like to see wild animals wearing ridiculous costumes I'm not fun? Anyway, it was stupid to come here. I should have said no. Lola lives somewhere around Portland. Look at all these kids. I keep thinking I see him. What if she's with him here?"

"You," she spoke slowly, "have got to move on." She said it more with sadness than anger.

I could feel my mouth grimace, and I held back my tears. We located her station wagon in the parking garage and drove home with no words, no radio, with only the clicking of her turn signals breaking the silence. I forced myself to sit up straight and keep my expression neutral. Arriving at my house, she put the car in park and we idled for so long that her gas gauge went from one-quarter full to near empty. Finally she whispered, "I'm sorry. I was an idiot to say that."

"I really love him," I answered.

Shell's face was wan. "I have to admit, I tried hard not to love him because I knew you were giving him away."

"Did it work?"

"No." She leaned her head against the steering wheel, hiding behind her hair. "My god, it was so incredible, watching him be born. Remember the sweet smell in the air? Sort of like—" she thought for a moment, and lifted her head, looking right at me—"a melon."

"That's real touching," I said. "But I need to get over it, right?" I slammed the car door and walked in front of the car, murmuring into the beam of her one headlight, "See you."

7

The hem of my cherry red sundress tore on the afternoon my mother and father dropped me off at college. The dress was dotted with pastel blue forget-me-nots and had a ruffle on the bottom. The top was a tube stitched with rows of elastic, and long strings that I tied into bows on my shoulders like shoelaces. I hated my skin when I took it off: My breasts rippled with pink indents from the zigzags of the elastic.

I focused on pulling at the loose threads on my dress because my dormitory, Quad 45, was so similar to Bird's. The carpets in the lobby had that fruity smell of spilled beer still drying in the fibers and the odors of too much living in a small area: spray starch, Cup-a-Soup, pepperoni pizza. A surge of guilt passed through me as if it were my fault I was making my parents stand in a dorm room again, with its patched sheetrock where holes had been punched with drunken fists.

My mother turned to me with her hazel eyes brightened with tears. I had longed for her face and yet, at that moment, I could not bear the closeness that holding her gaze might bring. I kept her on the periphery, her wide, bare arms hanging at her sides, dark shapes cutting into a day that was bright and lovely. As sudden hot gusts of late summer wind slammed doors shut throughout the building, I stared out of the big glass slider at the perfect view: Ithaca spreading down the hill, all the way to the lake.

My father squeezed me so hard he cracked my spine. "Be good," he murmured.

My mother unclasped her purse and handed me two twenty-dollar bills. "Let me know if you need anything," she said. Just like she had when she had carted me off to the nuns. But there were no nuns in this dormitory. Just the opposite.

My new roommate swooshed past me with a flourish. I stepped back into a tangle of coat hangers, stunned by her rudeness.

"I thought I requested a single," she said, turning on me.

"Freshmen don't get singles. Only doubles. And we should cross our fingers that they don't need to convert this into a triple."

"You won't mind me smoking," she informed me.

"I guess not."

"I'm Simone. But some people call me Flint."

"Why?"

"My mother's psychotic. Rich, but psychotic. She used to wake us up in the middle of the night and toss us in the back seat of the car in our pajamas to chase after fire trucks."

"Oh. I'm Hillary."

"Where you from?"

"Maine."

"You're kidding. You hardly have an accent."

"You do."

"So where am I from?"

"Long Island."

"Touché," she said sarcastically. She raised one eyebrow and offered me a cigarette. I took one and lit it. We settled cross-legged and hunched on the bottom bunk, trying not to knock our heads on the wire mesh above us.

"You don't really smoke, do you," she said.

"I never really learned to inhale."

"Then why bother?"

"Smoking is a graceful way to do nothing with your hands."

"Who said that?"

"My high school health teacher." Actually it had been Sister Joan, chastising Wanda.

Simone laughed with her lips pursed, smoke shooting up into the brown stains on the underside of the mattress. "God, I feel like I'm back at camp." Spotting the smoke detector above the desk, she rummaged around in one of her boxes and pulled out a washcloth, molded it over the smoke detector, and snapped it into place with a rubber band.

"Isn't it dangerous, doing that?" I asked.

Simone shrugged. "Sure."

Within the first few weeks I discovered the trails in the woods behind my dorm and the water tower on the hill. As I climbed the mint green ladder of the tower my mind swirled with the questions that my brainy professors were relentlessly asking. I took mental notes punctuated with question marks: *What is history? What is real?* My heart was pounding when I reached the top. I heard an infrequent car stereo in the parking lot far below, but otherwise only the late-summer cricket and phoebe duets interrupted the stream of questions in my head. *What is freedom? Who is free?*

Voices on the path below startled me. "Hey, there's a chick up there."

"No way. Chicks don't have the balls to climb to the top."

Then, vibrations came shivering up the iron rungs of the ladder. A face with a scruffy beard popped into view at the edge of the tower. "How ya doin'?" He scrambled off the ladder toward me, followed by his friend. "I'm Grant. That's Jared." They settled in, facing the lake, but Grant stared at me instead of the view.

"What is it?" I demanded.

He blushed. "Okay, I'll tell the truth. I was wondering. Are you—" his eyes scanned my tank top and cutoffs "—freckled all over?"

I felt a sparkle between my legs and then I panicked. "I have to go," I said, crawling backward onto the ladder and disappearing from their sight.

"Why did you scare her off?" I heard Jared say.

"I've heard if a girl is freckled, her skin is more sensitive to touch, that's all."

On weekends the girls in my dorm invited their boyfriends up from Long Island, and the boys padded with big hairy toes down our hallways, shy in the peach-colored bathrobes of their girlfriends. I could smell when boys were sleeping nearby, a faint spice seeping under the doors, but a dangerous smell, like smoke from a ragged wire.

Week after week the girls panicked, periods were late, more cigarettes were smoked, tough laughter, classes were skipped, then mint juleps appeared when their periods came. Celebrating as if they were at the Kentucky Derby. Talking about how you got fat thighs if you took the pill, how often they had their boyfriends pull out, how rubbers got lost inside their vaginas, and how hard it was to insert a diaphragm when you were really shit-faced.

One night Margaret, a girl who lived right below me, knocked on my door at midnight.

"I heard you were still up. You got any jelly?"

"What?"

"For my diaphragm. I've run out, and Eric's waiting for me in bed. I know it's tacky to ask, but could you help me out?"

"I don't have a diaphragm."

"Oh. Does Simone? Maybe you could check her drawer for me."

"I don't think so."

Margaret sighed. "All right."

I shut my door and heard her knock on Lisa's door. "Thanks," Margaret said. "You're a lifesaver! I owe you."

"How many people have you slept with?" Lisa asked me in the lounge a few nights later. Miles and I had never slept. Even at Old Orchard Beach. I made my decision. "None," I said.

From then on, they teased me about being a naive little hick. I did nothing to correct them.

Simone cut every class except art, lounging around in a jade silk kimono and blowing little smoke rings into already widening smoke rings. She'd get dressed around noon in freshly pressed Gloria Vanderbilt jeans.

"You Long Island girls are such prisses," I teased her. "Who ever heard of putting creases in jeans?"

"Our fashion sense is way beyond frayed dungarees."

"Hey, it worked on Grant."

We laughed. Grant had spotted me in the dining hall the night after we met on the tower, and he had been bringing me freshly picked bouquets for days. His flirting made me nervous. Though his face was plain, he wore sleeveless shirts that revealed his creamy brown biceps. I imagined circling my cheek over the contours of his arms.

There was a knock on the door. I opened it to Grant handing me a fistful of wilted daisies. "There's a party over at DK tonight. They're having like, eight kegs. You guys wanna go?"

"DK?" I almost shouted. "They have *DK* here?"

"Delta Kappa. Yeah."

"I'm not going."

"C'mon," Grant urged. "We can climb the water tower later, in the dark if you dare."

"I said I'm not going."

"Why are you so angry? Did I do something?"

"Don't you know they're a bunch of idiots in that messed-up fraternity?"

"It's a free buzz. I'll be looking for you if you change your mind."

Simone and Grant left without me. But later, around midnight, I was drawn across the courtyard to the dorm where the fraternity brothers lived. I spied on the party from the bench outside: boys and girls laughing into each other's ears, the light in the windows the color of flat beer. In another window a bare-chested young man did four shots in a row, throwing his head back, a ring of people cheering each time he victoriously raised an empty shot glass.

What had happened the night Bird died? What hadn't my mother and father told me? Were they protecting me? "They yelled at him to quit acting like a faggot," I had once overhead my mother screaming to Aunt Iris.

———

I remembered the summer before he died, pulling up to the takeout window of Goodwin's on my bike. Bird already had the waitress mixing my Awful-Awful in a tall silver cup. She tipped the bubbly foam into a paper cup. In small red letters it read AWFUL BIG, AWFUL GOOD. I sucked the straw almost flat before anything rose into my mouth, and when it finally did the cold, sweet shock of it was thrilling.

"*Mmm.* Vanilla. You always get the wrong flavor," I teased him.

Bird's friends Larry and Sean came around the corner joking with Charlie, the guy who swept and mopped the floors at Goodwin's. It was cold, even for August, so Charlie had the hood of his sweatshirt up. He was mentally retarded and joyful most of the time, not because he was foolish but because he had been discharged from Sweeny Hall, an institution where he had been frequently locked in a windowless room and sometimes beaten. He worked a few hours a week at Goodwin's and also picked up trash and twigs for free across the street at the high school. Smaller children especially loved him for his wide grin and how even his bald head seemed to slope up, his forehead wrinkles piling up like smiles.

"I'm gonna go tidy up around the schoolyard, then go get Gertie." Charlie smiled at me. He and Gertie lived next door to Goodwin's in a room over the lumberyard office. Gertie was in her seventies, older than Charlie, with white hair and big eyelids magnified by her thick lenses. I don't know why she wore glasses because she was blind and walked without lifting her feet, keeping her eyes closed. Charlie adored her, proudly holding her hand as he guided her around town.

"Gertie sure is purty," Larry complimented him. Charlie nodded. The screen above the takeout counter slid open and a hand holding a tall cone popped out. Sean took a long, hard lick of pink ice cream.

"That sure is some babe you got there," Sean said.

"I love Gertie," Charlie answered simply.

"She good in bed?" Sean prodded.

"You mean does she like to sleep?" Charlie grinned and then realized what they meant.

Larry and Sean cracked up. Bird looked down, not saying anything, sipping his Awful-Awful then biting his thumbnail.

When Charlie was nervous he repeated himself. "I was institutionalized for thirty-five years," he said several times, squinting at Sean.

"In-ti-too-ton-alized for tirty years?" Sean imitated Charlie's pronunciation.

Charlie began huffing, his left foot twisting in its plastic brace as he began loping through the group of boys.

Sean blocked his way. "I asked, is Gertie good in bed, you know—." Sean inserted his index finger of his right hand into his curled-up left hand and pumped. I had never seen a boy do that before, and it made my face hot.

"Lay off, Sean," Larry said lightly. "Birdy's little sis is here."

"Charlie, wait up!" I called out and trotted after him. I was relieved that Charlie still let me shake his hand. Our way of shaking hands was that I reached out to him and closed my fingers over the palsied knobs of his knuckles. That was our game: paper, rock, scissors. With Charlie I was always paper covering rock.

The wind began to blow hard, and he picked up trash quickly as it danced in the cinders of the track field. His bald head bobbed above his crooked body. "I have real bad memories of that place I lived," he told me. "But dat's da past. I try not to look."

My thoughts of Bird being too easygoing to defend a retarded man were suddenly broken apart by the realization that an older boy, perhaps a senior, was bowing in front of me, smiling. He held a DK cup and offered me a sip.

"No thanks."

He reached deep into his pocket and pulled out a small plastic triangle. "You look like you could use something special. Know what this is?"

I looked closely. "A guitar pick."

"This, believe it or not, was Bruce Springsteen's."

"You think I'm that naive? That could be any old guitar pick."

He looked hurt. "Why would I lie about something as serious as this?"

"Why not? You can't prove it anyway."

He tucked a dark curl behind his ear and looked at me. I didn't want to think he was good-looking. In fact, he was nearly gorgeous. My stomach fluttered and I closed my arms tightly over my chest.

"So," I said. "Is your frat seeking new pledges?"

"Not yet." Then he said very matter of factly, "For now, everyone's just trying to get laid."

Mick Jagger blared: "Start me up, start me up and never stop." Through another window dark mustaches danced with high, bouncy ponytails.

Simone's arrogance bordered on comical. She strutted through the student union with her pouty lower lip thrust forward, not caring who was there, not saying hello unless you were right in her path. Her round, beautiful breasts wiggled under her plush tops and she acted as if she were unaware of their movement. Groups of chatting students, male and female, followed her with their eyes.

"I think this guy Reed likes me," Simone said.

"Reed who?"

"Reed Sandburg."

"Reed Sandburg? Your teacher?"

"Uh-huh."

"Whoa. How do you know?"

"Because yesterday when I was drawing in the big studio, he came up to me and said, 'You wanna screw?'"

"How crass." I thought for a moment. "I can't believe he came on to you. What did you say?"

"I told him to get away from me."

"And did he?"

"He left and helped someone else with their still life."

"Do you like him?"

"Hillary, he's practically twice my age."

"That doesn't answer my question and you know it. You're interested. I can tell."

Simone raised her perfectly plucked eyebrows in that bratty look that meant *You are such a hick, Hillary.* "Have you seen him? He's so sexy. He's like Mick Jagger."

"But what about Theo?"

"Theo is a kid."

"So are you."

"Come on, Hillary. Get a grip here. How could you compare Reed with Theo? Reed's a man."

"But Theo is so sweet to you."

"Theo is a boy."

"But he's here all the time, waiting for you to come back after class. He treats you like a queen. He's gentle. He adores you."

"I don't really think there's a comparison."

"Simone, you are going to break Theo's heart."

"Yes, I am." She stuck her middle finger in her mouth, began biting away at the raggedy nail, and shrugged.

I stood at the turntable blowing dust off my Bruce Springsteen album when Simone burst through the door and fell onto a pile of damp towels, laughing.

"He got you pretty drunk," I said and cued up "Prove It All Night."

"So? It's my birthday. I'm nineteen!"

She hoisted herself up onto her boots, groped along the wall, then threw herself onto her rumpled satin sheets. Fumbling for her smokes in the pocket of her jean jacket, she slid one out, too drunk to taste the flakes of tobacco.

"He's fantastic."

I plucked the cigarette from between her lips.

"Hey!" she protested. I put the filter end in her mouth. "Oh. Thanks."

"So. Reed took you out for your birthday. Is he nice?"

"Nice is not a word you would use to describe Reed. He's wild. He's incredible."

"Do you think you'll go out again?"

"He's coming to get me tomorrow at six."

"That's fast."

"He knocked me right off my chair trying to screw me."

"My god, in the restaurant?"

"No, Hillary, at his loft afterward."

"Well, you didn't tell me that part. You liked that?"

"It was . . . passionate."

I got up to put the needle onto the cut of "Prove It All Night" again.

"Why must you listen to that same song over and over?" Simone moaned.

Why *did* I repeatedly play Miles's favorite song? I was sure he had moved on to a new Springsteen tune, maybe "Hungry Heart." I shrugged. "I don't know."

"Well, it's very juvenile."

"As juvenile as a thirty-four-year-old man hitting on a freshman? I just want you to be careful."

"Careful? Like you? Who wants to be a prune?"

"You mean prude."

She flung her arm over her head and passed out, the smoldering butt scorching yet another brown hole in her satin pillow. I blew out the embers before she set her hair on fire.

Simone and I had been placed in a dorm with drama majors, bold show-offs, emotional strippers who lived on the surface of their bodies like crayfish, joyous, shouting exoskeletons who would confess to anything as long you applauded afterward.

"Hillary, you have such an edge you'd be amazing in our workshop class. Come on!"

After they had dragged me to a class, I discovered that their acting teachers wanted me to break open by breaking down.

"What is the worst thing that has ever happened to you?"

"Nothing bad has happened to me," I lied.

"That's impossible. Dig deeper," the professor urged.

"No, really," I said. "My life has been boring."

"Okay." Professor Wall kept probing. "Then make something up."

The class watched me, waiting. I couldn't think of anything. Finally I shrugged and told the truth. "I'm a slut."

The girls from my hall burst out laughing.

"What's so funny?" the professor asked.

"She has a great imagination." Lisa Swartz clapped. "I mean, Hillary's good as gold. She's like Polly Purebred."

The Dramaramas didn't understand that I wasn't really one of them. While I fled to the water tower, they sought the stage, and if there wasn't a spotlight they stood singing under a streetlight until a crowd gathered. Lisa, for example, did an impeccable Cher impression: limp wrists, a rich, low alto vibrato, performing on Geneva Street after last call for the bleary-eyed students wandering up the hill.

Simone wasn't impressed with the histrionics of the girls, especially the star in the room next to ours. Georgette Martin had the enormous features of a startled puppet; her face looked like it was always behind a magnifying glass. You could see her expressions clearly from the back row of any theatre. Morning, noon, and night she played "What I Did for Love" from *A Chorus Line*. When she had to tear herself away from her turntable, she warbled in the shower, "Kiss today good-bye."

"Kiss my ass good-bye," Simone sang back.

"Check these pictures out." Lisa and Georgette were draped on the couches in the lounge. Lisa was flipping through her portfolio for her photography class. "You are so photogenic, Hillary. Look at these." I sat down beside her and was startled by what I saw.

I looked in the mirror only when rubbing a washcloth over my face. I had posed for Lisa on my way to class while giant, lazy snowflakes fell on me. Did I always look like that? So defiant? About to say "F-you?" And yet I could see my cheekbones were prominent, my face womanly.

Lisa stroked my head, almost petting me. "Intense little Hillary. What will become of you?" Her expression grew dreamy. "Let's see. One day when the sky clears after an afternoon of snow, you'll hop on a bus and disappear down the wet Ribbon Road. You'll go all the way to Hollywood on that road."

Maybe there were roads out there, places to find on maps. But maps showed only interstate highways, state parks, the dashes and dots where states ended and began. They couldn't warn you when a swing set or stroller might appear. That was the blessing of a college campus: I could avoid toddlers altogether if I went downtown only at night and if I went only to bars. When I accidentally spotted a baby who looked the same age as Tom, those longings rose up again in my heart.

The winter storms would last for days. Snow fell thicker here than in Maine. But I had radar for when the sky would clear. Sighting a confetti-colored snowsuit in the white noon sun, I immediately turned away.

Simone and I were falling asleep. Her smoke looped up to me in the moonlight, and lassoed her statue of David that glowed light blue on the coffee table.

"Isn't he so beautiful?" Simone mused.

"Yes he is. But I can't imagine letting everyone see me naked like that."

She laughed. "Everyone? You don't even let me see you."

It was true. I changed with my back to her so she would never notice the wrinkled little pouch of skin below my belly button.

"Maybe it's different because I'm an artist," she continued. "But I love the human figure. My mother, she would drive us around to these old burned houses. Nothing is uglier to me, nothing. The charred windows, the blackness in the empty rooms. Sometimes I had a feeling someone had died in the fire. Either from the smoke or the flame itself. It seemed so obscene for a body to be destroyed that way."

Simone's life sketches were glorious. Calf muscles, shins, heels, bony toes, pubic hair, hipbones, nipples, necks: Everything fluttered with movement. "The models drop their robes and my charcoal just begins gliding all over the paper. I don't think it's true that the female form is more beautiful than the male." Soon I heard her breathing evenly. I peeked over the edge of the bunk. She had fallen asleep with her chewed fingernails dipped in with the bent butts of the ashtray.

Simone was right. Reed was a clone of Mick Jagger. Reed even had the same long skinny thighs and pigeon-toed walk, head thrusting back and forth like a chicken. I felt very shy around him when Simone insisted that he take us both out for margaritas one Friday after her studio art class.

If you looked under the table you would be able to pick me out as the uncool imposter. Simone and Reed both wore three-hundred-dollar cowboy boots. Their boots were usually leather but every now and then Reed wore a pair of snakeskins. Neither of them cared when they splattered paint on the pointy toes. They traipsed straight into slushy puddles and never polished their boots, simply wearing them into the ground and then buying new ones.

I had cowboy boots, too. But ones with rubber soles. I had gotten them in Maine at the Bass Shoe Outlet in the little boys section. They read DINGO on the sides and were a real bargain for thirty dollars.

"I'm writing a haiku about Hillary for English class," Simone told Reed. "I have two lines of five syllables. 'Pale butterfly face' and 'lips wide line in pain.' I need a line of seven syllables."

"What is your favorite musical instrument?" Reed asked me, my mouth sizzling with jalapenos. I thought about how Frank Sinatra made my parents' house feel more full, as if we had a bigger family, with one more guy.

"I would have to say the human voice."

Reed's eyelids tightened into a serious look. "That's very esoteric, Hillary."

I had no idea what that meant. "Is it?"

Later that night I sat cross-legged on our floor with Simone's giant Webster's unabridged dictionary. *Esoteric* /es-ə-'ter-ik/ adj 1 a: *understood by or meant for only the select few who have special knowledge.*

Simone hadn't come back to our room. They dropped me off, then went back to his loft in town above the flower shop. I lay on the top bunk, my pale butterfly face staring out at the night, with my mother's favorite Billie Holiday song playing on the radio. Billie's voice seemed to be making the snow fall.

My sophomore year I studied both studio art and art history with Reed. I didn't learn how to draw or paint. Reed let me do whatever I wanted. One afternoon I shook out all the dried bits of autumn debris that I had collected in a pillowcase on my walks to the water tower: blonde oval pods, brown tear-shaped seeds, beige fronds like tassels. I arranged all the pieces in lines and patterns on a big piece of velvet. Reed declared it "delicate and beautiful."

Simone and I went to art openings downtown and at the gallery at Cornell to fulfill writing assignments for art history class. At the "American Voices" exhibit we encountered a set of black-and-white photographs of an old woman's naked bottom. The tag explained how this very rich woman from Texas had had an eating disorder her entire life, and it left her skin so wrinkled that it looked deflated.

"Gross. That is so unnecessary," Simone gasped. "What do you think of the show?"

"You've got every kind of bareness represented. But god forbid you show a naked pregnant lady."

Simone scratched off flecks of dried green paint from her knuckles. "That's a very odd thing to say."

"Why?"

"I don't know. But that wouldn't have dawned on me in a million years."

I quickly switched the subject. "I love this one, though."

Simone curled her lip. "Mary Cassatt? *Ew.* Too sentimental. I need more of an edge. Big deal, a mother washing a child's feet."

"But that's the point. Look at how neutral the faces are. It's not sentimental at all. I don't know where you see that. The mother isn't ecstatic or laughing. And she's not the opposite either, not annoyed, or tired, or sad. She simply is with her child. Easy and quiet. It's a symbol of the child's need, how basic that need is. A child needs a parent to do it. It's perfect."

"Yeah," Simone said. "Perfectly bor-ing."

So I never told Simone how many times I returned to the show in the two months it stayed. I couldn't get enough of *The Caress*, 1891.

In Reed's class, I learned I loved to write about art:

> Mary Cassat: The son is looking into the mother's face, he holds her chin, squishing her face almost. The mother is still, holding his little foot in her hand without squeezing it too tight. But without letting go either. They are an unbroken circle.
>
> She is not thinking of the past or the future. A pastel drawing can only show one moment, so it has to be the *right* moment. A moment that is filled with something true. And in this moment, holding her son, lovely colors fill the mother's face. Blue in her eyebrows, pink and ivory on her cheek. The shadow near her lips is a squiggle of slate blue. And the baby? A mocha belly button. Salmon and rose swirl around his legs in perfect spirals.
>
> The mother and son stare into each other's eyes. They will stay like this forever—they will never come apart.

Reed gave me As on my critiques. He especially liked my essay on a sculpture called *Hyberbooby* by an artist named Paul Perras:

> The white marble of this piece is so carefully polished that I wish I could lick it. Almost two feet high, the

marble is full with cool body parts flowing. The shapes
are so blatant, the piece is hilarious. The bottom of the
stand is made of white balls, perfect and exposed. The
balls flow up into what could be a female bottom, a female bent over. The male shape flows without any seams
right into the female shape. Who could look at this and
NOT want to touch it? When the security guards aren't
looking, maybe people are poking it. Or even tasting it.
I think the marble would taste like an old ice cube.

I asked my mother to forward the SMFS letters from Lola. I
now spent my summers in Ithaca, serving corn niblets and
burgers to summer-school students in the cafeteria. On my
days off I hiked in the state parks, along the pine-needled
trails that reminded me of Maine. Some nights I drank dark
beer in Micawber's and played darts with Theo. One night
after last call I spied Reed's angular silhouette in the window
of his loft. He gestured for me to come up.

"See you," Theo said bitterly. He detested Reed for stealing
Simone away from him.

I climbed the steep stairs past a drawing of a freshly dug
grave. The hole in the ground was the shape of a crucifix instead of the usual rectangular casket shape. The dirt was
shaded in very dark pencil so realistically that I suddenly remembered the cold, elastic feel of the clay around Bird's grave.
The small blades of grass fluffing the edge were long soft tri-
angles penciled lightly on the paper.

"That's beautiful," I whispered to Reed.

He shrugged. "That's my old style," he said and led me
into the studio area. It was like a huge office, a giant expanse
of mint green floor tiles, but devoid of cubicles.

"Heard from Simone?" I asked.

"She's having a ball in Paris."

The air smelled of pine sap, and I breathed it in deeply. "What is that?"

"Turpentine." Reed's canvases lined the walls: blasts of moving color, but with no shapes I could recognize. He nodded at his works. "What do you think?"

"Please don't put me on the spot."

"You're very bright, Hillary. Just look and tell me what you see."

Simone had warned me that Reed could be a prick. I took a deep breath and stared into the canvas he was just completing. Big red slabs cut across everywhere as if someone were painting a house and then just lost it, slashing with the brush like a weapon. But then underneath the red flowed a dark, bottomless blue.

"Well?" he asked.

I stepped closer to where the colors intersected. "I get it."

"How do you know?" he challenged, eyes squinting.

"I can feel it."

He smirked and stretched a sheet of Saran Wrap over the wet gobs of paint on his palette. In the corner of the loft was a small kitchen table. He pointed to a kitchen chair for me, then pulled one out for himself, straddling it backwards.

"Why don't you go home in the summer?" Reed asked.

I shrugged. "I don't know."

"Maine is so beautiful in the summer."

Shell wrote me all the time about Norway. *The summers you haven't been here have been nonstop rain. It's so damp my hair never seems to dry in its braid. I don't even bother to put the pots and pans away, there are so many storms.*

"I know all about it. Vacationland."

"Don't your folks miss you?"

"My father does, I think."

"Don't you miss them?"

"They come to see me here sometimes."

"They don't mind the long drive?"

"I don't think so. It's about eight hours. I've taken them to see all the natural sights. My mother says it's sort of like Maine here."

"Even so, aren't you homesick?"

"I was homesick even when I lived there."

He squinted his eyes like he was painting my portrait, figuring out what part of my face to fill in next. "Something happened to you."

"I beg your pardon?"

"I've watched you enter bars, when you're late to meet Simone and me. You move through a crowded happy hour with those little hands of yours held up in front of you as if to shield yourself from blows. I think someone broke your heart."

"Who hasn't had their heart broken? Besides, the past is the past. I don't look."

"That's impossible. I don't believe it. I think whatever happened to you helps you really understand the Venus de Milo."

I cracked up. "Oh, some secret trauma is why I think that sculpture is so tragic?"

"You looked at the statue and decided she must have phantom pain from her missing arms. That she's longing to hold what she has lost. You're wide open when you write about art. I can't help getting excited when I read it. Sometimes it's so easy for me to forget the passion of seeing new things, making new things, because of the bullshit of the art world. The greed of my art dealer in New York. The competition with idiots who have nowhere near the talent that I—"

I cut him off. "You love painting. You love it as if it were a person, right?"

"I suppose you could say that."

"So you're lucky, really. The one thing you love more than anything can't ever leave you."

He beamed with his boyish, dazzling Mick-smile. Then he slid his tiny butt off the chair, returned to his wet canvas, and pulled off the Saran Wrap to ponder his colors. He picked up a paintbrush and twenty minutes later was completely lost in his work, forgetting I was even there.

Fall semester came again, and, at Reed's insistence, Simone took six credits of photography. She came back from Rosh Hashanah with pictures of her niece, a three-year-old girl. "Geez, you must look just like your sister. Your niece is a carbon copy of you."

"Yeah. Except my sister can't wear a bikini anymore. She lost the weight after the baby, but her belly button's all wrinkly. Yuck."

The wet-haired little girl in the photo was tucked into a big thick towel like a white pea pod, fresh from her bath. "I love working with black and white." Simone laughed, looking at her niece again. "Look at Rachel. Isn't she a little doll? It's so great having her. I don't know if I ever want kids of my own. Probably when I'm old, like thirty. My sister said it hurts like hell, the birth part. I saw a movie in health class and I couldn't believe how gross it was, watching that thing come out. How about you? You think you'll ever have kids?"

"I don't know. Maybe. At least one, anyway."

"Or maybe you could just settle for nieces."

My face must have blanched because Simone cocked her head. "You okay?"

"I'm fine. It's just that . . . I won't have anyone like that. I'm not just an only child. I had a brother once. He died awhile ago."

"We've been friends two years and you never told me?"

"I don't know why I didn't."

Simone began chewing on her tiny, sore fingernails, staring intently at me, hiding behind her paint-spattered hand. "I'm sorry that happened," she said blandly. But I couldn't feel her sorrow at all.

Though Simone and I roomed together again our junior year it was like having a single because she lived at Reed's. She had returned from Paris with several long fur coats that she wore on snowy Friday nights when I met her and Reed for dinner.

"Why don't you take that coat off? It's boiling in here," I shouted in her ear one happy hour while Reed was talking with some girls from the intro to painting class who were gaga over him.

"I can't," she shouted back.

"Why?"

I looked at her shiny candy-apple lipstick that made her lips poutier, O-shaped, soft. She enunciated extra clearly. "Because I have nothing on." She lifted her eyebrows. "Reed likes it."

————

Sometimes I could see Reed and Simone from my dorm window, heading to the art building on the edge of campus; they were like twins in his-and-her fringed leather jackets. Sometimes I thought of her as a well-behaved pet. A dog that carries its own leash.

When they fought—which basically meant that Reed had gotten vicious and declared once again he didn't give a shit about Simone's drawings and paintings—she moved back into our room.

"He's a selfish bastard." I watched her pick at a whitehead on her chin. "Geez, this thing is as big as New Jersey. And there's something else."

I knew it before she said it.

She dabbed a wet tissue to her chin. "I'm late."

"How many days?"

"A week."

"What does Reed say?"

"I'm not going to tell him. He's made it clear he never wants kids. He just wants to paint."

"What do you want?"

"I want to get rid of it."

"But you don't even know for sure yet."

"I know. I just know. My breasts are so tender."

"Well, that's a sign."

She lit a cigarette and blew smoke rings. "I don't know how you do it, Hill. Don't you ever want to get laid? I mean, you do everything but."

"Who told you that?"

"Guys talk, Hillary. Come on." She gave a forced laugh.

I did fool around with boys sometimes, after parties, in dark lounges. I was ashamed to admit even to myself how much I loved the feeling of hands on my bare breasts. I could let a boy nibble on me for hours, back and forth, right nipple, left. It was even more shameful to admit that sometimes they grew bored with my refusal to go any further, and they would zip my shirt back up, take my hand, and take me home. Just that Friday, Dave Ripley and I rolled around on his couch in his apartment downtown. He was in all my philosophy classes, a rugby player who made me laugh when he rubbed his beard against my face. I was surprised at its softness. But when his hands tried to free the button from the buttonhole on my jeans, I guided them away.

"I'm just scared, I guess."

The little smoke rings floated through the center of the big ones.

"Who isn't?" she asked.

"Reed doesn't seem to be scared."

"Are you kidding me? He's terrified of getting close to anyone. Especially a woman."

"He can't be too terrified. He got pretty close to you."

My friend Becky would cut class to watch soap operas all afternoon on her little TV. Her door was always open, and every now and again I joined her, watching her inhale her cigarette. She sucked hard, then bit at the last tail of smoke as she pulled her lips off the filter. It made her look very cynical despite her fair skin, pale green eyes, and thin, flyaway hair cut into a childish bob.

There were rumors. No one was sure how many abortions

she had had, but I heard it was three. I needed to get help for Simone. No way could she go to the clinic on campus. Everyone knew she was Reed's.

"I have a friend who got in over her head," I said to the TV one afternoon as the plaintive piano music of *The Young and the Restless* began.

"Really." Becky indicated faint concern.

"I know you're a social work major. She needs to find—I don't know—some sort of clinic for women, I guess."

"I heard that the Buffalo Street Women's Clinic is pretty good."

"Okay. I'll tell her."

A week later Becky and I were bowing side by side at the row of sinks in the bathroom. She was hidden behind her hands as she lathered up her face. She mumbled, "How's your friend?"

"She . . . she's not good."

"Sorry to hear it." She rinsed the soap from her forehead and cheeks. Our sinks were always clogged with hair; the basins took forever to empty. "Tell your friend," she hunched tiredly over the cloudy water, "to ask for lots of Valium."

As I hurried across campus to the art studio to meet Simone and head to the clinic for her appointment, I heard Reed behind me. "Hillary, wait." The noon sun on a fresh snowfall blinded me.

"There's something I've been wanting to tell you." His legs dipped in his pigeon-toed strut more than usual. "I want to make love to you," Reed said quietly.

My stomach did a flip. "I'm going to pretend I didn't hear that."

"I do. I want to make love to you."

I was pretty, but I would never be a sex bomb. I wore a frumpy down parka all winter and would never be exotic and confident like Simone and all the other rich girls from Long Island. I turned to him and gritted my teeth. "What about Simone?"

"I care for her."

"Yeah? And?"

"She's not a challenge."

"You idiot." Other students on their way to class stared. I put a stupid smile on my face, pretending Reed and I were joking. I lowered my voice. "You said this same shit to Simone when you came on to her."

"Actually, I told her I wanted to screw her. But I don't want to just screw you."

"I cannot even believe we are having this conversation."

"I'm just telling you how I feel. I fantasize about touching you. I think you're extraordinary. I can't help it."

"What about Simone? She showed me the 'arty' pictures you took of her. Oh, it's just not challenging for you to photograph her looking all slutty? She does anything you ask her to. And you know why? Because she's in love with you."

"I know that. See that young woman over there?" He indicated a girl standing by the drama building. I knew her. Kate Garret. Addicted to coke. Wore sleeveless designer dresses all winter. She stood in the slush wearing no tights, just gold flats on her long skinny feet. Her gaunt face was tanned. "She's in love with me, too. So what."

"But you haven't been living with her. You've been with Simone for two years."

"Look, I want you. Is that so awful? That's what people do, you know, they have desires."

"You should keep your feelings to yourself."

"Like you do? And live cut off? Simone says you're a virgin."

"She's wrong."

"She's your best friend. She would know, wouldn't she?"

I wanted to tell him *Maybe I am Simone's best friend, but she isn't mine.*

"Why can't you just appreciate her, Reed?"

Just then Simone came toward us, the brown tips of her cowboy boots the color of wet paper bags. Her tight jeans looked even tighter and she had her nose higher in the air than usual, acting cool, faking it. I knew how scared she really was.

"Hey." She tilted her face.

"Hey." Reed kissed her cheek and swaggered with his rock-star walk into the building. Through the glass I watched him turn up the thermostat. He shot me a cold stare.

"You didn't tell him, did you?" Simone asked.

"Of course not."

"Then what were you talking about?" she demanded. "It looked sort of heated."

"I told him I thought Jackson Pollock was seriously over-rated." The truth was I loved Pollock's canvases: how the black burst all over, untamed.

"Uh-oh. You know Reed worships him." Of course I did. She held the studio door open for me. "Maybe someday you'll understand Pollock's work."

"Yeah. Maybe."

The Buffalo Street Women's Clinic was less dingy than the one I went to in Gray, but even with the bright yellow walls, the same horror choked the waiting room air. Simone had bitten off every fingernail and began chewing on dry tabs of skin. They called her in, and she raised her brows into her best haughty look as she disappeared into the back.

She had told Reed that she "needed some space" and curled up under her quilt in our room for a few days. "I am going on the pill after this. I used that diaphragm every time. And look what happens." I tipped a mug of bouillon to her lips, and she blew until it was cool enough to sip. Her breath stank. She drank a few mouthfuls then collapsed back onto her pillow and wept, purple half-moon shadows under her eyes.

"Is Simone sick?" Reed asked all casual the next day in the lunch line at the student union.

"Yeah. She's sick."

"Did you think about what I suggested?"

"No. There's nothing to think about."

It only made me want to take care of Simone even more. But by Sunday afternoon, when I came back from the campus store with her maxi pads, a ginger ale, and a *Cosmopolitan,* she had made her bed and was packing to go back to Reed's.

"Thanks so much, Hill. For all you've done. I've been thinking. I definitely have to go on the pill before Reed and I leave for the south of France." She plucked out the perfume samples from the glossy magazine pages, ripped open the gummed edges, and stuck her nose in the seams, sniffing them.

One beautiful May afternoon Simone came back to pack up the minks that she had never taken to Reed's.

"What the hell is this?" Simone jerked open the shower curtain to find me collapsed on the scummy drain of the dormitory shower, arms wrapped around my legs. The water was scalding me. I didn't care. The pain felt good. The letter had arrived that morning. My baby had begun to ask about me.

She gave me to you. She said you could have me?
Yep. She did.
She picked you and Daddy to have me?
That's right.
Picked you like how you pick pretty flowers?

I had ripped open the letter, left it on my bed, and then went to the annual Purple Nurple Party where a game of tag was played by first dipping your hand into a can of lilac-tinged Crisco and scooping out a big glob of goo. Then you smeared it on the closest person and they smeared it on you. Everyone was "it." I had been deliberately cruel to some Cornell boys, plastering their hair with lard, sliming them all the way down their backs. Kevin, a senior who looked like a middle-aged man because of his receding hairline and soft little belly, had given me a ride home. He had tried to slobber a kiss on me, but he couldn't get a grip on my slippery arms. That's when I had run to the shower.

Simone held one of the photos of Tom, his hands yanking a sword stuck in an anvil. *Disney World,* it read on the back in Lola's even, square writing. *Tom believed he could set the sword free if he pulled with all his might.*

I lunged at the photos. "It's a kid I know."

She pulled them away. "Really." She plucked Lola's letter from her back pocket and began reading out loud mockingly, "I fold the Batman suits in the top bureau drawer, next to blue-and-red Spiderman underwear."

I grabbed my towel and covered my front. I chased her down the hall back into our room.

"He's your kid," she spat.

"He's my nephew."

The loveliness in Simone's face vanished. Her eyes narrowed. "See, that's interesting. You're a goddamned liar. Your brother is dead, remember? But I shouldn't be surprised, should I, that you would tell one lie after another? Of course you're going to lie. Lie like you've always lied."

"You don't know anything about it."

"About what? That I turned to you when I was in trouble and you never breathed a word that you had been in the same sorry-ass situation? And on top of that, your little pure-as-snow act? Make me puke."

She pressed her thumb hard on the photo in her hand, denting the fleshy contours of Tom's smiling face. I growled through clenched teeth, "Give me that."

"No."

"Give it to me." I yanked the David statue off the table and threatened her with it, holding it aloft like a wooden baseball bat. I don't know if she laughed because she was nervous or because she thought the sight of me was really funny. But her smirk set me off.

I screeched in a sound I had never heard come out of me before and smashed David as forcefully as I could against the desk. His round white head spun off. I whacked and whacked until he was in pieces, his plaster arms and legs hacked into chunks, his penis a white pile of dust.

I picked up the head and tried to hurl it on the ground to crack it open like a geode. But it went sailing out of the room

and landed with perfect precision on the small red handle of
the fire alarm. Bells in the hallway and stairwell immediately
rang. Simone gaped at me, thrilled. She gently put the photos
and letter on the desk, picked up the head laying in the hall
like a dropped fly ball, plunked it in our trashcan, and swept
in the rest of the shards with her hand.

Fire engines wailed up the hill. As I pulled on some underpants, shorts, and a tee shirt, Simone stared at the stretch
marks on my upper thighs and the pouch of skin around my
belly button. She observed me as if I were an anonymous
model in her figure drawing class. I tucked the photos and the
letter into my pocket. I had the letter memorized. *Everywhere
Tom goes he brings James's calculator and pretends it's a walkie-
talkie. He speaks urgently, pressing his lips on the numbers, "Can
you hear me?"*

The sirens got louder. Simone and I dashed out to the
parking lot acting as if we were panicked that there might
really be a fire. We settled on the curb, near the tall weeds,
away from the tittering Drama Queens who had just returned
from a party all dressed up in strapless gowns with lovely
crinolines. The wind blew their skirts up in the back, giving
them sudden fairy wings.

"People look at you differently when they know," I told
Simone. "Every guy on this campus would think it was a free
ticket into my pants."

"You were how old?"

"Eleventh grade."

"Jesus, you were just a baby yourself."

"I didn't mean to lie to you, Simone."

But Simone wasn't fuming anymore. Her face lit up in a

rare open smile when the fire trucks ground to a stop in front of us. The sirens were deafening.

"I love that sound!" she hollered in my ear.

The firemen leaped off the truck, inspected the dorm, and returned to where we were, their five o'clock shadows flushed and sweaty from running in the spring heat wearing their heavy gear. The trucks went silent, but the ringing in my ears continued.

"Hey." Simone called to the fireman who had hopped onto the back of one of the trucks. "False alarm?"

"Some prankster," he replied tersely. "Very funny."

"That's awful." She pouted, lowering her eyelids into her Marilyn Monroe look.

"And what's your name?"

"Some people call me Flint."

"Flint. Now that's a name I'll definitely remember."

She exhaled cigarette smoke in a long stream and raised her eyebrows haughtily. "Everybody does."

I wrongly assumed several things about Simone. Since she had kept my secret from those beefy firemen when I triggered that alarm, I trusted that she would also keep my baby a secret. But I hadn't detected what raged beneath her nonchalant facade whenever she alluded to her "procedure."

Halfway through our senior year, she abruptly moved out of Reed's loft and retreated to a house by herself on Cayuga Lake (her mother eagerly paid the rent, because Simone convinced her that it was safer near all that water if an inferno overtook her one night). She told me that Reed still slept over sometimes, but I was relieved that she was spending less time with him. It seemed to me that since her abortion she acted more like him, sarcastic and arrogant.

I was delighted that she could spend her nights lost inside her drawings, filling long, wide scrolls of perfect white paper. She confided, "I'm drawing like mad. I can't keep my hand from moving."

My parents attended graduation. Uncle Billy drove down with them in a used car my Dad bought for me from Sloppy Joe. Uncle Billy was so overcome with emotion—blubbering that he was so goddamn proud of me, wringing me into a hug that smeared my eye makeup on the pocket of his shirt—that he actually had to sit in the car while I marched under a tent to "Pomp and Circumstance."

When my mother had arrived earlier that morning, I sensed from the way she had rubbed my back while hugging me that she had missed me. I could not relax into her touch. I pulled away and looked down at her sandals and the mushroom-colored toes of her queen-sized pantyhose.

Something had begun to unravel inside me. I didn't recall, as I listened to the graduation speaker and adjusted the bobby pins securing my mortarboard, that DeeDee Moore had ever hinted that it would be good to get on with my life and get an education. I don't even remember my parents saying that. And yet, somewhere inside me, I had believed that going to college would help, if only the tiniest bit, to justify my decision to let go of Tom. It justified nothing. I managed to go to classes, to write papers and take tests, but inside I was still languishing away, missing him.

I moved shyly across the stage, pumping hands with various faculty members. Balloons bobbed; CLASS OF 86 confetti shimmered in the air. I flipped open the cool, blue cover of my diploma. In fancy calligraphy I read:

Hillary M. Birdsong
B. A. General Studies

It meant zilch. The sleeves of my gown flapped like boneless wings.

At the close of the ceremony, after the cheers and all the family Polaroids, we shed our gowns and headed over to the Wallings Gallery for the opening of the senior art show. I recognized Simone's mother without even being introduced to her. An emaciated woman in black slacks and diamond tennis bracelets, she had such big teeth it was impossible for me not to think of the wolf in "Little Red Riding Hood," the better to eat you with, my dear. Her stilettos were pointy and high and yet she stood grounded and steady as if wearing ballet flats. She moved like a two-legged spider outside the gallery and lit a cigarette with what looked like a solid gold lighter, with a flame as big as a blowtorch.

The entire show had been hung, all except for Simone's work. A long, white wall near the floor-to-ceiling windows that faced the grass common was blank. The other studio-art majors milled around, uncorking bottles of wine the school had provided, stepping away from their work and viewing it with a critical eye. Reed had never come on to me again, and he stood angelically with his hands clasped humbly behind his back, a pose he adopted only to brownnose parents. I could tell he was anxious. Simone was his most accomplished and talented student.

A blue Volvo backed up to the entrance of the gallery. Theo (who had been in love with her since freshman year, had, unfortunately, not matured, and still could be easily mistaken for a smooth-faced teen idol) and Simone popped out and began sliding her giant canvases out from the back. She had covered them in brown paper to protect them. Reed excused himself from the swarm of parents. Simone let him kiss her cheek. When he tried to peek under the paper covering the biggest canvas, she wrenched it away from him. I helped Theo carefully drag four of the canvases inside.

She lifted the pictures until the wires caught on the nails.

"Let's see," Reed urged.

"Not until the official opening. In ten minutes." Simone poured white wine to the very top of a plastic cup and downed it.

When I went over to her to say, "Hey, we made it! We actually graduated," she turned from me as if she were too engrossed in her task to acknowledge me.

The gallery was crammed. The hilarity became shriller as more wine bottles were uncorked. Fathers in blue blazers got red-faced and mothers spilled on shirts bright with hibiscus-colored flowers. Younger siblings wandered around, wide-eyed but acting bored. There was an abstract painting with slashes of jarring color, a still life of lilacs, and one with only red cubes and blue spheres. My father, puzzled by a lithograph of a man's black hairy legs in ripped fishnets, shrugged and shook his head at my mother.

"Okay, it's five." Simone slammed down her wine and

clawed at the brown paper covering the first canvas. The crowd grew quiet, then gasped. "Good Lord!" a woman brayed. Everyone gaped at the naked man bursting from the dark charcoal wisps of Simone's drawing. It wasn't the fact that it was a nude that shocked us. It was the fact that we were looking at a life-sized, beautiful Reed. And then we all turned toward Reed. It was surreal, a gallery jam-packed with parents and graduates all looking at Reed as he looked at himself.

Then Simone went wild, snatching the paper off her other canvases. Reed's bare body kept appearing. Reed pressing his bare butt on a barstool, his penis and balls hanging over the edge. Reed naked and bending down, balancing on his toes, legs spread wide, thigh muscles taut. Reed viewed from the back, calves (always Simone's specialty) round and manly. Reed laughing hysterically, hand covering his face, penis swinging to the side.

The art students began exclaiming "Whoa!" and "Christ!"; they were astonished at Simone's technique, clearly admiring what she had achieved as an artist. Theo whispered gleefully in my hair, "Too bad it looks as if he posed for these."

But the parents were appalled. "This is outrageous!" one father bellowed. "What kind of perv are you?"

The girls who had the hots for Reed giggled. Kate Garret, dressed in her trademark gold slip-ons, snickered, "So, the rumors are true," and her entourage cracked up. They pointed at the long, smooth, shaded-in penis.

But then Simone uncovered her final piece. And there I was, naked, nine months pregnant.

The parents were so distracted by the naked teacher that they didn't notice I was the pregnant girl. But Theo knew.

"That's from Simone's imagination, right? I mean, it would have to be."

"They're all from my imagination. No one posed for these," Simone broke in. She turned to me and asked coldly, "Do you like it? You always thought pregnant women should be represented more often in discussions of the nude."

My mother tapped me on the shoulder and asked me to follow her and my father. We moved over to the plants under the curved stairwell that led to the library.

"Why would you subject us to this?" my mother hissed. "We got up in the middle of the night to come see you graduate, to celebrate, to drive back home with you, and you do nothing but humiliate us?"

"Mom, Simone is messed up. I had no idea she was doing this."

Not only was my father's face pink, but his entire scalp, under the wisps of hair, was blushing. "I think we'd better go," he said.

"Can we still go out to dinner? I made reservations for us at the Trolley House."

We didn't celebrate with filet mignon that night. At first I thought, *You know those Birdsongs. They manage to ruin every special meal.*

But then I realized if it hadn't been for Simone, my parents wouldn't have returned, defeated, to their room at the Ramada. I stormed through town, searching for her. All the bars were stuffed with shouting people who were spilling over into the streets. I finally spotted her in the back of Micawber's, pie-eyed and making out with Theo. When she saw me, she almost got punctured dashing in front of the dartboard.

Who would have known that she could sprint so fast in battered old cowboy boots? She headed up Aurora Street, past the frat houses, down Turner Avenue. I was not going to let her get away. The streetlamps were on, and her shadow looked like a little girl with spring fever chasing a hula hoop after supper. She cut across the long, tall footbridge that spanned the gorge. Chain link fences rose on either side of the concrete; the bridge looked like a wire tunnel in the air. Her boots weren't so great for traction after all: One of the pointy tips caught, and Simone fell hands first on the concrete. She kept crawling.

"Simone!" I finally caught up to her. She rolled over, then stood up. The knees of her jeans were slashed open, and she was bleeding. "You didn't even look closely at it," she said.

"Look at what? Your portrait of me? The way you completely divulged my secret to everyone? And on top of that, you fucked it up for my parents. Don't act like it was all in the name of art. You used your art to get back at me. For what, I don't know."

Pulling at the white tufts of thread on her knees, she spoke in a monotone. "I hadn't meant to show the picture of you. I was going to keep that one separate as a graduation present for you. I knew all along I would exhibit the portraits of Reed. But last night he told me he was attracted to you. And that you knew all about it. What is it with you and all your little secrets, Hillary? You get off on it? I mean, really."

"I never told him about your abortion. Seems to me you'd be delighted I know how to keep a secret."

She sighed and pressed her face against the fence. "You might not believe this, but I thought about telling him. But before I could let him know he had knocked me up, he said he wasn't sure if we should still see each other once I went back to Long Island. I know what's going to happen. He's going to get himself a new lay. In the fall he'll just begin all over again with someone sort of like me."

I remembered Miles's bragging, *She says she's in love with me, and she's beautiful.* It wouldn't have made any difference if she had told Reed. I listened to Cascadilla Creek washing over the giant boulders below. The temperature dropped. A misty wind cooled my face.

"I didn't mean to hurt you with that portrait, Hillary. In fact, I wanted the opposite. I was a jerk to ruin graduation like that."

"So are you saying you're sorry?"

She bit her lip and nodded. Though she didn't actually say it.

A few big raindrops plopped around us; the black sky opened. The raindrops fell on the links of the fence, then fell again. If it had been Shell, I would have linked elbows with her, gripping tightly. But it was Simone. She walked ahead with her back to me.

I wandered alone and shivering after midnight. The sudden downpour had passed, and the wet roads back up to campus shined red from the stoplights. The locked-up gallery was dark. I waited for my eyes to adjust to the spotlight that shined over the patio of the student union. Inside the gallery the pregnant girl stood silently, undressed shyly in bright moon- light. Simone had drawn me with full breasts, big nipples with dark centers, my arms folded behind my back, charcoaled wide thighs, and my belly drawn so round and soft. She had imagined my face full of calm and my lips turned up in the slightest smile. My posture indicated I was completely com-

fortable in my skin, even proud. The freckles on my face and
arms were the lightest of marks as if I had been waiting to go
into labor in the shadow of a polka-dotted curtain.

I turned away from my pregnant belly and looked out
over the lights of the town, knowing my parents were sleeping
there in a chilly, anonymous room. I was too exhausted to be
angry. A small plane passed overhead underneath the clouds.
The whirring propellers seemed to twirl so slowly that I feared
the wings might corkscrew down out of the sky.

8

At first I thought Sloppy's little secondhand Turismo got miraculous gas mileage. I was crossing bridge after bridge over invisible fresh-water rivers that fed into the nighttime blackness of unseen salt marshes, and the red needle of the gas gauge never moved. As I lost power in the center of a town called Camden, it dawned on me: Any car from Sloppy Joe would be damaged. I coasted down into a valley, steering sluggishly into an enormous puddle of a public parking lot. The sign read LINCOLNVILLE REACH, ISLESBORO FERRY.

I switched off my headlights. Tied to the pier, the ferry hulked silently in the water. I spotted a pay phone and stepped out into a puddle that seeped through my cheap boots. A stack of coins bought me three minutes of time with Shell.

"Shell?"

"Hill? You okay? Has something happened?"

"No. I'm fine."

"Where are you?"

"*Um* . . . Lincolnville?"

"With your folks?"

"No. I didn't follow them the whole way." With the putrid stink of the pine-tree air freshener Sloppy had strung from the rearview mirror for me filling the car, I had driven behind my parents up 495 back to Maine. When I read the sign for lake points along the Maine Turnpike—Exit 11, Gray, Norway, Paris—I remembered the milky blue of the hospital balloon, how it dissolved into the sky so completely that I could no longer distinguish what was boy-colored and what was sky. I zoomed off the road home and headed to the shoreline, deciding that I would stay in whatever coastal town I ran out of gas in.

I was waiting for Shell to speak when the recording came on, "Please deposit another fifty cents." I slipped five dimes into the slot.

"Shell? Are you mad at me?"

"Look, Hill, I was just really hoping you were finally coming back. I just wish it could be like it was. I hate it in this damn town without you." I heard rain dripping and bouncing into one of her aluminum pots. "All I'm saying, Hillary, is I'm disappointed."

"I know, I know. I'm going to try to find a place here. Will you come see me?"

"Of course. I love you, and I miss you."

I thought, *What's the difference? Aren't they the same thing?*

The recorded operator returned. I pressed the silver bar down. Disconnected from Shell, the receiver weighed more and became colder. I dialed again.

"Slop? It's Hillary."

"Good lord, are you at Shell's? I'm coming over."

"No. I'm not coming home. I'm in Lincolnville."

"Damn, that's like, two, two and a half hours away from Norway. And no direct route, only back roads."

"Speaking of driving, Slop, what's wrong with the car?"

"Nothing. That car's a cream puff."

"What's wrong with the gas gauge?"

"Oh, that. I did have a little accident with it. I was going forty miles an hour backwards up at the country club and slammed into the boulder by the first tee. I had to replace the gas tank. Just keep track of the gas and mileage when you fill it."

I sighed.

"Hill, your old man's been waiting and waiting for you to come home. You're gonna really hurt him with this."

"So what else is new?" Suddenly I noticed a tall man smoking about fifteen feet away. "Slop, I gotta go."

The man asked, "Your boyfriend?" Even in the minimal light from the one streetlight, he looked exceptionally handsome.

"Yeah," I lied.

"Then I guess you won't be coming to a party with me?" His eyes were dark as black leather.

"I guess not."

Another voice called out, "Leave her alone, Gary." A smaller man emerged from the shadows. I was out of a college town and back in Maine where all the men had scruffy hair curling over their collars. "Please excuse him. I'm Harold." He gestured to the post office across the street. "I work over there. This is Gary the Glutton."

Gary regarded me with an unblinking gaze, then disappeared into the night.

"Please forgive his rudeness. He's a fornicator."

I laughed and Harold's expression lit up. He was happy to have gotten a laugh out of me. "He's been one of my best buddies since second grade, and I love him, but . . ." He shrugged and looked out over the bay. "So where you headed?"

I collapsed on one of the big boulders that was probably covered with dog pee. I didn't care. I was suddenly so drained I thought I would faint. "I ran out of gas."

"I could give you a ride to the Cumby's up in Belfast. They're open past midnight." Harry opened up the door of his dented pickup. I had never seen so many empty Marlboro cartons.

He shifted gears as the truck jostled over some railroad tracks. "So what brings you through here?"

Crooked porches flickered past. He glanced at me quickly, not wanting to take his eyes off the spirals of fog swirling into the headlights.

"I'm messed up." It felt delicious to finally admit it out loud.

"Oh," he answered pleasantly, like it was the most normal thing in the world to chauffeur a lunatic chick to the nearest Cumberland Farms gas station. "I guess Gary and I were curious about you because we know all the gals around here pretty well. This time of year we get a lot of blondes from down south who come up to waitress for the summer months."

"I remember. It was the same in Norway."

He looked over at me. "You from Norway? I have a cousin up that way. Just bought a business. Ever hear of Woodman's?"

I nodded. "Albino porcupine in the window. Right on Main Street."

He droned on cheerfully about his family. When we finally pulled into the glare of the Cumberland Farms, I drank a giant cup of burnt vanilla coffee while Harold pumped a few gallons of gas into a small red tin tank. We drove back to the ferry. The moon rose and I could make out the sensuous curve of the bells in a church steeple. Harold adjusted the radio dial, and we listened for fifteen miles to broken-hearted love songs reaching us all the way from Nashville. Ballads transmitted from other mountain ranges where girls fall in love, and their boyfriends run away.

He poured the gas into my car as the waves lapped delicately against the little beach. The cables of the ferry creaked like enormous swings. I looked up at the stars in delight. How could I have forgotten how beautiful and abundant the stars are along the open horizon of ocean—all those nights at La Rosaria when everyone was sleeping and I stayed awake, my storm window open to the sea, watching my breath rise as soft white light? I was two hours east of Norway, two hours north of Portland now. Was Tom still there? Had Lola taught him to trace the Big Dipper the way Bird taught me? And the Little Dipper too, made up of fainter stars.

The next morning Harold knocked lightly. I rolled down my window to find him in a dove gray United States Postal Service uniform. He had tall, bright white socks pulled up to his knees though it seemed too chilly for shorts. He smiled at me. His teeth were beige in the sunrise. "You slept in your car? You really *are* messed up," he announced pleasantly. "Listen, are you going to stick around? I spoke with my aunt last night. She has a place you might be able to stay." He walked over to the passenger side and pointed at the lock. I lifted it and he climbed in. Pointing to a black shack on the hill overlooking the ferry landing, he said, "She just bought that property behind the antique store she owns. She said she's tired of looking at that eyesore and wants to fix it up. No one's lived there in a long time."

"How much is the rent?"

"I don't know. Dirt cheap, I would guess, since it's sort of a dump. Actually not sort of. It's a dump."

Later that day Harry and I waited for his aunt in the driveway of the shack. Black tar paper covered the outside walls. Windows were boarded up. Gutters hung off the roof. It reminded me of a cardboard box that had tumbled in a fierce wind and gotten lodged there in the triangle of birch trees.

"They've always called this the Bat House, but it's just kids making up stories. I opened this place up a few weeks ago, and there's not a single bat anywhere."

"That's right," Harry's aunt Rhana agreed. "None of those rumors are true. Not the ones about the Satan worshippers living here either. It is simply an abandoned house."

Aunt Rhana unlocked the padlock on the front door. In her early sixties, Rhana surprised me with her strength when she slammed her humped shoulder against the door and it opened with a slow ripping sound. We stepped into darkness. She yanked up the torn window shades with a snap. We all blinked in the sudden light of the tiny kitchen. I surveyed the living room and the bedroom, where I flicked dead flies off the windowsill and strained to pull out the nails of the plywood covering the window. I slid the storm window up. The laments of seagulls blew in on the breeze. Their shapes rose and descended, flapping up over the post office, a few shops, the red-shingled antique store, and the fishing shacks folded into the basin of the valley.

The color of the bay switched suddenly, the way a scrap of blue velour darkens and grows rougher when you brush your finger against the nap. Simone had taught me that Monet painted the same river at six a.m., then at seven a.m., then at eight a.m., and that the change in light on water was enough to nourish him. *Tom is still gone. This view of the water is so beautiful. Uncle Billy gave me $500 as a graduation present.*

"I'll take it," I decided.

"Remember, you can't drink the water from this tap. Rinse out a couple of your milk jugs and head over to the Petunia Pump near the Country Store. Freshest water in the world."

Heavy boot heels echoed in the kitchen. Gary the Glutton announced, "I can't believe she is going to live in this rat hole." Then he was gone.

"Ignore him," Rhana said icily and unfolded the lease from her pocket.

"I'll be back later, kid," Harry announced on his way out. "I have some extra wood. I'll cover the tar paper up, and we'll make your new abode a sweet little seaside cottage."

All that afternoon there was only the crying gulls, the whistle blasting as the ferry left and returned, and my sponge wringing and soaking in the suds of Murphy's Oil. I emptied gallons of brown gritty water from the bucket. All the Bat House needed was some tender loving care. TLC—it sounded like a drug.

With Harry's carpentry skills, curtains from Kmart, and threadbare furniture from Rhana, my Bat House was transformed. Certain it would be my home for a while, I wrote Southern Maine Family Services to alert them that 15 Beach Road, Lincolnville, Maine, was where Lola's letter should be forwarded to on Tom's next birthday.

I was scanning the help wanted ads on my front stairs the evening of the first really boiling day of late spring when Gary pulled up in his souped-up old car and got out. "Those jeans look good." He nodded at my legs.

I could feel the pulse in my throat fluttering and hoped he couldn't see that his good looks made me nervous. "Most people say hello. But thank you."

"'Sittin' in her black jeans, soakin' up the sun.' Isn't there a country western song with lines like that?"

"Not that I can think of."

"There should be."

He bent his long legs to sit down on the lowest step.

"Sometimes when I wear black jeans in the sun they get so heated up it almost hurts to keep them on."

"I'm doing fine, thanks."

He spoke to my inseams. "I asked Harold's cousin if he knew any Birdsongs up there in Norway. He said there was a sign in town for the Bradford Birdsong Memorial Field."

"Yeah. So?"

Gary waited for me to say something about the field. I didn't. He continued. "He said he had heard that the Birdsong kid had a little sister but that she had moved away in high school. He heard she was in New Jersey."

I burst out laughing. "That's right. I'm in New Jersey."

Gary took my amusement as a cue that I might agree to go for a ride with him. "Come on, I just tuned this baby up for the summer. I'll show you the sights around here. Don't you want to know where you've landed?"

The interior of his car had the scent of hot, old oil. I relaxed as I inhaled deeply. We headed out off the gravel of my driveway onto Beach Road, which led down to Route 1. Gary barely blinked. I wondered if he even needed tears in his eyes. He kept them open so long that he must have won every single staring contest (*made you blink!*) when he was a kid.

"Lincolnville has no main street." He shifted gears. "Route

1 connects all the sea towns north and south. Camden has a Main Street. That's where the rich folk dine. I can't complain because I fix their Mercedes and their Beemers. It's quiet now, but the tourists will be here next weekend for Memorial Day."

In the daylight I could see the town of Camden was crowded with well-kept Victorians—bed-and-breakfasts with purple front doors ruffled with wreaths of dried hydrangeas. I caught our reflection in the windows of delicatessens and boutiques. At red lights Gary jerked the Firebird into park and gunned it over and over like a stock car at Oxford Plains Speedway.

"How old are you?" I shouted over the engine racket.

"Twenty-seven," he shouted back, accelerating under the light as it turned green. My head snapped back. A police siren swirled behind us.

"Jesus, not the Terminator," he yelled.

We edged next to a curb near a French restaurant. The cop who peered in at us was a fleshy woman with her hair in a bun that looked painfully tight. "Gary Snow," she snorted, gleeful to have stopped him. "Had a sudden little burst of *testosterone*, did we?" She wrote out his ticket and handed it to him like a waitress giving him his bill.

My tour that night included biographies of the locals as Gary showed me the shortcut behind Mount Battie. "There goes Earl the Pearl, the local Triple-A guy. He makes money by totally gouging out-of-staters in the summer when their radiators explode in the heat. In the winter he helps jump-start all our dead batteries."

I had a sudden stab of missing Norway when we slowed down by the Lincolnville County Firehouse No. 1. They, too,

had a Smokey Bear cut-out that the volunteer firemen changed
to indicate the fire danger every day. A short fat man sitting in
a plastic beach chair waved automatically to us. Gary called
out, "Hey, Raj-ah!"

"That's Jolly Roger. He's a bit slow, but he's a good guy." I
had never seen so much denim used for one pant leg—each
side was as wide as a pillowcase. Along Newton Road, a neon
raised hand twitched in the window of a brick garage. TAROT
CARDS, the sign read. He rolled his eyes without blinking.
"Laura Twitchell. Local 'astrologer.'" A woman with a long
pink scarf draped around her neck and over her back tipped
her watering can to shower a pot of geraniums. As we whizzed
by her, I saw her beaded earrings that hung to her shoulders.
Gary added, "*Major* Stevie Nicks fetish."

I watched her pretty face in the side mirror turn longingly
toward the sputter of his car. "You were with her, weren't you."

"You could say that." He grabbed the thin cardboard ticket
and let it fly out of his window.

I worked cruddy jobs early that summer, the worst one involv-
ing a long commute to a doublewide trailer that served as the
office for a telemarketing business. I dialed all the exchanges
in Augusta, politely asking if the lady of the house would like
a year's subscription to *TV Guide*. I quit one morning when an
aged, warbly voice answered me, "Oh no, dear, thank you, but
I can't read. I'm blind now with the glaucoma."

Around that time, Rhana finally had enough of her main
clerk, Dorothy. "I don't believe in retirement," Rhana had
sniffed. "But I am in need of a little support here." Dorothy
was a washed-up ballet dancer with a great need for, and reluc-
tance to take, medication. She sobbed constantly, even while

waiting on customers at Rhana's store, the Red Barn. Rhana was too kind to actually fire her, so she simply hired me to take her job and kept Dorothy on, letting her be the maid. Her tasks included Windexing all the cobalt bottles that illuminated the south-facing windows. This served two purposes: keeping Dorothy away from customers and letting her sop up her tears with a roll of paper towels cradled in her ropey ballerina arms.

If you drove along Route 1 you might have thought that Maine's state flag was blue and white and read ANTIQUES. The first thing I learned at my job was to put the giant OPEN flag out every morning. Red Barn Antiques wasn't really a red barn, but rather an old two-story bread factory crammed with a hodgepodge of junk in all its nooks and crannies. The rusty horse sleigh bells on the front door rang with the steady peal of customers. The job was ridiculously simple: Work the old-fashioned cash register, record sales in my neatest handwriting in the daily log, change the records on the record player constantly so that the creaky floors were accompanied by nonstop tunes from the 1940s.

"It isn't just that the music reminds me of when I fell in love with my husband," Rhana insisted, pulling out of a dusty record sleeve. "It sets a mood." She was right. I spent that summer observing how people pushed through the door. When they slipped out of the sunlight and entered our cool shadows they sighed, fern-like, unfurling a little to the strains of Bing Crosby or Judy Garland. I selected Frank Sinatra and Billie Holliday albums because, even though I had left Norway, I missed my parents' music.

I had always loved antique stores with their scent of crumbling old paperbacks. My mother used to take Bird and me with her to junk stores. Bored, Bird and I always managed to find the fresh batch of wild kittens that always lurked under tarps in the back, mewing and purring. That was how we got our cat Lucky. Birdy had concealed a kitten in his baseball jacket and it had remained there, content in the dark pouch of satin and quiet the whole ride home.

Rhana was recently widowed and had lived in Lincolnville all her life. Despite her drooping posture, people in Lincolnville were a little afraid of her, with her haughty look like a searchlight poking at you. Even though she was still in mourning, Rhana swished around in long, cascading Indian skirts flecked with sparkling gold. She kept her graying strawberry blonde hair feathered back, and she had sparse eyelashes coated with dark blue mascara. Somehow she still appeared elegant even when her plum eyeliner blurred like a doodle of waves over her large, wrinkly eyelids. Her eyes reminded me of the centers of peacock feathers.

"You're always so alert," Rhana announced one morning after the summer had passed. Lincolnville had thinned out, fewer cars, more eighteen-wheel trucks passing through. The diesel sounds became as natural to me as the soft, small waves lapping on the narrow town beach. We dug into a cardboard box full of packing popcorn, pulling out bowls of pink Depression glass. Even though it was still early, Dorothy had already cried herself to sleep upstairs on a red velvet love seat. "Like you're waiting for something. Or someone."

I was waiting. I was waiting for the endless ocean wind to blow so hard that it pushed time, pressuring twenty-four hours to pass more quickly. I thought, *If only the wind could blow the hands of the clock forward.* "I guess I'm just getting used to a new place. I know how small towns are. One false move and I'm labeled forever."

She let loose with her shrill laugh. "One false move? Honey, you've been here almost five months and haven't gone out on a single date. Nor do you seem to have any family."

I don't know why but I had forgotten that even not making a move could get you talked about. "Who am I supposed to go out with? Gary the Glutton?"

She slid her pocketknife into the tape of another box. "Of course not. He's an SOB. But what about my nephew? Harold has a good, stable job over at the post office."

"Harry's become my friend. But I'm not attracted to him."

"He's very smitten with you. He says that you two are very compatible."

"Yeah." I laughed. "We're both a couple of lunatics, taking walks on the railroad tracks at midnight."

"Well, it's a start," Rhana pointed out, placing one pink saucer on the next so they wouldn't chip.

I scanned the childless beach. The shrieking kids in bathing suits had vanished. Tom was a kindergartner with a Batman backpack rattling with smooth, unused crayons. Did his new sneakers have enough room for him to grow? Could he tie them himself, or did he point his foot forward so Lola could kneel down and spin the laces into double knots? I ached to press my lips and nose on his fresh haircut. "Hey, Haircut Boy," I'd tease him.

A yellow school bus shifted gears down the hill. I caught a glimpse of little boy ears, pink in the morning sun. My heart pounded, believing that Tom, in the front seat, had just sped by me.

9

April 20, 1987

Dear Hillary,
Now he is six, but envision him last summer, wearing a tie-dye shirt and wading in the edge of a slow-moving river, dunking in cool water. He stands up, finding his footing on the little rocks, then exclaims, "How come water seems like it's your friend?"

April 25, 1988

My dear Hillary,
This is what I wanted to share with you, his wonderful b-mother, this year. An image of Tom, almost seven, late afternoon in the tub. He is bare and shiny. His plastic pirates, named Pork-chops and Rumbelly, stand on the deck of their ship, taking aim with cannons at the bubbles on the bar of soap. Outside, geese pass above, crying, honking.
He calls to me. "Mom! I want to get out of the bath."
"Why? I thought you wanted to play in there a while."
"I want to get out to see the shapes," he says.

"What shapes?"

"The shapes the birds make."

I wrap him in a towel and wipe circles of steam off the windowpanes. Still dripping, he gets my blouse wet. He peers up into the sky and smiles at the geese, the crooked V.

May 1, 1989

Dear Hillary,

I say, Happy eighth birthday to our boy! I hope this finds you well, wherever this finds you. Enclosed, as usual, is this year's school photo. As I reread my diary, I will write down for you my favorite conversation that I had with him this past year.

He is fascinated by how eyeballs move.

He shuts his eyes. Pulls the lids tight and moves his eyeballs around. "Can you see them moving?"

"Yes."

"Now you do it," he asks. I shut my eyes and wiggle my eyeballs.

"Eww!" he cries in delight. "Is this what is called rapid eye movement?"

"That's what your eyes do when you sleep. I've seen your eyes moving. It helps you dream."

He cracks up with his silly laugh, falls dramatically on the bed, pulls his lid over his one eyeball again, and moves his eye around. "You can feel my eyeball, Mom," he says cheerfully. "Go on. It's okay."

I press my fingertips gently on his eyelid. It's supple and warm. I feel his eye underneath, strong and searching, like something wild.

Love always, Lola

10

While I waited for my letters, the years in Lincolnville passed. I spent hours sitting on an overturned putty bucket while Gary lay underneath cars. I talked and talked. He was a good listener, only occasionally sliding out and asking, "Wanna go lie down?" I never said yes, even though I loved to watch him roll around on his creeper in the cold air of his garage. I admired the way his arms tensed with strength from fingertip to shoulder as he manipulated the undersides of exhausts and transmissions, which he called "trannies." He lived alone in the apartment upstairs of his auto shop, which sat on about twenty acres. His field sloped all the way down to Hollow Lake. Right near the water's edge an old shed sagged, soggy with wind and rain. Barn owls peered out, their faces shaped like apples cut in half, eyes like seeds.

Gary was working on another BMW. "These a-holes," he mumbled under the car. "They can't get out of their leases and they don't want to pay the $450 a month anymore. I was up near Augusta getting an exhaust system for that Mustang Earl the Pearl gave me. There's this chick outside Augusta who asked me if I wanted in on a chop-shop scheme she's working on. It's pretty elaborate. It's set up so that the owner knows someone is going to 'steal' his BMW, then the car is taken away and stripped. The owner gets the insurance; the girl gets the car and sells it for parts. I'll tell you, she shouldn't be flapping her lips like that. She's one crazy chick."

I watched as he arranged his tools carefully in a tall red cabinet. "I thought you liked crazy chicks."

"No ifs, ands, or buts. Wanda Chute is shit-ass *crazy*."

How many Wanda Chutes could there be? I licked my lips and croaked, "What does she look like?"

"Oh, she's a big ole gal. She could kick my ass."

"Dark hair?"

"Yeah. Spiked up like a blowfish. Why? You know her?"

"I might. How old is she?"

"About your age, I'd say."

"Damn. I bet it's her."

"How the hell would you know her?"

I closed my eyes and took a deep breath. "Can you keep a secret?"

"You know I can."

I opened my eyes. "Wanda and I were in a home for unwed mothers together."

"You had that happen?"

"Yeah."

He stared at me for a long moment, then walked toward me very slowly, almost cautiously. He crouched down, his legs spread open like wings. His face was close to mine. The sharpness of his features seemed less harsh. His taupe jumpsuit made his eyes appear a warmer, kinder brown. "I don't know what to say," he whispered. I could smell cinnamon gum on his breath. "It seems you turned out okay. This Wanda, she's burning up with anger. At least you're not like that."

His face, near mine, looked more beautiful than ever. Suddenly I wanted to shove his broad shoulders away. "I wouldn't be so sure."

Gary wrote out the directions on an envelope. I teased him, "Are you sure that's spelled right?" I was headed to the outskirts of Cobbosseecontee Lake. At the end of the ride, as I crested a hill and first read the sign for Magic Wand Automotive, the hair stood up on my legs and goose bumps flew over my skin like a wind.

I don't know how so many dreadfully crumpled cars had gotten towed to Wanda's flat, barren property, but there were junkers with roofs sheared off, driver's-side doors pushed into the passenger's side, trunks punched through to the dashboard. No way did people survive these accidents. I counted more than eleven cars in this section near the barn.

Next to these metal ruins were mountains of tires, a small mound of fat exhaust pipes, and about thirty cars parked this way and that, with cats sunning themselves on the bumpers, or leaping in and out of the rolled-down windows. Creamsickle-colored shorthairs, black longhairs, tailless coon cats, white cats whose fur was dingy like sooty snowbanks. The low tones of a radio commercial hummed from inside the barn. The big doors were flung open. Two cars were nestled side by side. I tiptoed in and found Wanda bending under a hood. I said cautiously, "Hello?"

She looked up at me while continuing to tighten something on a hose, nodded slightly, and said, "Hey, Hillary. Long time no see." Her hair was still cut short and spiked up, she looked stronger than I remembered her, and she had steel-toed shit-kickers on, unlaced. "Something wrong with your car?"

"No. It runs pretty good."

She peeked toward the parking lot. "Turismos are pieces of shit."

I shrugged. "I don't drive much."

She continued to tinker with the car. I waited with my hands in my parka pockets.

"So, I guess this is the point in the conversation where I'm supposed to politely ask something, like 'Hey, what do you do?'" She stepped back from the car and wiped her hands on a rag, holding my gaze.

She wasn't going to bully me with sarcasm. Being near her brought old feelings of rage to the surface, and it felt good. "Sure, go ahead and ask me what I've been up to. I work in an antique store. It's a job any idiot teenager could do during summer vacation, except for the fact that I do it year round and I've been there almost five years."

"So you dropped out of high school after?"

"No, actually I went to college. What about you?"

"After La Rosaria?" She hesitated, then forged on. "I gave another baby girl away."

My face must have clouded because she asked, "Shocked? Don't be. It's not as uncommon as you might think."

I shot back, "Don't talk to me like I'm ignorant of the facts about girls like us. I'm not thinking anything less of you just—"

She cut me off. "Why are you here?"

I thought about it. "You just left. I never got to see you again."

She grabbed a giant wrench, pulled over a stool, and began struggling with a bolt on a rusty tire. "I don't know why you have those big crocodile tears in your eyes. I haven't cried in years," she bragged.

"You're telling me you never cried over your daughters?"

Wanda's lips pursed. She lay down her tools and rubbed her hands all over her face. When she took them away her skin looked gray from the grime. "I don't cry anymore. I just scream."

She was telling me the truth, and I knew without even asking her that she did a lot of screaming.

"Well, I cried," I admitted quietly. "I cried my head off the first few weeks without him."

"Him," she said. "So you had a son."

I nodded. "But I chose parents for him. Right after you left. I lucked out finding a couple of really nice people."

"Nice? You mean boring."

"No, I mean nice. As in kind, caring."

She returned to her masked self. "Oh. How cute."

She moved around the car, picking up other tools, making adjustments. The sleeves of Wanda's work shirt were rolled up past her elbows. On her forearms I saw the lines of black downy hair that I remembered. Her dark arm hair that she claimed to not care about as a teenager was smoothed down like thin fur. But then she flicked the wrench, and I spotted something else along her wrists. White scars, each about an inch and a half long, carefully spaced along the inside of her arms where the softest smoothest skin was. She had cut herself repeatedly. I knew those lacerations had not been there when we had disco-danced at the home. We had passed many hours doing the bump. And I remember thinking then that her arms were pure as Snow White's, with milky skin and blue veins at the wrists, like Miles.

"You're not the first one I've seen," Wanda said. "I ran into Sunny a couple of years ago. She still smells like Double

Bubble gum, smiling that little troll smile. No more braces though. She hugged me and almost lost her balance on her high heels. She didn't want her husband to know where she knew me from. I don't blame her for that."

"Rodney?"

Wanda rolled her eyes. "Oh please. If it hadn't been for the fact that she was knocked up when we knew her, I don't think I would have believed there even *was* a Rodney."

"It's true. We never saw him. She had a boy, you know, and named him Rodney."

Wanda sighed. "Jesus."

"What was her husband like, if not a Rodney?"

"Some Greek guy. Powerful handshake. He had their baby in a backpack."

"What baby?"

"She had another kid."

"Oh."

"She lied and told him she and I knew each other from marching band in high school. Then we talked in code about the marching band. I said, 'I never really liked being in the marching band, did you?' 'Oh no, I never really liked the marching band either.' She asked me if I had seen you, and I told her no, and she kept the lie going by saying she always really loved how beautifully Hillary played the flute."

"Yeah, that's me, the flutist."

So Sunny had never told her husband that she had had a previous child. What was that like, snuggling in a bed with a man, your new baby suckling in-between, and lying, not letting him know that there was another son before this one?

"Was her baby cute?" I asked.

"I didn't look."

"I never seem to be able to look at any baby either." The radio played a few more songs. I held some tools for her, handing them to her when she asked. "I made it so my kid could come find me at eighteen."

She slid under the car. She growled. "I eventually signed away my rights. Same with the second kid. Who would want to find out they had a mother like me? The poor kid would be traumatized after wondering about me all that time."

I secretly wondered if that was what Tom would think. I had heard how adopted children wanted their birthmothers to be famous. Why would a child want that? For him to find out that I was just this ordinary woman, would he be disappointed? Lola was an original. Was I? I never felt that way. But I loved the way Lola perceived me. Lola had such faith in me. I never understood why.

I didn't want to tell Wanda about my letters and photos. Wanda saw herself as so unworthy that she hadn't even bothered to find out what happened to her daughters. "You were always angry. You're still angry," I said.

Sliding out from under the car, she said almost menacingly, "What's your point?"

"All I'm saying is you're angry. So am I."

I stood up stiffly. My back hurt. My toes were frozen. I don't know how she stayed out in the barn so long and so close to the cracked, cold cement floor.

"Hey, where you going?" she called out.

I turned to her. "Wanda, you know you could do other paperwork now. You could write a letter to the state adoption agency. So that your daughters could find you someday, if they wanted to."

"They're not going to want to."

"Why wouldn't they? *I* wanted to see you again."

"I have no idea why you came here."

"I've been worried about you."

Wanda looked incredulous. "You've been *worried* about me? For *nine* years?"

That was about right. I laughed. I knew it sounded absurd. But it was true. I was relieved to find out that Tiny was adopted, and relieved to have found Wanda's snaking rawhide laces.

I lay in bed late that night, looking at Tom's most recent picture. It was black and white, the contours of his cheeks illuminating the creaminess of his skin. I imagined that his temples near his short sideburns smelled like sun and white soap. I fell asleep with that year's spring letter still folded open between my breasts.

April 29, 1990

Dear Hillary,

Sometimes my eyes play tricks. I think I see you walking all alone in your winter coat, your reddish brown hair blowing, and you are looking up at the sky. I never met anyone who loved wind as much as you!

You'd be surprised how much I think of you, how often. The image in my mind as I write you now is from a tranquil summer evening, August, when we were picnicking on a cool, still lake. Tom kept calling out. His own voice kept coming back to him. He would say, "Yip," and then a few seconds later we would hear yip yip yip *like a stone skipping across the surface. Who are you? He asked himself, and that came back as well.*

Writing you these letters feels like that. I have no idea if you are on the other side. And if so, can you hear me? I send this out to you, as if shouting over water.

11

"Of course it's like being cut in half," Rhana was saying into the phone on a rainy afternoon at the Red Barn. She allowed herself and me personal calls if we had no customers. I knew she was consoling Mrs. Molson, whose husband had died earlier that year after forty-seven years of marriage. "*Mm-hmm.* Yes, I know. You hang in there, darling. I'll give you a jingle tomorrow."

I was sorting the antique postcards that Rhana had purchased in rubber-banded stacks at a big state auction. I saved cards of Norway for my own collection, watercolor sunsets and birch canoes. Nosy person that I am, I loved reading the intimate messages on the backs: "Will arrive next Tuesday at 2:00 P.M., hope to finally meet your beloved Edward." Or: "Have to cancel for Easter, Eleanor getting sicker with pneumonia."

Way back in the early 1900s the average person's penmanship was striking and delicate. I realized how atypical Birdy's writing was. Folded in my bookshelf, next to my photo album of Tom, I saved Birdy's five letters, written while he was at college. I have no idea where he had learned such exquisite penmanship. Even the brainiest girls from Oxford Hills didn't write with the flourish Birdy did. *I'm sorry it took me so long to write you, little sister*.

"Rhana, did you ever wonder if your Wendell would have lived—if only—"

"You mean if only he hadn't smoked, would he still be here, instead of dying a long, ugly death from emphysema? I can't do that to myself. 'If only's will eat away at me. I see how they eat away at you. Harry told me how you wait for that letter every year."

"Yeah," I answered. "I felt better after I told Harry. Now he helps me look for the letter that should have come already. It's the first time in ten years I haven't gotten the card before his birthday. Today is my son's birthday. And you know what, Rhana? I have a thousand if onlys."

Her eyes became more triangular, and she looked very sad. "A thousand if onlys are too many."

I began to name them, ticking them off on my fingers. "Well, let's start with the first one. If only my brother hadn't died. Then, if only I hadn't gotten knocked up, or if that had to happen, if only Miles had helped me. If only my mother and father had done what Priscilla Nix's mother had done. If only I did—"

She made me stop counting by covering my hands with hers. She still wore her wedding ring.

"I want you to listen to me. No, look at me so I know you hear me." I was embarrassed by the intimacy of her holding my hand. The Man in White had held my hand but his had been encased in a seamed glove. In the rainy light Rhana's gaze gathered strength, became even wiser. "You were just a slip of a girl. You did the best with what you were handed. You were a *girl*, Hillary. You weren't even old enough to drive."

I shook her hands off of me and snapped a rubber band from another dusty stack of postcards. She sighed and walked slowly up the stairs. "I am talking about having compassion for yourself."

The wild, wet breeze trembled the spring morning glory vines that pressed on the front window. With the day so underlit, the flowers remained twisted in tight cones. Defiant, soft, and lovely.

Her words rang in my head, *a slip of a girl, girl, Hillary, just a girl,* for the entire month of May. After Memorial Day I spent long nights on the overturned bucket in Gary's garage, lamenting Lola's missing letter.

"Has Lola forgotten about me? Did she get tired of writing? In her last letter, she—no, that *can't* be it. Something must be wrong."

Harold ignored regulations and allowed me in the sorting room as he whisked through bags of mail, his yellow fingers flipping along white paper. "Some days it seems like I sort a thousand missing children. I get these constantly. What's with this huge increase in Jiffy Lube coupons? Ads on one side, missing kids on the other. Endless HAVE YOU SEEN ME?s All these children are just taken? Who are they, do you think?"

"Lots of times they get taken by their own family members. Mothers running away from abusive dads. That sort of thing. But not always. Some of these kids have been gone a while. They use computers to show how they might have aged—this is the kid at five, and this is what they think he might look like now that he's eleven."

"It's sad," Harold agreed. "I say a quick prayer for each of them."

I couldn't imagine not knowing where Tom was, couldn't imagine his gorgeous face printed on a cheap postcard alongside a red hotline number. I was desperate to hear from Lola. But it could have been worse. To not know where your child was, that would be the worst pain of all.

Finally, just after Father's Day, Harold stopped flipping through a pile. "I got it." He grinned.

The envelopes always came with the outer envelope addressed to me from Southern Maine Family Services. Inside was the envelope that Lola sent to them with her letter and his photos. As soon as I tore it open I knew something was wrong. Lola's square, playful handwriting, always in black felt-tip, was replaced by a messy blue-ink scrawl.

6/12/91

Dear Hillary,

I must write as Lola is unable to; she had a horrible accident but she is going to be okay. Her hand is still healing. She was burned in her studio. The school where she teaches had the Sparax acid and water mix that she uses after soldering heated too high and when she added cold water to it, it exploded. Thank god she had just put on a long-sleeve shirt because she would have been even more mangled. The doctors put her in the burn unit (where firemen go) because the burns were third degree, and since there is so little fat and flesh on a hand, she risked an infection and losing the hand. After eight days in the burn unit, they did skin grafts. She told me to assure you she will write when she can.

I'm not sure what else she tells you in her letters. He is healthy, bright, beautiful, and went for his annual physical, weighs seventy-two pounds. Let's see—Tommy—he is an amazing little kid.

Take good care,
James

That afternoon I made a call from my kitchen.

"Southern Maine Family Services," a voice answered.

"I need to speak with DeeDee Moore."

"She no longer works here."

"Where is she?"

"I can't disclose that."

"I need to talk to someone about my case."

"Are you relinquishing?"

"No. I'm a birthmother. I just found out that the woman who adopted my child was in an accident. I was wondering if the liaison knew whether or not Lola was really okay."

"How did you find out this information?"

"Her husband wrote me. My son's adoptive father."

"What is your name, please?"

"Hillary Birdsong."

"Hold one moment, please."

I listened to a sanitized version of "You Are the Sunshine of My Life." The woman clicked back.

"Ms. Birdsong, I cannot give any other information. I'm sorry."

"But this is an emergency. I need to know if Lola is okay. I'm not asking so I can find her myself. If you could do what you always do, just be the go-between!"

"I'm sorry. Communication initiated by the birthmother is, and always has been, against our regulations."

"But Lola—"

"I'm sorry."

The rest of the summer was poisoned by my nightmares, parallel to the ones I still had about Tom. Not only did the hallway have a baby whimpering at the end, a baby I could never reach, now I heard Lola's voice bleating, "Hillary?" I heard them both so clearly and ran toward them, but the dark brown hallway, a rectangular tunnel, was never ending.

12

With Lola hurt, my waking hours darkened. That summer all the tourists seemed more disrespectful than ever of our beach. In the mornings before I went to work, I put on latex gloves and collected trash. Of course it was soda can after soda can. Coca-Cola, Tab, Sprite, Diet Iced Tea. Receipts from the Sugar Shanty, and white paper blown from plastic straws.

The most crucial trash to collect was the plastic circles that held six-packs together. These were dangerous to birds. It was sickening to spot a seagull with his legs twisted up in one of those. Unable to land on their legs, able only to fly, these gulls were sometimes seen hanging upside down, dead in the tops of pine trees. The worst case I had ever witnessed was that July, when two cormorants, tangled together in a plastic ring, their heads threaded closely together, struggled in the wake of the Islesboro ferry and drowned.

The colors that fall were dreary, the result of too much rain or not enough, I never knew. The leaves shifted quickly to brown then plunged to the ground. Hunting season began. I had out-run Norway, but I could not escape the bottomless, swirling pupils, the whirlpools of hunting season—the parade of deer slung on top of cars. Because of the hunters near Mount Battie, Gary and I had to wear orange hats as we hiked so they wouldn't shoot us.

The empty trees always reminded me of Bird's death. Sometimes the surface of the bay was scored with nicks of wind, the water looking like a field of crops, wind rustling the water, ripples high as small leaves with the tips turning over.

One evening in late October, fifteen minutes after sunset, when the hunting was over, I slipped off my orange wool hat. I had been walking for over an hour and was headed back to the railroad tracks near Harry's church when suddenly a doe stopped right near me. She snorted like a pony and lifted her head, her brown eyes aimed at me, liquid and beautiful as a deep quarry pool. Her ears twitched, alive and busy. Then she dashed by me, leaping in graceful semicircles. I heard her cracking twigs, lumbering through the falling dusk, and then she was gone.

A few minutes later I heard pounding and dry acorns splitting. The doe was aiming for me, running back along the trail. Her front legs bent sideways, weak looking, like the way a handicapped child walked with armband crutches. She was snorting, and then her head banged on the ground and her jaw clumped with a hollow sound. She gathered her strength again and rushed under the dead branches of the pines. Horrified, I saw why she was losing her equilibrium. An arrow stuck out of her hide. Blood was leaking out in several directions.

I was hurrying to catch up to her when I heard more branches snapping and a deep voice calling. Then a man popped out along the trail with a little boy right behind him who looked about Tom's age, with beautiful skin made pinkish by the cooling air. The boy's eyes were wide, and he looked terrified.

"Did you see that doe?" the father asked frantically.

If I said yes, would they simply follow her and pierce her with more arrows? He gave me an angry look for not responding and stayed very still until he located the sound of thrashing down a small embankment. "Luke, let's go, buddy," the man said quickly. "We need to go find her. Your first deer! Good thing I brought Mom's camera."

I dashed behind them to where the deer had fallen. Her white belly was striped with red. In a final effort, she raised her rump in the air, tail twitching, her back legs trying to run but only scraping the spongy loam of the earth.

Her breath quickened and she fell over. The little boy burst into tears as her hooves pawed the air. The father kept his eyes on the doe. I could not bear to look at her face and instead watched the boy's mouth spread wider in grief. The father began to speak, as if an even, modified tone could coax the boy out of his despair.

"You did good, buddy, figuring out how to find the deer, from when you hit it to where it disappeared. That's called the line of flight. And you did good not aiming specifically for the heart," the father rambled on. "The heart is a bit too small and too low a target to count on. That sound right after you let your arrow fly, well, that was a rib. So what do think of your new birthday present? Don't you just love the tension on this PSE Spyder? Yeah, I remember my first deer."

The boy wept with his eyes squeezed shut so he wouldn't have to look. The father refused to comfort him. "Come on now, son." I detected a spike of agitation in his voice. "Isn't this what we've waited for? You're not a little kid anymore. You waited to turn ten! Come on! Youth Hunting Day! You've been counting down the days."

The boy opened his eyes and cried out, "It's different when you shoot it." He threw down his bow and stalked off along the trail. I looked at the father's face: an average-looking man with dark brown hair sticking out from under his cap. But as he grew angrier, his features became sharp and ugly. He took off after his son and spun him around by the shoulders. "You knock this off, Luke, or I'll knock you into next week."

The father shook him. "What are you, a momma's boy? Look at me!"

The boy coughed from crying so hard.

"Don't be a faggot," the father said coldly.

They were yelling at him to not be a faggot.

"You're an asshole," I yelled.

"Get the hell out of here, you nosy bitch," the father answered back.

"That's how you're going to make him be a man? By treating him like shit? He's just a kid."

In the dwindling light I saw Luke's face. He had stopped crying and now just looked stony with rage. He glared down at the ground, still keeping the deer on the periphery.

"Grab a leg. Let's get this doe out of here," the father demanded. "Now!"

Little Luke gagged as he touched her bloody front leg. They both pulled. Her massive body pressed a long, dark trail in the pine needles and the leaves. They pulled her up the embankment, then back along the curve of the trail. I took one last look at her face. Her eyelids were slits, the pupils completely black. I didn't understand how she could still be so beautiful even when she was dead. Luke glanced back at me as they disappeared around the curve. When I saw the father wasn't looking, I waved. Luke didn't wave back.

I couldn't bear to leave the woods and see them bungee her carcass to their car roof. Then, as the woods darkened, I panicked, thinking I had waited too long to find my way home. I rushed along the trail with my hands held in front of me.

13

December 29, 1991

Dear Hillary,

I hope you received James's letter. I am finally writing, able to tell you that I am recovering after my accident and that Tom is okay, too! It has been so awful and so terrifying. But my hand is healing. When they removed the staples from my skin grafts it was weird: The skin was attached, but it was so thin you could see right through it. It made me feel faint, but I forced myself to look. It was kind of beautiful in a way, so thin and transparent like a waxed-paper window into my hand.

Ever since my accident, life has seemed even more fragile. I never wanted to be one of those parents gripped by fear after the loss of their child. But I was kidding myself to think I could out-run it. Sometimes I have so much anxiety about wanting to pro-tect Tom from how hard life can be. I'm telling you this a-mother to b-mother because I know you too want to protect him. There's so much we can't protect him from. All we can do is love him.

Love, Lola

This was the Lola whom I loved. Lola, the mother I wanted for Tom. A woman who could see the tragedy of her fragmented, burned hand, but who could also detect some-thing else, something beautiful: a wax-paper window.

I curled two loops of Scotch tape to hang up the card she had included from the Metropolitan Museum of Art. The card was cut out in the shape of a shoe and on the back it read ANKLE-STRAP SANDAL, FLORENCE, ITALY, 1938, CORK PLATFORM COVERED IN RAINBOW SUEDE, GOLD KID UPPER. I pressed the shoe to the wall next to my bed near my pastel Norway post-cards and hoped that Lola had purchased a shoe card for her-self. A pair of funky platform sandals. I felt lighter knowing she was all right. I kept rereading and laughing out loud at Lola's P.S.

Tom: "Was there anything funny about me when I was born?"
Me: "Like what?"
Tom: "Like did I have a conehead or anything?"

I called Shell to tell her.

"Thank god Lola's okay," Shell said.

"Shell, I need you to take a trip with me."

"Cross-country? See the sights? The Grand Canyon? Uncle Zee never would have done this, but now that it's mine—well, I'd close up this drugstore right now just to have a goddamn adventure!"

"No. I'm not going west. I'm headed north. To Caribou."

"Caribou." She did not disguise her disappointment. "You're kidding."

"No."

"You've been living in that little shack—"

"Cottage."

"Excuse me. *Cottage.* You've been holed up in that cottage

since you graduated from college. And now, the first time you venture out, you want to head up into no-man's-land?"

"Yes."

"Because?"

"I'm going to go talk to the boy—the man—who was there when Bird died."

"How did you find him?"

"Rhana helped me locate the Orono yearbooks from the years Bird would have gone there. His name is Thomas Jason Shea. He goes by TJ now, since that's what his wife calls him." The section on fraternities and sororities had been nauseating. DK's motto was "Friends from the Heart Forever!" They had gotten kicked off campus because of what had happened to Bird. There were a few snapshots of the inside of the new house, one with a photo of a tall stack of beer cans that spelled out DK. "I was able to locate him by making a few quick calls."

"And he remembered you?"

"He remembers me as a skinny little kid. He was sort of blown away by the fact that I named my child after him. He really didn't have too much of a choice in agreeing to meet me. I certainly didn't want to do it over the phone."

I could tell she was thinking. "So, we're taking the Turismo?"

Whenever Shell visited me, it was like being girls in pajamas again. Rhana had given me a gorgeous antique oak trundle bed so I could draw it out and have Shell sleep near me. I felt happiest when Shell's hairbrush, always swirled with lost strands, was resting with her toothbrush on my sink.

I slid out the bed and tucked the elastic corners of a fresh sheet around the mattress. I unfolded the heavy quilt, another

big-hearted present from Rhana, a patchwork of bright orange pinwheels.

"Is my drawer ready?" Shell always joked that the trundle
was like sleeping in the bottom of a bureau.

We scrambled into bed. I turned off the light. "I hope I
don't have that bad dream."

"You have that hallway dream? *Still?*"

"A couple of times a year at least."

"Shit," she said. Then she yawned. "I'm nervous about
tomorrow."

"Me too."

She dozed off. She always lay on her back with her face
lifted by the pillow. My eyes adjusted in the dark and I could
trace the outline of her cheek. I lay awake, thinking that had
Shell's mother been alive, she would have loved to watch her
daughter sleep.

I suppose there is no good time of year to travel and find out
about a death. So it might as well be January. We drove the
four hours up to Caribou, snowbanks piled along the edges
of I-95. "It's like a dream," Shell mused. "We're the only ones
on the road, and it goes on and on before us, then behind
us, but it looks exactly the same, like we're not even getting
anywhere."

We followed 95 to the end, drove up Route 1, then turned
onto 161. Gliding into Caribou wasn't any different than enter-
ing any other small Maine town with a freshly painted white
steeple in the center. TJ was keeping warm inside his car, waiting on the main street of Caribou as we had arranged. TJ
looked like I remembered him, though he had aged into a
man with gloomy purple circles under his eyes. I pegged him

as a chronic insomniac like Uncle Zee. I didn't know how to greet him so I extended my hand and he shook it while we formed a one-armed hug. He nodded when I introduced Shell, and I guessed that he vaguely recognized her from Bird's wake.

In the Bear Claw Coffee Shop, Shell and I settled in on one side of the booth and slipped off our parkas. We all ordered coffee. The men at the counter spun their stools so their ears were aimed in our direction but TJ kept his voice low. He stared into the blackness of his cup and said, "I haven't ever talked about this to anyone but my wife. She thinks maybe if I tell you, I'll be able to sleep better. I need to tell you this straight through or else I won't be able to say the words."

My heart began pounding and for some reason Lola's words came into my mind—"I forced myself to look at it . . . a waxed-paper window into my hand."

"Your parents didn't tell you because I think they were just trying to protect you. I have two daughters of my own, and . . . well, I've been going over this in my mind ever since you called. And one thing that stands out is the pledging that night was more intense than it had been when I had joined." He spoke gradually, pacing himself, not rushing the details and not leaving anything out.

"The night your brother passed on, the pledges were dressed in plastic pants and jackets. Same as always, from what I had been told. We were in the bathroom with the steam going from the showers and the pledges were doing sit-ups. They had to say 'Yes, sir!' to everything that Joey said. Joey was the pledge captain. When Bird started to slow down the pace of his sit-ups, Joey put his boot on Bird's back, pressing him down into a curl. As Bird came up, he had to fight even harder to keep going because of the pressure on his spine.

"I had to do the exact same thing the previous year. So I didn't think it was all that dangerous. I did know that Joey had a mean streak in him. He had suggested once that we make a peephole in the girl's guest bathroom. We were like, 'Man, you're a sick fuck.' Joey had been drinking all day. I think he was also popping Black Beauties."

"Speed," Shell said dully.

"Yeah. Uppers. So he was very hyped up that day. He talked us into having the pledges wear diapers and making them suck their thumbs. Then that night we had shots of gin and grain alcohol all lined up in paper cups on the toilet seats. Bird wasn't used to drinking much. He loved to play games, though! I didn't know him long, but I knew that about him.

"Joey wanted to see what Bird was made of. 'C'mon, keep going,' Joey yelled, shoving his foot on Bird.

"'Yes, sir!' Bird answered. He was almost done with the three hundred reps. Joey wanted to see him fail. He shouted, 'Birdsong, you faggot.' Bird lay back and didn't finish the final few sit-ups. The other five pledges were done. Bird was in better shape than they were, so I didn't understand what was going on. Joey taunted him, 'Birdsong, you're not man enough to be one of us.'

"Bird collapsed on his side. I saw his eyes roll up in his head, and through that hot misty steam, I saw that his lips had turned bluish. I pushed Joey and shouted, 'Back off!'

"He shoved me back. 'Shut up, you pussy.'

"I knelt down to cradle Bird's head. Joey shouted again, 'He's a faggot,' and kicked Bird in the ribs. Several other brothers went after Joey and pinned him against the tiles. 'You fuckin' freak,' they screamed at him.

"'Everyone shut up,' I yelled. I loosened the string of Bird's hood and pulled it off his hair. Someone turned off the showers. The bathroom became very quiet. Bird lay perfectly still, his eyes almost shut. I pressed my ear to his chest. There was no sound, no vibration. It's strange, the thoughts that go through your head in a crisis. I thought maybe my left ear wasn't my good ear. So I zipped open his warmup jacket, turned my head to the other side, and listened with my right ear. I heard nothing. I gathered him into my arms. He was dead weight. I burst out crying. I don't know who called the medics. It was a rare medical situation, from what we were told later. Alcohol poisoning, inducing a heart attack."

We sat for a long while. Finally he said, "I dream about it still. Horrible nightmares. Listening for his heartbeat and not hearing it." Our coffee grew even colder. "You drove such a long way to hear this. I'm sorry."

Shell looked stricken. "Goddamn," she whispered. "No wonder Janée went nuts."

We made sure we filled the gas tank before returning to Lincolnville. With the windows rolled down, we turned up the heat full force to keep warm. We drove with our hoods up, craving the bitter bite of the wind, the very alive feeling of a desolate night blasting our faces.

14

I turned twenty-eight and Rhana decided that since I was nearing thirty, she should fix me up with a "decent man who could provide." Not only that, I had been depressed ever since my trip to Caribou, without much appetite for food. Rhana hoped that romance might snap me out of it. She invited Kevin Roark to the Red Barn one snowy afternoon. He wore the brightest red cable-knit sweater I had ever seen on a grown man. He had a pleasant face and shook my hand with a warm "Hello, my friend." And then said he had to head back up for recess duty in Belfast.

"He is cute," I admitted to Rhana later.

"But what?" she demanded.

"I don't know."

"You mean he doesn't seem cool. Seems to me you would have had enough of cool. You need to face facts, darling. Grown women have needs. One of life's greatest pleasures is waking up with a naked man in your bed. Don't look so shocked, Hillary. I know what I'm talking about."

Kevin asked me out to Christmas-by-the-Sea in Camden. I didn't want to face Rhana's disapproval, so I went. Though the bells in the Congregational church steeple rang my favorite carol, "Have Yourself a Merry Little Christmas," I still felt no Christmas spirit. Carolers strolled in top hats. We threaded our way into the crowd through the fruity steam from mulled cider. I greeted Jolly Roger and Dorothy, who, in one of her manic episodes, gushed about how much she loved and admired me. Just then I felt a tap on my shoulder.

Gary leaned his face next to my ear. The low hum of his voice made my stomach flip. He mumbled accusingly, "You're not planning on getting serious with this Poindexter nerd from Belfast, are you? I've been trying to get you to lie down for years now. And you might be giving it up for Mr. Egghead Principal?"

Kevin was craning his neck to see if Santa was arriving in the lobster boat. I hissed back, "You and I decided a long time ago that we were just going to be friends."

"*You* decided."

He was with Laura Twitchell. She waited until Gary pulled her away, his arm extended behind him, the fringe from her pink shawl pulled forward. He didn't hear her say to me, "You may be very pretty, but you're not all that."

As Santa glided up in his boat, Kevin slid his hand underneath my ponytail. I felt nothing sensual as he caressed the short hairs there. I broke away, heading toward the darkness beyond the dots of tiny white Christmas lights.

I was rude, and yet he called out to make sure I was okay.

Why did I see him again? I had no desire to see him anywhere near naked. But maybe there was more to love. After all, he was a "nice guy." So I went on date after date with Kevin. Unfortunately, every morning when I woke up, my dreams blew out like the fog in Penobscot Bay, the disappearing mist of dreams of Gary's hands sliding down my bare back, stripping me. On the edges of a forest (in Norway!), I danced with Gary. He glowed, too, and in the cooled meadow grass, he entered me and filled me with warm light. We made love standing up while slow dancing under orange globes, papery bright.

I thought the dreams would stop if I didn't go see Gary anymore. I was unable to look Gary in the eye when I ran into him at the town water pump. "Why haven't you come to see me in a while? It better not be because of Poindexter." He teased me, "I miss your yakking." I was grateful I had on my winter hat to cover the blushing of my ears.

One day two women, obviously mother and daughter, came into the Red Barn pushing a stroller. The older woman was an old friend of Rhana's, and I eavesdropped, rewinding all the cuckoo clocks, while she explained to Rhana how her daughter had just adopted this baby from China. I dared myself to look down and was shocked at how sunken the baby's cheeks were. She was listless in her stroller, held up only by the down of her red parka.

"It's going to take some time to get her healthy," the grandmother offered. "Her hair was all matted down when we first saw her. She was totally lifeless because of malnutrition. She's eighteen months old, but she's the size of a nine-month-old. She also had ringworm, but she's okay now. She just needs lots of TLC. Her middle name is Chinese for 'summer sounds.'" She beamed at her daughter, who leaned over and kissed the little girl. "She'll fatten that baby up. Before you know it, that baby will be running around flying kites on the beach."

Rhana bent closer. I heard her knees crack as she peered down. The grandmother gushed on. "With an international adoption like this we have a little information about her family, but not much. The likelihood of the birthmother coming to knock on my daughter's door is slim. That's one of the reasons China worked. This is *my* grandbaby. The way I see it, the birthmother had her chance."

Rhana's eyes blazed. The daughter opened her mouth to correct her and then shut it again. The little baby looked up at her new mother with a direct, steady gaze. The women left, pausing together in the brisk beach wind outside.

Suddenly the cuckoo clocks whirred. The hour struck. *The birthmother had her chance.* Tiny birds with lime-colored wings popped out, like party blowers unrolling all the way. They thrust their heads out three times, then curled back up all alone in their cottages, locked in the dust, muffled by the dark.

I drove up to Belfast Elementary the night of Kevin's spring concert. I arrived late, and as I neared the door, I heard the choir singing about cherry blossoms falling. Their high-pitched voices were so innocent that they brought tears to my eyes. Tom was in middle school now. An adolescent. I had missed his childhood. The doors to the auditorium were open, and I wandered over to the elaborate playground, a real train engine where the kids could play, painted red and blue, a dopey face on the front with rosy cheeks decorated with hearts. I settled into a swing, my hands grabbing the chains and my bottom barely fitting on the black rubber arc. I heard Kevin thank the parents of the singers, and then a string instrument sawed away at "Twinkle, Twinkle, Little Star."

After more applause the kids began skipping out, shrieking, white collared shirts on the boys and chunky heels for the girls. The lights of the school went out, window by window. Kevin emerged and locked up the side door. He spotted me on the playground. He didn't smile as he neared me.

"Why didn't you come in?"

"I could hear fine from here." My voice sounded forced. I sensed that he was angry with me, or maybe just disappointed.

He turned his head to the empty slide and asked, "Do you even like kids?"

"Why are you asking me this? I thought we were just dating."

"I need to know where we're going. It's important to me."

"We haven't even slept together."

"I want a family," he confessed.

"I've been in a family. It wasn't that great."

I knew then how Kevin had perceived me. I was, in his eyes, the sweet little clerk from the antique store, a girl to bring home to Mother. He mistook my lack of ambition and my unexpressed desire for girlish innocence. How wrong he was. A coldness overcame his expression as my supposed virtue seeped away, replaced in his mind by something twisted and unfeminine. He struggled to maintain his gentlemanly exterior. "I think we should just remain friends," he declared.

"You're not looking for a friend. You're not even looking for a lover. You don't care that I don't even like kissing you. You're just looking for a breeder." *Breeder.* I hadn't heard that word since Wanda had snarled it at one of the sisters.

He drove off. The vacant playground was tranquil as I dangled on the swing, listening to the wide iron chains creak. Then I heard the far-off honking of geese coming home. The half moon was luminous enough for me to make out the long, imperfect V.

The odor of metal clung to my palms as I drove past Gary's. I spotted a bar of light from underneath his garage door. I knocked lightly. He lifted the door up, and I took my usual seat on the overturned bucket.

"What brings you out at this hour?"

"Kevin broke it off with me. Want to know why?"

"Because he's a douche?"

"No. He wanted to talk about having kids. It's ridiculous. He can kiss my ass, that's what."

Gary didn't answer.

"Maybe it's good for me to know that I don't want another kid. Just admit it to myself. I'm sure of it now. Does that make me evil? I'm twenty-eight. Oh sure, I have lots of childbearing years ahead of me. But I admit it, I just couldn't go through with having another. It's hard enough being separated from the one I do have. Like last year, I get the annual letter. I open it. My boy is now questioning: Is the Tooth Fairy real? He wants to know. He lost a molar and his mom, Lola, gave him an envelope to put it in. He thinks he's tricking the Tooth Fairy by putting an acorn inside instead of his tooth."

A smile flickered on Gary's face. He had quietly put down his tools and was sitting on a stack of rubber tires, listening closely, pulling a little on his moustache.

"But every single year, I look at his picture, and I lie down and cry. I try not to get the photo wet. I try not to smear the ink on the back. I smell the paper. I do everything but eat it. And I still feel so empty! I feel so much love for him. But I never, ever, *ever* get to tell him." Exhausted, I felt lighter with the release of these words.

"You'll meet up one day. I know you will. From what you say of this Lola, she sounds decent. But at least you have a kid."

"What do you mean?" I asked. "What, you're like Kevin, you want a kid to ful—"

He cut me off. "I shoot blanks."

I laughed awkwardly. "Excuse me?"

"I can't have kids."

"You had a vasectomy?"

"Believe it or not, I've been cheated on. A long time ago. I was like, nineteen. I was with this girl. She got pregnant. I thought it was mine. I tried to be good to her. Anyway, around six or seven months into it, she starts telling me how she was still in love with her high school sweetheart and that she had been driving over to Nashua to meet him. She wanted to know who the father was. She had paternity tests done. It wasn't mine. I had these other complications. Which I don't want to go into. To make a long story short, I shoot blanks."

"Did you love her?"

"What's love? I mean, can anyone really say what it is?"

And I laughed, relieved. "Then you didn't love her. Not with an answer like that."

During the months following my trip to Caribou, Gary had listened to my preoccupation with the horrific details of Bird's last night. So the least I could do for him in return was to keep him company one summer night when he made his monthly trip to visit his mother in Lewiston-Auburn, the twin cities. Package stores and Cumberland Farms, kids with that god-awful hairdo they called "tails." Hair feathered back with one long strand hanging down the middle of their backs, pointing down off their round heads like the tails of horseshoe crabs. Some of the kids bleached it white, or braided it, or twisted it into a springy curl. A bossy, dark-haired girl put her hands on her hips and screamed at a group of boys as they played hide-and-seek. Whatever had happened to Wanda's first daughter? Could that be Tiny? A tough expression on her face, the girl looked around thirteen, a box of Marlboros tucked into her overalls. Too young to have just crossed over that line of learning to inhale without coughing.

We came to a halt in a parking lot, scattering a flock of pigeons. "That's her." Gary pointed up at the silhouette of a woman in the window. Her apartment building, five stories of wood, was a tinderbox. One staircase, no fire escapes, and no smoke detectors that I could see. The stairway was dark brown, illuminated only by an orange bulb. Gary led the way up the steps. I couldn't see clearly where the edges were and held on tight to the banister.

His mother's room had no lock on it. Gary knocked and walked right in. She stood up and came toward him, her arms out, her round face stretched tightly in a grin. "*Mmm, waahh.*" She made a loud, affectionate noise as she kissed him and fluttered her hands on his back. They looked like the paddles inside a pinball machine. He flinched.

"So how are ya?" she asked cheerfully.

She pointed to a broken couch for us to sit down on. A crack in the wooden frame forced us to sit right next to each another. She had the same rich brown eyes as Gary, and his stare, though her medications made her irises appear brighter than her son's.

His mother pointed at me. "She looks nice."

"She's not my girl," he said tiredly.

"Oh." She nodded her head vigorously as if he had just told her the most interesting news.

"I got taken away in an ambulance the other day," she said.

She was looking right through us. It gave me an awful feeling. She acted like I was there, like Gary was there, but she was in her own head. Like someone sleeping with her eyes wide open.

Gary was looking just to the right of his mother's head at a picture of himself at his First Communion. In the photo he wore a suit with squared-off shoulders, his hands were pressed together as he prayed, and he looked up so innocently. You didn't see that hard look in his eyes then.

"Hear all those pigeons?" she asked. Trucks outside went grinding by, the kids with the tails hiding and shrieking when they discovered each other, the pigeons sounding like they were saying *toodaloo, toodaloo.*

"I caught a disease," his mother went on. "From them pigeons. I couldn't breathe at all. They had to take me away in the ambulance. Did you know my hands are coming apart?"

"No, Mom, I didn't know that." Gary poked around in his ear with his index finger, pulled it out, and looked to see if anything was on his fingernail. I was shocked. Gary hated for anyone to see him fixing himself up. He never picked his teeth even after eating popcorn. He wiped his moustache obsessively to make sure no crumbs were in it. He would only go around town with very clean, perfect hair—he was the first man I knew to use hair mousse.

"I'm better now, though." She began to laugh. Her face looked as though she was about to cry, but she was laughing very hard. "Can you believe it? Pigeons!"

"We gotta go, Mom." He stood up and leaned down. She made the same loud *Mmm-wah* noise as she kissed him. "Nice meeting you," I lied. She attempted to rub his back as he hugged her but he pulled away. Gary ran down the tenement steps so quickly it looked like he was doing a simple but perfect soft-shoe step.

"Do you know how many times she's been in Sweeny Hall?" he demanded.

Sweeny Hall. The institution where Charlie had been, where Charlie had been hurt. Where they housed retarded people and the mentally ill. "No."

"Over sixty. She goes nuts, she goes in, they medicate her with something new, she comes out. This whole apartment building is for people on state aid."

"How old were you the first time she—went?"

"Seven."

I took one last look at her up in the window. The pigeons on the sill were shiny gossamer colors—dusty rose and lichen green. They clung to the rain gutters. I could still see the spacy glaze in her expression as she tilted her face in the orange glow of the setting sun.

15

Through my white, sheer curtains, I recognized my father's large head and massive shoulders. I threw the door open, peering behind him to see where my mother was.

"So she's not coming?"

"No."

"I invited both of you. She's only been here a couple of times to visit me. You, you manage to find your way here more often. This is the first time in my whole life I've cooked for a holiday. I wanted her here."

He held out a pizza delivery bag he had borrowed from the End-of-the-Lake store. "Happy Thanksgiving! Mom sent this pie for you. Extra pecans, the way you like it." I gave him a hug, patting the soft pills of his old sweater. "Smells good in here," he said. "Yep." It sounded like *yip*. Tom's yip over the water.

I slid the pie out and steam rose from the sugary nuts. My mouth watered. My father bragged, "Over one hundred miles, and it's still hot."

"The turkey needs another hour or so. Should we be decadent and eat dessert first?"

"Why not? It's just us."

"Let me make a pot of coffee. Then we'll dig in."

He pulled out a chair and straddled it with his legs spread wide. The Birdsong brothers, I thought; he sits just like Uncle Bill. Even when my father folded his beefy arms over his chest he still filled up the kitchen. Shy and unsure together, we watched the stream of coffee pour into the carafe.

"I wanted her to come." I sounded young, almost bratty.

"Your mother's going through a lot right now."

"So much that she can't come see her own daughter? For a holiday?"

"I guess you guys have that in common."

"What do you mean?"

He shrugged. "It's not like you ever come home to see us." He said it factually. I was grateful he wasn't angry. How could I explain to him that the silhouette of Mount Battie at night, a black cutout against a salmon sunset, had befriended me? "I live here now. This is my home."

"You don't have any family here."

"You're here now," I teased him, trying to lighten things up. I gave him his cup and the cream and sugar.

"You could come home with me," he mused. "Tomorrow night is your high school reunion at Oxford Hills. People have asked if you're coming."

Shell had been calling me, also trying to coax me home. "It would be good for you to face the demons of your past," she had argued.

"Dad. No one even remembers me."

"That's not true. Don't say that. Everyone asks about you. And your uncle Bill still cries about you not living near us."

"Dad, Bill turns on the waterworks about everything. Is that where Mom is today? At Uncle Bill's?"

"Yes."

"She didn't mind you leaving?"

"Not at all. She knew how much I wanted to see you."

"Doesn't she want to see me?"

He didn't answer.

"Oh, that's right," I said sarcastically. "Hillary is always so difficult."

My father ate his pie slowly. Thirty-five years of eating my mother's pies, and he still concentrated on every buttery crumb. "You are difficult," my father finally answered. "So am I. So is your mother. Who isn't?"

"Bird wasn't." I always hated when my mother brought Bird into every conversation; now I was doing it.

My dad nodded. "He was a good kid."

"Do you think we act like he's a saint, that we forget his faults?" My mother believed that my brother had had a few minor, irritating habits at most. Burping long and loud after guzzling a can of soda. Biting his nails and spitting them out of the side of his mouth.

My father ate his crust. "He wanted to get along with everyone. Please everyone. Maybe that's not always such a good thing." My father pressed his lips together so hard they disappeared. It was always such a strain for him to let words out. One thing about my father, he was so cautious with language that I don't think he ever regretted saying a word. This was one of the longest conversations I had had with him since I had been pregnant. I held my breath, woozy with closeness, wondering if I could bear it.

"Dad, I went to see one of those boys . . . you know . . . one of those brothers who was there when Bird died."

My father put his fork down and swallowed. I waited for

him to adjust to the news. Finally he picked his fork up again, but he still didn't eat.

"I had to know. But I don't blame you for keeping it from me." We sat in silence, then the oven timer beeped. I slipped on mitts and pulled the turkey out and placed it on the counter. It glowed a golden brown. I sat down again, waiting for the juices to cool.

"You were so little when it happened. Your mom and I saw how much you had suffered losing him. We figured you didn't need to know everything. That it would be best to just—move on."

"Why didn't Mom come today?"

"Your mother," he said slowly, "thinks maybe that the nun was right."

"What nun?"

"One of those sisters when you were in trouble."

"Sister Joan? The one Mom and I met with for counseling?"

"That's the one. Joan thought Mom treated you like a pincushion."

"Sister Joan said that?"

"Your mother feels bad about that. She has regrets. She's ashamed of how she acted." He stared into his mug, swirled the last drops around, and sighed.

I tried to observe my father's technique for carving the turkey, but my mind was far away. *A pincushion.* We ate in silence. "I know I haven't been home in so long," I began. "That doesn't mean I don't think about it. You want to know something? I picture in detail what will happen someday if Tom comes back. All of us together in Norway. Mom laying out the wedding china. Lace cloth. You dozing in front of the football game. And Tom and me in the kitchen, laughing. It's strange, though, I never really picture us actually eating the meal. I spend hours envisioning us cooking. Stirring pots. Measuring."

"Is Small Fry okay?" I loved that he had a nickname for Tom.

"Yeah. He's doing great, I guess. You know, it's the little things I want to know about." I picked at the remaining turkey on my plate. "Like whether he likes white meat, or dark."

There was a knock on my door. "Dad, I do have good friends here." I opened the door and let Gary in. "Dad, this is Gary. Gary, this is my dad . . . Ray."

"Nice to meet you." Gary shook his hand. "I'm sorry to interrupt your dinner. I was wondering if you were coming to Harold's carol sing later."

"Yeah. What time?"

"Seven."

"I'll be there."

Gary nodded politely at my dad and left.

"You realize that he is in love with you," my father announced.

"What makes you say that?"

"Isn't it obvious from the way he looks at you?"

"He stares at everyone like that, Dad."

"No. I'm right."

We stacked up the plates and piled the leftovers in Tupperware. "That turkey was delicious. Great job. Hey, is it always this freezing?" he asked.

I pointed to the baseboards. "Electric heat is so expensive." My Bat House, though it was bleached clean and white, whistled just like La Rosaria had, the unceasing sea wind blowing in between the window caulk. A sudden wind sounded as if a handful of dust had been flung at my window.

I peered into the dark behind the window shade. "Uh-oh, Dad. Sleet."

Sadness flickered on his face.

"Do you want to stay over?"

"No. I can't. I'd better go. I can't leave Mom alone all night."

I flipped the rest of the pie into a Tupperware container, then rinsed my mother's pie pan, wiped it dry, and handed it to my dad. I remembered helping him string pie pans in the vegetable garden to protect it, attempting to keep the hungriest, darkest crows away. It never worked. He hugged me good-bye, squeezing so hard he dented the empty pie pan that was pressed between us. "Take good care of yourself, Hill." He pulled out his wallet and handed me five crisp twenty-dollar bills. "Warm your toes." He patted the top of my head with his big bear paw, clumsily, like Uncle Bill.

The kitchen seemed emptier without him. If my dad could be an object, he'd choose to be a heavy paperweight, happy to keep pages from flying away. I leaned my elbows on the counter, alone, eating the same plump, syrupy pecans and melt-on-your-tongue crust that had earned my mother blue ribbons year after year in the pavilion of the Waterford World's Fair.

The phone startled me. I let my answering machine pick up. "Hillary?" It was my mother. "Are you there? I was just wondering if Dad left yet. The snow's coming down pretty hard here. I wanted to wish you a happy Thanksgiving. I assume you're not coming back for your reunion. Well, I guess high school wasn't the best time for you." Was she trying not to stab me? "You—" I decided to pick up. I rushed to the phone, but she was gone. The dial tone droned.

The sleet lightened, but the wind increased as I walked down the railroad tracks over to Harold's. He had asked a bunch of us to come begin the Christmas season with a sing-along at his house. All Harold's coworkers bitched about Christmas. How it got earlier and earlier every year and people were shipping bigger and more fragile gifts. Too much crystal, too many ripe pears, and teddy bears that were too tall. Harry disagreed. I had never met anyone who loved both Valentine's Day and Christmas as much as he did.

Harold belonged to the Light of the World Fellowship Church. I entered his living room and said hello to Gary and Rhana, and then was introduced to an odd assortment of choir members from his church. Ruth, in her nutty-looking wig, which she took off and on like a fur hat, readjusting it so it sat backward. Eddie, a WWII veteran with a limp. Jane, a very nice woman from Belfast with a blond moustache and a sweatshirt embossed with kittens dancing with candy canes.

Harold passed out sheet music. I am an alto. I have a good voice but I am no good at counting. I rush ahead with the music, not wanting to wait for the beats to be over before starting the next note. We sang "O Little Town of Bethlehem," "Angels We Have Heard on High," and "The Little Drummer Boy." I stole a look at Gary. He was so completely engrossed in singing his bass notes of *Rum pum pum pum* that I was embarrassed by how vulnerable he looked.

Then we began the first verse of "Silent Night" in unison. When we took parts on the second verse, I realized I was having the best Thanksgiving since I was eleven. This year I had basted my very own turkey; I had spooned stuffing with someone from my family; I had heard that my mother realized how harshly she had treated me. With a full belly, the music swelling, I had a feeling of serenity. I heard the wind whistling as usual from Penobscot Bay, but it circled around us like a cocoon, and inside the cocoon there we were, a glowing four-part harmony.

Gary offered to drive me home as we buttoned our coats and hugged Harold goodnight. "I'd rather walk," I said.

"Then let me walk a little with you." We headed up the train tracks that lead back to the ferry.

"Do you believe in God?" He stopped for a moment.

I thought about it. The only unchanging part of my entire life was the wind. Nothing else had remained the same. If anyone ever asked me, that would be my definition of God: wind blowing the same direction as the lone headlights on the road, blowing wild.

"Maybe."

He reached out and tucked a few loose, blowing strands of hair behind my ear.

16

Gary told me later that his New Year's resolution was to finally get me. On January 1 I heard a knock as I was rinsing my face clean before bedtime. "It's me," he called. I patted my skin dry and opened the door. I had my hair twisted into a topknot on my head. I wore an old stained sweatshirt, blue snowflake long johns, and, over those, Wanda's big black shorts. The polyester fabric shone with pills, and the waistband was slung low on my hips with barely any stretch of elastic left.

"Hey," he teased. "Nice shorts. So, is this what you look like getting ready for bed?"

"It's freezing with this damn door open. And to answer your question, yes."

"Okay. Just wondering." And he turned and left.

Three, four nights in a row, he knocked on my door around eleven, said hello, and left. On the fifth night, I couldn't help laughing, and I pulled him in out of the winter cold and into my bedroom. He emptied out the pockets of his jeans, placing coins and a pocketknife on my dresser. He lay down in his jeans on my bed. We kissed for hours. "I feel like you're teaching me how to kiss, and I'm teaching you how to kiss," he said. Sometime deep in the darkest hour of the night, I shed the black shorts.

Rhana was right. There was nothing quite like waking up with a naked man in your bed, and there was no way I was getting out of that bed. I called in sick to work.

"You're not sick, Hillary," Rhana said snottily. "I am looking out the back window. I see Gary's car in your driveway."

"I have the flu and his car didn't start last night," I lied. "Earl the Pearl is coming with his tow truck."

We made love and dozed all morning. I finally understood Simone's drawings of Reed. You can look at a naked man from so many different angles. Like all beautiful things in nature, no two glimpses are the same.

I was "sick" the entire week. Trying to fool Rhana, I had picked up Gary and brought him back to my cottage. I loved glancing over at him when he was my passenger; he sat like a polite little boy, his hands pressed between his knees, daydreaming into the trees he had passed a thousand times before.

When I finally returned to work on Saturday, jangling the sleigh bells on the door of the Red Barn as I came in, Rhana greeted me with "I bought that little cottage so it wouldn't be an eyesore. Now I have to look out and see your appalling taste in men." When I didn't answer, she softened. "All I'm saying is you deserve a *true* love."

"Yeah, I know all about it, like you and the great Wendell," I said tiredly. Wendell smiled at me from his photo, his bow tie forever pointy and crisp. "My life isn't like other people's, especially yours. Gary's kind to me. Don't I deserve kindness? Isn't that good enough for you? You're the one who said I shouldn't be so hard on myself. Why are you being so hard on me? People change. Things change. You want to know what's changed? I'll tell you. I read an article on La Rosaria in the Portland paper. Did you know those girls settle in for up to eighteen months now, because a lot of them keep their babies? They have little apartments now. I saw the request in the paper at Christmas, how to donate to a needy charity. 'Here at La Rosaria we need diapers; baby clothes, newborn to three months; formula; and gently used baby items.' I'm trying really hard here, Rhana, to keep it together. Gary's been my friend for years. So I went to bed with him. You're the one who said grown women have *needs*."

She unfurled the OPEN flag. Her lips were pursed. She nodded her head up and down. "Fair enough." Then she looked at me closely.

"He's good, isn't he?"

I blushed. "I don't know what you mean."

"Yes, you do. He's good. I can tell by the way you're glowing."

"What's that song we listen to sometimes? 'Woman be wise, keep your mouth shut, don't advertise your man.'" And we both began to laugh.

A new bar called The Haunt opened in town a few doors down from work. Though the owners had redone the inside of an old delicatessen with brand-new hardwood floors, within a few weeks of opening the place had the permanent odor of a dive: cold popcorn and flat beer. I often heard the high-pitched feedback of sound checks before the bands played. There was a new, nonstop flow of rock-star wannabes checking out the stuff in our store. The wild lead singers had a bad habit of accidentally busting our porcelain figurines when they swung their long girlish hair around to fluff it up.

Sloppy Joe came down sometimes and joined in late-night jam sessions with his mandolin. He and the band members talked big when they were really drunk. After inhaling mega-hits of pot at the back of The Haunt near the Dumpster, they babbled on about how they were going to fly out to L.A., how they would remember us all when they made it big, going on tour in their busses. I usually drank ginger ale, rolled my eyes at Sloppy Joe, and thought about my dream of Tom. If you only got excited about your dreams after doing a few shots, those dreams were never going to come true.

I waited outside The Haunt that November for Shell and her new husband, Christian. In the pale yellow light, I watched Shell in her cloth coat, red buttons pulling on buttonholes, a coat not meant for being so pregnant in. Her husband instinctively grabbed her elbow and guided her up over the curb. Her slim gold band shone in the sun. They were a family already.

Gary, Shell, Christian, and I grouped together and watched The Haunt's twist contest. Harold was an excellent twister. All the girls fought to dance with him. He always won because he could drop closest to the ground and not fall on his butt, still shifting his elbows and shoulders back and forth. I wondered why someone didn't fall in love with him while he danced. He looked his best then, flushed and free.

"Your new beau is gorgeous," Shell said to me when Gary went to the men's room.

"I suppose."

"You suppose?"

"I don't think about it."

She smiled. "You are such a liar. You have chemistry, don't you?"

Chemistry. What did people mean by that? I had done poorly in chemistry at Oxford Hills. I don't remember any actual experiments we did, only that we had to wear geeky glasses to protect our eyes from sparks and explosions.

"Yes. Gary and I call each other three, four times a day, every day. He's the first one beside you to ever call me honey. I like cooking for him. I know it's sexist to want to cook for a man. But I like feeding him." I could have gone on. He brought me hawk feathers, blue jay feathers. Tiny empty snail shells. Huge gold hoop earrings like a city girl would wear. Big barrettes strong enough to hold back the thickness of my hair without popping open.

"With a name like Gary the Glutton, what did you expect?" Christian joked.

"He didn't get that name from his love of food."

She eyed me suspiciously. "What do you mean?"

I shrugged.

She pressed on. "You mean he's a *dog*?"

"If that's the word everyone is using these days, fine."

"Oh, Hillary. Has he changed?"

"You mean does he cheat on me?"

"Well, does he?"

"No."

"How do you know?"

"I haven't heard a thing from any ex-girlfriends. And this county is crawling with them."

Gary slid back into our booth. Unaware that Shell and Christian were studying him, he smiled at me and reached out, trailing his knuckles around the curve of my ear.

17

In muted shadow, hiding in the dusk, I returned to Norway with Gary—a slow homecoming working up to a harsher glare. My trip down Main Street began with the familiar sight of teenagers roaming under the burned-out streetlights, cheap six-string guitars on their backs, holding cigarettes awkwardly, glaring at the passing police cars from underneath their shaggy bangs. Smokey Bear still waved near the fire station. With hardened winter snowbanks, the fire danger read LOW.

The albino porcupine was gone from its window, but the log-cabin exterior of Woodman's was still nestled in the shops along Main Street, many of them now empty and gray like shoe boxes with loose lids. I rolled down my window and told Gary to follow the roads around the lake, Round-the-Pond back to Crocket Ridge. The edges of the lake smelled of brown pine needles soaked with melted snow, and I breathed that coolness deep down inside me. I directed him to the furrowed roads out at the edge of North Pond where Shell was living in her childhood home with her new family.

Shell's life had deepened so suddenly. She had fallen in love, eloped to Las Vegas, and had a baby. I was supposed to be present at the birth, but the baby had come so fast that

Shell had given birth to her daughter in the back room of Carlton Drugstore.

"I'm so sorry you weren't here." Shell had phoned me after they had taken her and the baby to St. Stephen's. "But I have some other good news for you."

"Besides that you have a wonderful brand-new baby daughter?"

"I'm naming her Ellary. It's a variation on Hillary."

"Really? I never heard of it."

"I made it up."

I teased her. "Ten thousand baby names in that book I gave you and you had to make up a new one. But you know it means the world to me."

We pulled up the long, unpaved driveway to the shack of a house. I could see inside, a bare bulb illuminating Shell's bright blonde hair. As I watched her stir a big spoon in a pot, I thought how my very first memory in life was of the day I met Shell, when her Uncle Zee enrolled her in the three-year-olds' program at Lucky Charms Nursery School. He had gotten custody of her within days after her parents were buried side by side. Shell and I were dressed alike but not because the school required uniforms. It was just an odd coincidence. In matching plaid skirts with navy and pumpkin-colored squares and thick elastic waistbands, Shell and I had eagerly toddled to each another.

Dogs barked furiously in the chill air as I opened my car door. Shell peered out of the window, then she smiled wide and burst out of the squeaky screen door. She gave Gary a little hug, then rushed at me and hugged me so tight it hurt my breasts. I grasped her meaty arms and said, "Hey, Miss Muscles!"

"Oh, god, no, I put on a lot of weight with this babe." She pulled away and stuck her hand inside her turtleneck and adjusted the pads inside her nursing bra, laughing. Her long hair, which she usually brushed one hundred strokes each night, was snarly. "I know I look a fright. The baby was up all night and cried all today, too. She's finally sleeping. Come in, come in, come in!"

She guided me into the house, still damp, slightly sour, the kitchen walls stained brown with raindrops, past bags of re-cyclables overflowing in the pantry and into the living room, where all her uncle's musty *Reader's Digest* books lined the warped shelves. The piano sagged in the corner, the keyboard drooping like an accordion. The creepy cowboys still stared from the bottom of the stairwell. I turned to Gary. He raised his eyebrows, like *What the hell is wrong with this place?* I shot back a look that said *Keep quiet.*

In the center of the room a white wicker bassinet gleamed under the one section of roof that didn't leak. The bassinet swirled with bright eyelet lace, fresh pink flannel blankets, and gingham bumpers. Settled in the middle, sleeping on her belly, was Ellary. Her perfect little fists on each side of her perfect face.

I leaned closer. Her powdery sweetness flooded me with a longing. Before I could calm them, tears pooled in my eyes. I hid my face. This was Shell's joy. I did not want her to help me carry the burden of my heartache. I prayed my voice wouldn't catch when I exclaimed, "She's awesome. Look at her skin. It's flawless."

"I know. And did you know they have a chicken pox vaccine now? So no scars for this little princess."

"That's excellent." Before Shell could ask if I wanted to hold Ellary, I blurted, "My mom and dad are waiting for me. I'd better go."

She agreed. "I've started back a few hours on the morning shift this week. Your dad's been eating breakfast at the counter and bragging that his little girl is coming home. You know he's excited when he actually *talks*."

"Speaking of talking, how's Uncle Zee?"

She sighed. "The stroke took its toll. But the doctors say that with more rehab he has a shot at a pretty good recovery."

I nodded. "I'll see you at the church at noon?"

"Of course."

Gary and I returned to town. "Take a left here. Now right onto this street. Slow down. That's it on the left." I tried to spy my father through the window. The light was on, but his chair was empty. Maybe he had to go to Uncle Bill's for something. "We don't have to stop, not just yet. We can drive around some more." But as we passed my house, I saw my dad planted on the porch steps. Gary threw the car in reverse, and, going backward, I finally returned home.

"Hillary!" My mother rushed out. I barely recognized the bony shoulders jutting in her workout suit. "I wasn't sure what time you'd get here. I'm so embarrassed—I just got back from my run and haven't showered." She flipped back her pointy hood and wiped the sweat on her face with her arm. She had colored the gray out of her hair. I remembered the contours of that face, the mother who had buckled a life preserver on me and rowed me along the edge of the lake, except now the face had looser fitting skin.

"My god, Mom, when did you start running?"

"A couple of years ago. Not bad for fifty-seven, huh?"

I smiled. "Not bad at all."

"Mom, this is Gary."

Her eyes lit up. She had always loved good-looking people.

My father insisted on carrying my bag upstairs. *What is the smell of this house?* I wondered. *A scent of supper lingering in checkered curtains.* I crossed into the parlor's familiar maze of my mother's braided rugs.

"This is a real treat." My dad beamed. As I passed their bedroom I inhaled the smell of my dad coming from his bureau, a peppercorn smell, the smell of his white undershirts. On my father's nightstand was a Polaroid of Tom crying in his snug little hospital cap. Lola must have given them that picture the day we said good-bye—but I had never seen it before.

"Here's where you guys are staying," my dad huffed.

I stopped, peering into Bird's room. Instead of the soldier-blue walls and the grinning Farrah Fawcett poster and the trophies, I discovered a tranquil reading room with a foldout couch and beaded lamps with bright bulbs.

"Your mother and I hang out. . . . " My father shrugged. The thin sections of that week's *Advertiser-Democrat* lay spread on the floor.

I flicked on the light in my room. Now it was my room they had turned into a shrine. Nothing had been altered. It was a little girl's space, with the same white eyelet curtains, oval dressing mirror, and my Barbies arranged on a shelf in strapless gowns.

"This is kind of weird, Dad. I'm thirty now."

He shook his head. "Thirty. Where did the time go?"

"I don't know, Dad. But all isn't lost. Don't forget there's a new little girl."

He nodded. "What a little peanut Ellary is. That little baby fits right here, just like you used to, from my elbow to the tip of my hand. No bigger."

We had that in common. Memories of holding our children. I wanted to give my father something. "It's so good to be back." I smiled. My father nodded happily, but Gary looked me in the eye, questioning. My father turned and, behind his back, I shrugged. I had no idea what I felt—if I was telling the truth or lying.

Christian, Shell, Gary, and I, with Ellary tucked in her car seat under a mountain of knitted pastel yarn, mingled in the parking lot outside the church. Christian had on a little blue wool coat. He could almost be described as petite, if anyone ever called a man that. When he and Shell had come to visit me in Lincolnville, my first impression was that he wasn't manly. He was so tiny that he and Shell could have both easily fit into the bottom of the trundle together, no problem. But within a few moments I realized I was wrong. In fact, Christian had an unusual masculine beauty, with his high forehead and green eyes that drew you in. I trusted him immediately. Mostly I loved his voice, which was a rich, melodious bass polished by his years training as an actor. He had met Shell when he moved to Norway to be the high school's first drama teacher.

"There's something I want to tell you." Christian's brows were lowered.

"What?"

"I'm not going to let us stay living in that rat hole of a house. We're moving out. It's a dump. Shell deserves better."

"That's real sweet." I was touched by his desire to shelter her.

My mother pulled into the parking lot followed by my father with Uncle Zee waving eagerly in the back seat. Uncle Zee's stroke had altered his personality in odd ways. Even though he now had a sunnier demeanor since his stroke, Shell missed Uncle Zee's more familiar somber self.

My father unfolded a wheelchair and set the brakes. Leaning down into the back of the car, he slipped his arms under Uncle Zee's armpits. He gave him a big bear hug and lifted Uncle Zee as effortlessly as if they were practicing a Red Cross water rescue.

Inside the church Shell slipped off Ellary's bonnet and saw me staring at the furrows of Ellary's skull. "It's called a fontanel, remember?" The silver ribbons of the bonnet undulated in the drafty air.

Shell was pale with sleeplessness and yet looked more beautiful than ever. She was no longer the big-eyed waif. She had swept her hair into a high ponytail in an almost '60s mod style and wrapped it in an emerald sequined elastic band. My mother had given her one of her vintage suits, a green wool Evan Picone that showed off Shell's pretty, muscled calves.

Christian's best friend, Ned, also an actor, was the godfather. He was a handsome, doughy man with a blonde goatee. I only heard a smattering of the words the priest invoked. "The light of Christ . . . cleansed . . ." When Ned handed Ellary to me, I couldn't refuse in front of everyone. I had to hold her.

I had to hold her even in front of Priscilla Nix, who sat a few pews back, without pigtails, her thin hair covered in a beret. With her beady eyes on me I felt a sudden flash of

shame, and then I lost myself in Ellary's warmth. I couldn't
believe the relief I felt at holding a baby. Her gentle heat made
me drowsy as I cradled her. Ellary opened her eyes and shivered when the holy water droplets doused her dark wisps.

Uncle Zee had never made anyone laugh in his entire life.
But since his stroke, he emitted strange and whimsical frag-
ments. When the priest asked, "What name do you give this
child," he hollered, "Watermelon Starburst."

After the ceremony I waited for everyone to leave, wanting to
rest in the church all alone, smelling my palms to see if Ellary's
scent was still there. For a moment I wished Gary would leave
so I could be as solitary as I was when I climbed a pine and
swayed with the blue jays. The church quieted, the sounds
slowly draining away like water. Finally I heard no more banging doors as everyone exited, and the murmuring ceased. I
realized we weren't alone. My mother was behind us, bony
hands clasped in prayer.

"May I?" she asked, coming to join me in the pew.

"Sure," Gary said.

She sat, crossing her legs a few feet from me and picking a
thread off of her skirt. She stared into a canoe-shaped hollow
where a life-sized pietà gleamed. Mary wept for the son in her
arms, both of them carved out of the same perfectly cool,
white marble.

"I think your brother is in heaven," she whispered.

I couldn't help staring at her. She was a stranger, so thin
with barely any breasts. Her flat chest released a deep breath,
and when I sniffed the familiar scent of White Shoulders, it
carried with it the memory of feeling close to her while playing dress-up with her silken powder puff.

"I've read about that theory that you might see a light when you die. Maybe Birdy saw that light. Do you think he might have?"

"I don't know, Mom."

"I have stopped going to his grave so often. I began imagining light that had the magic of opals. A gentle place that warmed you up and where you never felt hunger. Where you could wake up with your family and feel full." She pointed to Mary. "Did you ever notice how you don't ever see Mary with a blotched face, howling? I'd like to see a pietà where they show that." She stole a look at her watch. "Shall we go?"

We followed my mother, her velvet stilettos clacking on the marble floor, the high heels I hadn't seen her wear since I was a little girl. When we stepped out into the February light, she squinted and then slipped on tortoiseshell sunglasses.

"You two are heading over to Shell and Christian's for the luncheon?"

"No, we're heading back. We've already packed."

We all stood awkwardly. I held my breath then blurted out, "You'll come to see me?"

"Do you really want me to?"

I searched to find the outlines of her eyes behind her dark glasses. Even through the brownish lenses I could see her eyes tense with doubt.

"Yes," I reassured her.

"I'll come."

I watched as she drove out of sight.

Who was my mother, now? Wiry in stretch pants, ready to jog or lift weights, her face wind-burned, her body more liquid. She had surfaced, dormant for years in the earth, pushing up out of darkness. Like the first spring flowers that bloomed in slush even before the crocus, she was a small white blossom: a snowdrop.

Gary and I left for Lincolnville.

"Whoa," I said. "Look at that. Norway Drive-In died. God. I saw a ton of movies there." The movie screen still stood but with gray patches like strips of ripped paper. Somehow the decay seemed beautiful. All the speakers were gone, only a hundred metal posts remaining. Queen Anne's lace, dried out and fallen in curved brown bunches, blew lightly, bouncing across the ruin.

18

I stared out of the window at work, watching Mr. and Mrs. Legendre catnap in their big, old Cadillac parked in the ferry parking lot across the street. Sometimes they dozed so deeply that their mouths fell dark and open, and I was afraid that they had died in their sleep. The jangling of the phone startled me.

"Red Barn."

"Hill."

I knew instantly that something was wrong. "Shell, what is it?"

"I have to tell you something."

"I'm getting a weird feeling here."

"I'm working the morning shift here at the soda fountain."

"Shell, just spit it out."

"Miles."

My stomach turned. "What?"

"He was just in here."

"Doing what?"

"Looking for you. Shit. He's hardly changed. That cocky walk, remember?"

How could I forget?

"Hill, when he ordered coffee my hands shook as I lowered the cup and saucer. I can't even believe I served him. 'So, how have you been?' he asked, all casual. I turned my back to him. I felt like beating the crap out of him with my spatula. Can you believe it? He saunters in after all this time and asks how I've been like it was only last summer."

"What did you say?"

"'Gee, Miles, you mean, how have I been after fifteen *years?*' And he says, 'You know why I'm here.' Of course I knew he was looking for you. But I was like, go ahead, I dare you, say it out loud. I said, 'No, actually, I don't know why you're here. Enlighten me.'

"'I want to see Hillary.'

"'She doesn't live here anymore. In fact, she hasn't lived here since she went off to college. She hates coming back here, if you know what I mean. Too many bad memories.'

"So he says, 'I know I once acted like a jerk.'

"Then I leaned closer until our faces were almost touching. I said, 'I'm pretty much assuming you're the same asshole you've always been.'

"He tilted back and adjusted the hood of his sweatshirt. He still wears a denim jacket like he's a damn teenager. 'This doesn't concern you.'

"'Doesn't concern me? You don't have a clue what she's been through.'

"'You're not the only one who knows where she is.' He pulled a wad of cash out of his pocket, flipped through some hundreds and fifties and crumpled a couple of ones at me. Just then I spotted Sloppy Joe's bald spot. Sloppy waved to me, but his grin disappeared when he saw Miles. Sloppy pushed open the door, ready to kick butt. Sloppy says, 'I cannot believe what I am seeing.' And he slams his hands into Miles's chest and shoves him into a rack of postcards. They stood there breathing hard, snorting at each other.

"'Sloppy,' I shouted. 'He isn't worth it.' Miles pushed past him. Sloppy pulled off Miles's hood, grabbed Miles by the hair, and bashed his face into the metal doorjamb. Oh my god, it was horrible, the blood gushing from his nose. Miles tried to sop up the blood by pressing his face into his jacket sleeve. He shouted at Sloppy, 'You fucking redneck!'"

We all knew that Sloppy hated more than anything to be called a redneck.

Shell continued. "Miles dashed away and took off in his car with Sloppy running after him. The last thing that Miles must have seen in his rearview mirror was Sloppy Joe flipping him the bird with both hands."

I heard a door creak. I knew Shell was trying to hide in the back hallway of the drugstore, as far away from the counter as the cord would reach. She whispered, "The Man in White tried to help me by using a dishrag to clean up Miles's blood. He had taken off his white gloves and laid them carefully on the counter. Think about it—have you ever seen the Man in White's hands?"

"No."

"Well, when he saw me looking, he blushed and quickly pulled his gloves back on as if I had just seen him totally nude. It was awful."

I took a deep breath and shut my eyes tight. "Miles is coming to Lincolnville, isn't he?"

"Goddamn it," she said, sounding distracted. "I got a run in my brand-new tights."

The lilacs outside my kitchen window had small, cold buds. As I lifted my hands from a sink full of bubbles, Miles came toward me, framed by lavender and deepening blue. He strode up the hill in jeans that fit him just the same as the last time I had seen him in New York. I remembered the summer I spent stroking those thin thighs. He had never beefed up, remaining boyish. He still looked light enough to lie on top of me with all his weight and not crush me.

But as he neared I realized that years of beer and pills had dulled his handsome edge. I wiped my hands quickly on a dish towel. I opened the door and stared at him through the crack.

"Who told you I lived here? My mother?"

"Yeah."

"I'm not inviting you in."

Premature gray hairs lessened his beauty. He may have been confident with Shell, cocky with Sloppy Joe, but when he was in front of me white balls of spit stuck like glue to the corners of his lips. He stammered. "Well, why . . . then w-will you c-come out?"

I slammed the door shut behind me and sat on the bottom step. Miles joined me. He began talking, banging the steps with his palms, repeating simple rhythms. I listened, crumpling up dried leaves that had blown into the spokes of the banister. The ferry blasted its horn, left the shore, and then returned from the island. Miles still kept talking, filling in the years. He was finally making money. He had gotten married, then divorced. He was lonely. It killed him to know he had a son out there; he struggled with insomnia, wondering if his little boy was okay.

My voice sounded as if someone far away was speaking. "You think I feel bad for you? It didn't have to be this way."

"I was an asshole. A real asshole. When they called and told me you had filled out the adoption papers, I didn't want to feel anything. I did nothing but go clubbing that summer. I partied nonstop. That's when I started freebasing."

Something in me shifted at this new idea that Miles, too, had suffered. But I was not ready to let down my guard.

"Your drug history bores me."

"It's the only history I've got."

"But you're clean now, supposedly?"

"Almost two years clean and sober."

"So why are you wired? Banging on the steps like you're playing bongos?"

His hands went still. I refused to look up from my pile of shredded leaves.

"No other girl's ever gotten as close to me as you have."

"If you call this close, I feel bad for you. What about your ex-wife?"

"I married her because I was twenty-four and all my other friends were getting married. It was wrong from the start."

"And what about Tina?"

"Tina?"

"You know, the girl you were with when I told you I was pregnant."

"Oh, Tina." He shrugged. "I don't know."

The memory of Tina nauseated me. I had felt so ugly standing in that phone booth. "You ended up being nothing but a sperm donor," I said flatly.

He winced. "You weren't in love with me?"

"Yes, I was in love with you."

"I was young, Hillary. I was stupid."

I wiped the dried oak leaves off my hands. I spotted Gary's car down on Route 1. I couldn't see his face clearly, but he obviously had figured things out. He inched slowly up the hill then drove into my driveway, got out, and slammed his car door hard. He had his hands tucked casually in his back pockets and yet walked menacingly toward us. Miles put out his hand. "I'm Miles."

"I know who you are. Hillary, may I speak with you for a moment?" He pointed to a spot down the hill. I followed him.

He whispered angrily, "Why are you even sitting here with this prick?"

"I can handle it. I need to talk to him."

"Why?"

"I am not discussing this now."

Gary didn't take his eyes off Miles as he skidded away in a blur of exhaust.

"Your boyfriend?" Miles asked.

"Yeah."

The ferry chugged out to the island again. "I guess I'll be heading back to Boston now. My car's parked down in that lot. Do you have pictures of . . . ?"

"Of?" I wanted to hear him say it.

"Of Tom."

"I do."

"Can I have a look at them sometime?"

I stood up. "I suppose."

Then he attempted to slide back into the old Miles, sucking in his cheeks to look cool. He hesitated then asked, "Do you know what I noticed about you?"

"What?"

"After all this time your hair still looks like it's being blown back in the wind even when the air is completely still."

"Really. That's fascinating."

"Why do you act so bitchy toward me? How many times do you expect me to say I'm sorry?"

"That's the interesting thing, Miles. You haven't ever said you're sorry."

He stood and took a few steps. He stared a long time at the water, then whispered to himself, "I am sorry." He sighed, then turned to face me. "I am sorry." Then, almost inaudibly, "Could I see his pictures?"

"Wait here."

I got Tom's album then went back outside. Miles continued taking in the view. "It's beautiful here," he decided.

"You want to see him chronologically?"

He thought for a moment. "I want to see what he looks like now."

There were about fifty blank plastic pages. I had only enough pictures to fill up the first few. I flipped to the page of Tom in tenth grade. He gazed at Tom for a long while, then broke out into laughter. "He's a gorgeous kid. He looks a lot like you. He doesn't have wavy hair like us, though. He's got straight hair like your brother."

I couldn't help smiling.

Miles turned backward through the album year after year all the way back to the beginning—my big belly under Lola's hand.

"So that's who has him?"

"Yep."

"Lola? The ditzy artist?"

"Is that what my mother told you?"

"Yeah."

I shook my head, incredulous. My mother had changed but not completely. "My mother never even knew her."

"So where does this Lola live?"

"Maybe Portland. I don't know."

"He was really cute, wasn't he?"

"He was incredible."

He clapped the photo album shut. "Tom is about the age you were when you and I met." He sounded wistful. "I wonder what happened to the *Blue Blazes*."

"It's still running."

"You're kidding?"

"No. It's had a bunch of different owners. It's not the fastest boat on the lake anymore, but it still runs."

Miles smiled. "Damn. That was a beautiful boat."

I remembered Miles pressing the levers down, full throttle out of the bog and the thrill of hitting sixty miles an hour as we passed the totem pole. "It really was."

Miles descended to the ferry parking lot where fishermen in olive-colored jumpsuits were swinging lunchboxes into their trucks. Driving off, the inside of his car lit up like the ferry, Miles fumbled hungrily to light a fresh cigarette.

19

Two years passed and Tom turned eighteen. No letter came. Not from Lola, not from Tom. I stopped sleeping, haunted by the phantom sounds of my phone ringing in the middle of the night.

I'd bolt upright, disturbing Gary. "Who's calling?"

He'd mumble, "Hon, I don't hear a thing."

I had forged that deal so long ago that all the HoJos had vanished, the slick orange roofs covered over with the black shingles of Friendly's.

Still, I staggered in Wanda's shorts, pinned now at the broken elastic waist, and grabbed the receiver. "Hello?" Every night was a dial tone. No one was calling me. Wind chimes dangled from the apple tree. How lonely they sounded at 4 A.M., metal tubes clanging in the gnarled branches, barely like music.

Sometimes it was so silent that even the withered apples that had never fallen stopped spinning. Then, I moved slowly in the light of the lamps. That was the hour I clung to, when no one along Route 1 was exchanging words. No talking, just listening. Gary breathing in the bedroom. The crows waking up the gulls.

20

One afternoon in June I spotted Gary and Harold running up my hill like little boys racing. I knew they had the letter. My face felt feverish, my hands were shivery, and goose bumps raced over my arms as if I were skinny-dipping in the autumn wind.

The stationery was folded up into a thick cube—like a note you'd pass in school.

Dear Hillary Birdsong:

It's very hard to begin this letter! I first wrote "How are you?" But even though my mom has told me a lot about you, for me it's "Who are you?" My mom said I should tell you the truth and not worry about anything else. I hope she's right. I have a lot of emotions inside me about who you are. There's always been this voice in my head asking "Where is your other mother?"

I'm nervous about writing you. I know my mom has written you every year and that you wanted those letters. I hope you want mine. My mom assures me that you do.

I am writing to say hello and I also hope you will say hello back.

From your son,
Tom

Gary and Harold waited on my steps while I called Shell.

"Carlton Drugs, will you hold?"

"No! Shell? He wrote me!"

She squealed, "What? Oh my god. What did he say?"

"He wants me to write him back. Can you believe it? He wrote me. Shell, he wrote me. My kid wrote me."

She laughed. "Honey, he wrote you."

"I have to go. I love you."

"Love you, too."

I grabbed a blank notebook and a pen. I wrote "Dear Tom." Crossed it out. Wrote "Dear Tom, I can't you tell the joy" and crossed that out. I quickly filled an entire page with "Dear Tom, I love you," "Dear Tom, I've always," and "Dearest Tom, it's so difficult to"—all scribbled over and every other line erased.

Gary and Harold gathered around my kitchen table. "I can't do this," I lamented. "All this time I've waited, and now I can't do this."

Harold sighed. "Just take your time. People write letters every day. It's simple. I'd hand deliver it to him for you if I could."

Good old Harry. The world's most committed, most dependable United States postal worker.

Rhana told me that times had changed, that there were tons of books about adoption. I went to the Camden library and checked out *Adoption Reunion: Guide for Adoptees, Adoptive Parents, and Birthmothers*.

I skimmed the chapter headings and sank back to the ground as if Tom's letter had given me temporary flying powers that were now fading.

Chapter 9: To Hug or Not to Hug? "Birthmothers, refrain

from telling your child, 'I've loved you since you were born,' as the intensity of your feelings might frighten your child away. If you meet with your child, avoid acting clingy."

I found Rhana dozing upstairs on one of the big brass beds for sale. I shook her awake.

"Rhan? Rhana?"

She opened her eyes and looked at me softly, then she curled up and slid out of the bed. Even with her osteoporosis, she moved in a very ladylike way. "I'm so tired lately," she said, perplexed—as if being seventy-five wasn't reason enough for wanting to catnap. She resumed her work, humming along with Bing, standing up the cobalt bottles on the southern facing window ledge where the morning sun made the color burst.

I was grateful that, although tourist season had begun, the Red Barn was free of customers.

"Listen to this advice I just got," I sputtered. "'No gushing. For adoptees considering a reunion, remember that relationships are not built quickly. Your birthmother, should you meet, did not raise you. There are many years missing between you. Keep your expectations realistic.'

"Meaning low," I said sarcastically. "Okay, so some of these stories did turn out horribly. Drug addict birthmothers. Needy birthmothers. Drifting apart after meeting. But 'don't gush'? I don't understand. That's like advice Dear Abby would give to a sophomore girl who had a crush on the captain of the football team."

Rhana tore off another section of paper towel, grabbed the Windex to squirt it, and then stopped. She studied me closely.

I continued. "'How to sign the letter to your child. Fondly, Always, Sincerely, but not Love.' Fondly? Who uses that word anymore? I'm supposed to write 'fondly' to my own son as if he were a pet?"

"Why do they recommend that?" Rhana asked.

I quoted. "'You don't want to scare your child off now that he's initiated contact.' Don't you think I'd scare him off with a 'fondly-always-sincerely'? Isn't that what he would be afraid of? That I was able to give him up because I was only *fond*? That it wasn't love?"

She rested her veiny hands in her lap and looked at me, her purple eyeliner squiggled over her loose-skinned lids. "You're afraid."

"I am afraid. But I'm also completely happy. How is that possible?"

"You're his mother. Of course you just want to run toward him. The book is just saying to slow down, that's all. Trust a little."

I had to laugh. "I'm not sure trust is my strong suit."

"Well, you can get better at it now. Trust that things can work out if you give them time. It's like the wildlife refuge up near August Fields."

"You mean those poisoned wetlands?"

"They're not poisoned anymore. An environmental agency has spent the last few summers tending it. Now the great blue herons are reestablished. There are a hundred of them up there now." She stood up and stretched. Her spine cracked. "We haven't had a customer all day. Let's go and see the herons."

"You'd actually close *early* for me?"

"Yes, darling."

"Can Gary come?"

"Certainly."

We headed north. It *was* a miracle. Where there had been only red-winged blackbirds, the marshes were now teeming with tall, twig-legged birds plucking fish out of the water lilies. And if that weren't enough, bald eagles had begun to nest.

Gary and I helped Rhana walk the bumpy, long wooden bridges through the cattails in the refuge. The sun heated up. Rhana pushed her sweater sleeves up. I cupped one of Rhana's wrinkly elbows; Gary cupped the other. I suddenly wanted to cry really hard as I thought about what an excellent mother Lola had been to my son.

"My old friend Simone told me that the human eye could see two thousand shades of green. Do you think that's true?"

Gary surveyed the marsh. "Yes."

Rhana agreed. "I'd say at least that many."

21

Dear Tom:

I can't tell you the joy I felt on getting your letter. There has never been a day or a night that I haven't thought about you.

The main thing I want you to know is that I love you, Tom. I always have and I always will.

It never got any easier, losing you. I would like to keep writing. Would you? I am finding this hard as well, saying the right things. Having you write me is a dream come true—the only dream I've had since I lost you.

Love,
your birthmother, Hillary

Dear Hillary:

As much as I love my mom—and, of course, I love her forever—I have always wondered about you. And dreamed about you, too. I feel like a missing piece of me is being found.

I have heard people say that a baby can be given up or given away. You said you "lost me." Could you tell me what you mean by that? I asked my mom and she said I should just tell you what I am thinking. I think that's good advice.

My mom said that you never truly said good-bye to me, that it was too hard for you. Is this true?
    Tom

Dear Tom,
    Lola's right about several things. First, I did have the idea that maybe if I didn't actually say good-bye, it wouldn't hurt as much when I had to let you go. But that was naive. I was naive. It didn't matter what I said or didn't say. When I handed you over to Lola, it was the hardest day of my life. Brutal, actually. Is it wrong to say I lost you? I really don't know. Of course I don't mean to imply that I ever forgot about you. I need you to understand that I have missed you since the moment I left you. And I did leave you. Tom, I have carried your absence everywhere.

Dear Hillary:
    Thank you for your letter. All these years, my mom told me you were a special person, but I was sort of suspicious. I thought my mom was just trying to help me feel better about being adopted. I am afraid to ask you this because what if you say no? But I'm a pretty strong guy, so here goes: I was wondering if maybe you want to get together? I'm an okay writer, I guess, but it seems so hard to do this on paper, with envelopes and stamps, when we could do it face to face. I would like to meet you. Would you want to meet me?
    Tom

Dear Tom:
    I can't put into a letter what it means to be able to see your face soon! And not just in two-dimensional photos. Each year, your teeth changed, but not your eyes. Your eyes were the same

*eyes I gazed into the first night I held you. But your teeth—I
never even knew you with teeth. In the first photo I received from
Lola, you had four teeth. Then for a few years, a perfect, white
baby-teeth smile. Then front teeth were missing. Then new front
teeth, too big for your little face. Then braces, then a young man's
perfect smile.*

*I cried the year I received your ninth grade picture with that
faint mustache. Because that meant I would never know you as
a boy—only as a baby. I hoped with all my heart to see you as a
man.*

Love, Hillary

Dear Hillary:
*This is my phone number. If you call me then we can figure
out when and where we can finally meet. (I mean, meet again.)*
Tom

When I was finally able to call my son, it made me sick to
realize that I was so afraid. I put it off. A hundred times a day
I heard an inner voice urging *Call Tom!* Fear and shallow
breathing. Having his number, dialing his number, was like
shattering a sheet of glass. But if I waited much longer he
would think I was never going to call. I dialed.

My heart beating as if I had climbed a mountain. A rasp-
ing old man's voice. "Hello?"

"Is Tom there?"

"Tom? Young lady, I believe you have the wrong number."

Misdialing was like a bad dream—needing to call 911 but
unable to dial the right number, 557, 884, everything but 911.

I dialed again, double-checking that I had the correct dig-
its in the proper order.

And if I got an answering machine? I was not to leave a message, that advice I agreed with. But if Lola or James answered?

Two rings, then I heard Lola say "Hello?" like it hadn't been eighteen years, her voice as if I had just called her recently. I felt her beautiful face right there in front of me, and I hung up on her.

Oh shit, oh damn, why did I do that? Should I call back and admit I'm an idiot, or wait until maybe Tom is home?

I waited a few minutes. Called back. "Hello?" This time even more curious.

"It's me," I said in a faint voice, like I was a mousy little sixteen-year-old again.

Lola recognized me. "Hillary! I am so glad to hear from you. Tom's been waiting. How are you?"

"Thank you for all the letters over the years. You never let me down."

"How could I? I thought about you all the time. I'd really like to see you."

A flash of anger jolted me. *She* would like to see *me*? No, this was about Tom and me. Nothing to do with her.

"I mean after you and Tom—you know, get together."

"I can't wait. Is he . . . home?"

"He'll be back in a few minutes. Do you want to leave your number so he can call you?"

"I don't know. What do you think?" I had regressed back into a lost child: thirty-four-years old, unable to decide if I should call someone back or have them call me.

"You okay?" Lola asked.

"Why wouldn't I be okay?" I shot back.

She didn't match my anger. "I missed you."

I burst out crying, my words barely understandable. "I've missed you, too. All of you."

"I'm just so glad I can talk to you now. You could write me, you know."

A door slammed in the background. Lola covered the receiver, muffled talk in the background. Then Lola said, "Tom wants to talk to you. I'm going to leave the room. I know you want it to be just you two. Don't start talking for a minute, so I can go all the way downstairs."

I heard a rustling, then breathing.

We both spoke at the same time, "Is this you?"

"Why? Why don't you want to be with me?" Gary was pouting the afternoon I packed to go stay with Shell on the eve of my reunion with Tom.

"I just need to be with my best girlfriend. I'm not trying to hurt your feelings."

"Will you call me?"

"You know I will."

I met Shell at the new Kohl's department store that had opened on the edge of Norway. We flipped through the clothing racks together, searching for a new outfit for me.

"How about this black sweater? You look good in cowl necks." Shell held the hanger up, her thin eyebrows raised.

"It's too casual. Too blah."

"Aren't you just meeting for lunch?"

"Yeah. How about this?" I laid a blue shirt over a creamy beige blazer and a tailored skirt.

"Uh, Hill? It's not a job interview."

"Sure feels like it."

What if we have nothing to say? What if he's angry with me? What if we never see one another after this?

"Well, it isn't, honey. Try that black sweater on. It'll look good with your gray trousers."

"What about this?" I held up a navy blue dress. It flounced, the filmy ruffled hem tapering out. "I'm just afraid he won't like me."

Shell squeezed my shoulder and said softly, "Of course he's going to like you. No matter what you wear. You're his mother."

"He has two mothers."

"Don't you think he's nervous too?"

I had thought about this. "Yeah, but I need him more than he needs me. He's had another mother. I don't have another son."

"How about this?" She held up a pink fuzzy sweater with three-quarter sleeves and pearly buttons. "Just like the one you had in high school."

"Yuck. Give me the black one."

Shell waited outside the dressing room. I had to raise my voice to be heard over the twittering of the teenage girls who were stuffed into a dressing room farther down. "How should I wear my hair? Pulled back or down?" I opened the door and walked toward my reflection.

Shell adjusted the floppy collar. "Get this. It's you. You look pretty." She pulled my hair up. "Wear a high ponytail. Gold hoops. You're all set. See?"

Three giddy teenage girls came bursting out in strapless gowns of pink, lilac, and silvery white, vying for room in the mirrors. One pushed me by accident.

I smiled. "Prom?"

"Yes."

Shell admired their lithe, satiny bodies. "Girls these days are so sophisticated."

The girls were manic with excitement. "*These* days?" the one in lilac teased. "It wasn't that long ago you guys went, was it?"

Shell laughed. "We're over thirty."

"No way! You both look like, maybe twenty-five." Exposing white ankle socks, they daintily lifted the hems of their gowns and pranced back into the dressing room. Shell and I were left alone in the mirror. With Shell still coaching gymnasts and me still walking back roads for hours, we were as trim as sophomores.

I called out to them, "In fact, I have a son your age."

"Get *out!*" they shouted.

Over the sounds of unzippering one asked me, "Hey, is he cute?"

Shell had just moved with Christian and Ellary into a brand-new modular home. I helped Shell hang up Ellary's clothes in her new room, which already smelled of her, a light powdery smell like fabric dryer sheets. I organized her Little Mermaid bath toys, and then Ellary asked me to play outside with her.

She wanted to trace my outline on the new front walk. Swinging a bucket of chalk filled with thick pastels, Ellary chose a new white piece as I lay down. I looked up at the clouds, which were moving quickly as if they had tails snapping them along. Ellary started with my hand, going around the fingers, giving me mittens.

"How's it going, Aunt Hill?" Shell rocked on the porch.

"You do some, Mommy!" Ellary demanded.

Shell kneeled beside me and traced around. "Whoa, we might need some more chalk for around these hips."

"Shut up." I laughed.

"Mommy says shut up is bad." Ellary breathed graham crackers into my face.

"She's right. I'm sorry."

"Shit is bad, too," Ellary continued.

"Yes, it is," Shell agreed, handing me the chalk. "You can do that part, if you don't mind." I drew in the V between my legs, connecting the lines she had drawn up my inner thighs. Then Shell and I switched places; she lay down and I followed with the chalk along her torso up to her hands arced over her head.

"Look at me!" Ellary called out, balanced in a perfect handstand, her plump little feet pointing up.

"How do you do that?" I asked, amazed at how she had inherited Shell's gymnastic gift.

Ellary let her knees fall to the grass and squatted, her face blushing. "Easy. I pretend I'm air and I'm filling up a big balloon."

That night I took out the garbage in the rain and stood near the cans. Even though the house was brand new, a film of Ellary's handprints already covered the windows.

We all went to bed around ten, but I lay there, my heart pounding. *What if? What if?* After midnight I moved quietly through the house and hunted down Christian's cigarettes. I figured I might as well help Shell in some way so I unpacked boxes for hours until I heard the swish of her slippers.

"At two A.M. you're organizing my Tupperware?" She yawned in the doorway.

"I'm matching up the lids. They're a mess."

"You're the one who is a mess. You have got to get some sleep. You will be exhausted in the morning."

"I'm too excited. I can't sit still. I put all the silverware away. I alphabetized your spice rack. Shell, what if he changes his mind? What if he stands me up?"

"He won't."

"How can you be so sure?"

"He's your kid, isn't he?"

"Of course."

"If he inherited half of your intensity then he's waiting in the damn café already."

I considered this, trying to keep a cigarette pressed between my lips as I grinned.

"You still smoke like a wuss, you know that?" She loosened the sash on her robe and pulled out a chair.

"Not everyone sucks it hard like they're drinking out of a straw."

"I quit, remember? Maybe you should go back to those artsy-fartsy things you smoked in college."

"Cloves," I reminded her.

"Shit, it's raining hard." She yawned again.

"Shit is bad," I reminded her. "But at least you're dry."

"Yeah, it's amazing. Even in this downpour I can keep the pots in the cabinet where you put them. My god, did you even organize all the magnets?" she said, looking at the refrigerator.

"I straightened them out a bit."

"I've got to go back to bed. Will you please try to get some sleep?"

"No."

I spent the rest of the night watching raindrops in the

porch light. At three in the morning I called Gary. "Is it rain-ing there?" I asked.

"I love you," he answered.

At sunrise Christian came down in his bathrobe.

"This place is spotless," he croaked, filling the coffeemaker with water. "Thank you."

The realization that the day had finally come made me temporarily mute. Christian sat across the table, staring at me. That felt comforting. He broke the silence. "This is such a big day for you. It's phenomenal."

I nodded. I loved the deep kindness in his voice.

He got up to pour our coffee, then he pulled back the cur-tain, staring at what was left of the outlines on the sidewalk. His voice reflected his training as a Shakespearean actor and made ordinary morning words seem even more lyrical. "The chalk ran in the rain, a tie-dye stream. But you can still see them—the arms from yesterday."

I stopped by my parents' before I left town. My dad looked scared, yet excited. My mother stood on the porch, holding her sweater around her, pulling the buttons tight. Her hand was clammy. She smiled, embarrassed. "I'm nervous for you."

I rolled down my windows as I passed the Gray Family Clinic on Route 26 and let the wind rush up my sleeves. I gunned it onto the Maine Turnpike; even the clouds seemed to be going over the speed limit. Those flat-bottomed clouds always reminded me of old wooden rowboats, warped and creaking. Words from Lola's letters passed through my mind. *He always sleeps on his back, face up, arms over his head. I watch him, then turn off the hallway light. Tom hoards things. Has al-ways hoarded. He just won't part with anything. He saves single playing cards that he has found blowing in the wind. He still has an art project from preschool taped to his wall: a windsock made of faded crepe paper.*

I squeezed the paper with the directions between my thighs so it wouldn't blow out of the window. I pulled into the East Street municipal parking lot, didn't bother to lock my car, and ran.

three

22

And there my son was, alone at a table for two.

I gasped, like the shock of the very first moment after giving birth to him: Tom, still miraculous. *That is the same baby I carried, the baby boy I held.* He tipped his wrist to stare at his watch, then flicked his hand and adjusted the wristband. I was mesmerized by how familiar he was: eyes dark chrome blue, like Miles, but with sun-bleached highlights in his hairline like my mother used to get. Though his coloring was not mine, the shape of his face was, the strokes of his eyebrows, the dip in his cheeks.

He looked up, recognized me, and smiled. My heart radiated. We could have been any mother and son meeting for lunch. Didn't other mothers, the ones who raised their child, also find it strange to feel so small inside a grown child's arms? Didn't other mothers squeeze their eyes shut to keep back the tears of delight when their son lifted their feet right off the ground?

"You're so small!" he exclaimed. Though it was the first time I was hearing his voice directly, it was achingly familiar. Still.

"Especially compared to Lola." I laughed.

He lowered me, and we shyly pulled up our wrought-iron chairs. I slid a paper napkin out from underneath a fork and pressed it to my eyes, then covered my whole face with it so he wouldn't see my mouth quiver. "I'm sorry," I whispered. Then, feeling how near he was, stillness descended, and I opened my eyes.

"Hiii!" He sang it out so cheerfully that we both laughed.

I had to force myself not to stare. I looked down through the glass table at his big feet in new white Adidas sneakers. *May I tie your shoes?* I wanted to ask. *Just let me be your mother and let me tie your shoes.*

But I remembered the reunion book's advice: Allow small talk. I asked, "Have you been waiting here long?"

"All morning."

I laughed again. "Shell was right."

The waitress came. Weren't Tom and I at that moment like an ordinary mother and son being greeted by a waitress writing down our soup orders on a pad?

"Shell." He looked me right in the eye, held my gaze. "The one you wrote me about."

I could stare into your face forever.

"Right. My best friend. She was there when you were born."

He pinched a fold of skin near his watch, kept plucking at it. *Wow,* I thought, *he's nervous, like me.* He turned his palm up, exposing pale wrists tangled with blue veins, exactly like Miles's. His hands were not pudgy and soft like a little boy's. They were strong-looking, solid, with fingernails scrubbed pearly pink. He leaned back and smiled, and the loose denim wrinkles of his jeans gathered below his waist and made him seem suddenly boyish. Already I knew I couldn't bear to say good-bye to him when lunch was over.

"Tom, there's so much that I want to ask you about. But I don't want you to think it's like an interview. I just want to—"

"Get to know me?"

"Yeah."

"I want to get to know you, too. But I don't even know what to call you."

I had secretly hoped he would call me Mom. But he didn't offer that. "Call me Hillary, for now," I suggested. "How's your . . . Lola?"

"She's great. We talk a lot. I can tell her anything."

I used to love to talk to Lola too. I wanted to see them together in my mind. "Where do you talk?"

"On the couch, in the kitchen, ten at night, two in the afternoon. Sometimes for a few minutes, sometimes for hours."

"She loves you."

He nodded. "Deeply. Yeah."

I thought, *What eighteen-year-old boy would use the word "deeply"?* "She did an amazing job raising you. She and your dad." Could I dare feel good about having chosen these parents for him? That I had been, in a small way, a good mother for selecting her? There was no "if only" about Lola.

Tom said, "She used to tell me something I thought you might like to know. A couple of years back I was really pissed off at you. I called you bad names."

My mother's words came back to me. *She's making our family look like trash.*

Tom leaned forward and clasped his hands together. His muscled biceps bulged under the short sleeves of his white tee-shirt, and he looked very manly. "Even though my mom is really great, you know, I was still mad. I was mad that you gave me away. I said I could never forgive you after what you did.

But my mom said that you loved me. And that you had given me the love that counted. That when a baby first comes out, the best love of its life is in those first few days."

"I hope that's true," I said softly. "I know you can't remember. But I sure do."

"You had me at sixteen."

"Uh-huh."

"I didn't kiss a girl until I was seventeen. I don't want to make the mistake you did."

I had never thought that my giving him up would make him afraid of anything. He must have seen the shock in my face because he quickly said, "But I have a girlfriend now." Tom stood up and flapped open his wallet. "Want to see her picture? She's my first major girlfriend. I'm very good to her. I bring her hot chocolate with lots of marshmallows. I buy her little pink roses. We've been together eight months."

He waved a photo of a beautiful dark-haired girl in front of me, and then one of them in satiny clothes, standing extra tall in their prom picture.

"She's nice, but she has her wild side," Tom said.

I must have flinched because he asked, "What?"

"Miles said that about me." How unafraid I was to jump into that black quarry water.

"Oh." His face clouded.

"I have to ask you this, Tom. There are people—my mother and father, and your birthfather, too—who want to meet you. Are you even interested in that?"

He spun his watch around on his wrist, plucked at the skin. "You know what? I'm curious. I do want to meet them. So yeah. Out of curiosity."

A dread filled me. My cheeks grew hot.

"You okay?" he asked.

"Of course."

He watched me, then lifted his brows. "You sure?"

"Will we have another meeting?" I whispered.

"Of course. I mean, yeah, why wouldn't we?"

"I don't know. Your curiosity is satisfied. You'll go back to your life as it was."

"But you're my b-mother!"

I took a deep breath, steadying myself. "Yeah. I am."

You're not the baby I knew, but that's okay. I tried not to stare at him and failed. All those yearly photos were lifeless now. I might as well have been sent his fingerprints for how little they had to do with his energy, his beauty. Everything about him fascinated me. He wiped his mouth with his napkin then gulped his water, his Adam's apple moving up and down. He lifted his bowl of soup to slurp from it, then plopped it down quickly, embarrassed that I was watching him so closely. He carried a little bit of all of us: his wide shoulders exactly like my father's and Bird's.

"You look like my brother."

Tom took in my whole face: the flyaway hairs, the spread of my cheekbones down to my chin. I lifted my head higher, like reaching up to receive sunrays. "I look like you," he said simply.

I lingered with him long after my second cup of coffee grew cold and the table had been cleared. The waitress was waiting for her tip as new customers, two old women with canes, were seated near us. I grabbed the check as Tom reached again for his wallet.

"No, please, let me pay," I insisted.

I was in love with the world and left a forty-dollar tip.

The lady next to me warbled, "You have a lovely son."

We met at the same café two weeks later for another glorious lunch and met again two weeks after that. During our fourth visit, Tom walked me to my car, and we were engaged in a drawn-out good-bye in the parking lot. I couldn't bear to drive away from him or watch him drive away from me. I still detested parting from him, even though we were becoming closer.

Tom's cheeks reddened in the chilly early evening air, the stubble on his face growing more pronounced. The sky darkened, seeming almost autumnal. Tom said, "Well, it was definitely good that you got to finish high school and get a college education."

I gaped at him. How many times must he have heard that about me? That it was good that I gave him up so I could embrace all that glittering opportunity.

Shifting his weight from foot to foot, he said tentatively, "You're not saying anything."

Finally I spoke. "Tom, I never, ever want to lie to you. I never want to sugarcoat—"

"So don't," he said slowly.

"There's no other way for me to say this. I know people think that it's best when a teenager gives up her kid. Yeah, I finished high school. And went to college. But I don't feel anything about that. I never did."

He dropped his gaze, then. Even though his hair was shorn, he looked up exactly like the way Bird used to from underneath his bowl cut. "You're saying you gave me away for nothing?"

"My god, of course not."

"Oh, then I guess it was worth it for you to spend your whole life working in a shitty little junk shop."

My hands began to tremble and my mouth went dry. I swallowed, trying to moisten my lips and shape the words more clearly. "I'm saying that there were many reasons why I chose adoption." I had said the words "lost you" once to him in a letter and would not say them again. "And despite everything, I would have given up everything to be with you."

His eyes suddenly silvered with tears. He looked terrified, lost. "This getting to know you is a lot harder than I thought it would be."

"Sweetheart," I said. I reached out my hand to take his. Is this who I would have been if I had raised him, a woman who freely sighed *sweetheart, baby, honey* like Shell?

He jerked back. "No, no, it's okay, Hillary." He spat out my name.

I wanted to hold him. It broke my heart to see him so full of anguish. *Don't be too intense,* the book had warned me. But how could I be otherwise?

There was something else he wanted to know. He said, almost accusingly, "Your big brother died."

"That's right."

"When?"

"I was twelve. He had just turned eighteen."

The thought saddened him. He said wistfully, "He would have been my real uncle."

I pictured Birdy turning forty, sideburns stubbled with gray, calves still muscular. "It just didn't work out that way." I wrapped my arms around myself, my right hand squeezing my left bicep, left hand squeezing my right bicep. I flexed my muscles, feeling my strength. I leaned against my car. We both turned and watched a truck loaded with lobster traps rattle by.

Our parting was terrible and awkward. I drove up the coast. I arrived home and Gary said nothing as I obsessively picked up the phone to call Tom then put it back down. I didn't want to pressure my son. The phone rang a few hours later, startling me. Tom didn't say my name or even hello when I picked up.

"You meant it, didn't you?"

"Meant what, Tom?"

"That you would have given up everything to be with me."

"I meant that."

"I want to tell you something. I'm not as angry as I used to be. About you giving me away."

"Tom, don't feel sorry for me for what happened with my brother, or anything that followed. I don't want pity."

"No, it isn't that. I've been thinking about this since this afternoon. I know you didn't just dispose of me. I get it now, why you couldn't keep me. I mean, my mom explained all this to me. I knew about Uncle Bird's death. I know all about the home you had to go to, how your mom and dad couldn't deal with you getting in trouble. But it's different hearing it from you."

"But I'm not asking you to forgive me, Tom."

"I don't know about forgiveness. But I want to tell you I am really glad you had me."

Raw sounds broke open from deep within me.

"Hillary?" Tom asked.

I was unable to speak.

"Hillary," Tom shouted. "Are you still there?"

Gary stepped closer. I let him hug me. He said into the phone, "She's here."

Later that summer I received an invitation in the mail that read LOLA VINING and then in smaller letters underneath, 1999 EMERGING ARTIST AWARD WINNER. Next to Lola's name was a photo of a brooch she had made out of two huge garnets, one a bit larger than the other, both rimmed in gold and connected with steel.

Tom and I agreed to meet at the opening reception in Lenox, Massachusetts. I drove down the Mass Pike early, found my way through the Berkshires, and searched for the gallery's landmark that Tom had told me to look out for: a figurehead from a ship hung high on the brick front to attract tourists. The carved wooden girl was completely exposed, arms lifted over her head, her long hair flowing wavy and thick. Seaweed was carved around her wooden hips. She looked surprised to find herself so bare. Her skin was painted a honey tone. She was cracking along her weathered collarbone down to her nipples.

The gallery was filled with light but was empty of people when I walked in and was surrounded by Lola's extraordinary work. I read a little sign next to a ring that said, ARTIST'S STATE-MENT. "My designs with these garnets mimic how they occur in nature—how these amazing things just appear, growing out of the earth."

It was dizzying, being surrounded by a sea of stunning, unusual jewelry. Lola had two styles, the heavier, darker garnets connected in clusters on necklaces dangling in glass cases, and a lighter, airier style, necklaces and rings of stainless steel filigree.

I heard heels behind me on the wooden floor and turned to see Lola, her hair swirled into a topaz knob on the top of her head. She looked like a queen, with huge bejeweled glasses like Elton John had in the seventies. She was simply dressed in a red tank top, jean miniskirt, and red flats. When we hugged, it all came back to me, how much taller she was, how long her willowy arms were.

"I am so glad to see you."

I just kept holding on to her.

"I want to spend time with you from now on. You're an amazing person," she said.

We pulled apart.

"If I'm so amazing, why have I felt like a nutcase all summer? One minute totally elated and grateful, the next minute completely depressed?"

"I think reuniting with Tom—all your old feelings are going to surface. You might think this is nuts, but I've had fears of Tom completely abandoning me because I'm not his first mom."

"But he really loves you! And he knows how much you love him."

"I know. I'm just telling you what it's like from my position."

I stole a look at her hand. The scar from her accident was faint, like the outline of an island on a map.

A woman entered carrying a platter of cheese cubes and purple grapes. "Barb," Lola said. "This is Hillary. Hillary, this is Barb, the gallery owner."

"God, Lola," I apologized. "I'm being so selfish. I didn't even mention your work. I am so proud of you. It's amazing."

Barb smiled at me. "Brilliant, isn't she? And are you one of Lola's students?"

Lola and I looked at one another. I raised my eyebrows to indicate "Go ahead."

"No," Lola said. "This is my son's birthmother."

"Oh!" Barb peered closely at me like I was one of Lola's pieces and she was scanning my body to see if she could find my clasp.

23

That autumn Tom invited me to go hiking with him at Acadia National Park. "You call yourself a Mainer, but you've never been to Acadia?" he teased me.

First he drove me around the long loop of Mount Desert Island. I finally understood why people raved about the park. I had grown up inland, now resided on the coast, and the two places were separate lands. But in Acadia, seascape and woods overlapped. Massive ocean rocks stretched under acres of skinny birches; pine trees sprouted in beaches of white sand.

We parked near Thunder Hole, a carved-out rock that boomed with air and water when high tide came in. "Low tide," Tom said. "Let's hike and come back in a few hours."

It was intoxicating being with Tom when he was climbing. He knew the trails intimately, explaining how he had spent his high school years exploring the island with his buddies. "We won't take the Beehive," he said. "There are iron ladders over the ravines. That's for more experienced climbers."

Instead, we followed a clear stream up a flat path to a tranquil pond. I kept asking Tom to stop so I could take his picture.

"You've already taken a whole roll," he protested.

"Actually, I've taken two." I couldn't help it. He looked so capable in his hiking boots, shorts, and windbreaker, poised at the start of his life. He had taken one semester off and was starting college in Boston in January. My son—looking right into my camera with fawn-colored leaves floating down onto him.

I didn't mind that a storm was approaching with a light warm rain. Fog soaked our hair.

The park thinned out of people as we hiked back.

"We should do Cadillac Mountain. We can take the wimpy way and drive." We hopped back into his truck. Round and round we went, our ears popping.

"We can't see a damn thing with this fog," Tom said. "Usually the view is spectacular."

We circled up over the top of the mountain, the wind pushing the truck toward the guardrails. "During some times of the year, this is the first place in America that the morning sun touches," he said, almost bragging.

We got out, and the wind swept through the truck in a giant cold whirlpool, lifting all the gum wrappers, paper soda cups, and fast-food napkins. Both of us scrambled to grasp the pieces, but the paper escaped too fast.

I had never encountered such a forceful wind. As it hit me sideways, it threw me off balance and I stumbled. We were both shocked and thrilled by its strength. I had never seen Tom laugh so hard. He must have looked like this when he was little.

Suddenly I realized that if I turned and faced the blast it just might support me. I opened my arms and stood on tiptoe, leaning right into it. Tom tried, but he was too muscular and he had to catch himself. He cheered me on while I hung there, both of us laughing in astonishment at the power of the wind. And then I just let go entirely and, with arms outstretched, I was flying.

acknowledgments

My thanks to Money for Women/Barbara Deming Memorial Fund for supporting this project early on; Ann Santell, for her honesty, beauty, and strength; Karen Caffrey, for her truth and insights; C.C., for everything, including Acadia; Betty O'Hare, RSM; Lynn Kanter and Robin Parks for endless sustainment; Tim Cybulski for helping me with Tom; Abbe Miller for her exquisite guidance; Lola Brooks for over fifteen years of friendship and for letting me build a character from her; Kim Silcox for her cheerleading and support; my neighbors—forever welcome on the porch; the Panella and O'Brien families, especially my mother for her enduring love of the Maine landscape; colleagues and students at the Academy; the breathtaking women of Fatal Rebellion; my dreamlike Ohana Sisters; Mark Sullivan, Lee Sachs, Julie Janiszewski, Kristin Blanchfield; Jen Charat, Sloane Miller, and David Hough for such intelligent and intuitive editing; Benee Knauer; Victoria Sanders for opening the door and calling me in; Madeline and Max for being exactly who they are.